ON ANY GIVEN SUNDAY

ON ANY GIVEN SUNDAY

A NOVEL BY
Pat Toomay

DONALD I. FINE, INC.
New York

For Michael, Ted, and Jack
with thanks to David

We don't want to admit that we are fundamentally dishonest about reality, that we do not really control our own lives. We don't want to admit that we do not stand alone, that we always rely on something that transcends us, some system of ideas and powers in which we are embedded and which supports us. This power is not always obvious. It need not be overtly a god or openly a stronger person, but it can be the power of an all-absorbing activity, a passion, a dedication to a game, a way of life, that like a comfortable web keeps a person buoyed up and ignorant of himself, of the fact that he does not rest on his own center.

ERNEST BECKER, *The Denial of Death*

God is an intelligible sphere whose center is everywhere and whose circumference is nowhere.

HERMES TRISMEGISTUS,
The Asclepius

PART ONE

CHAPTER | **ONE**

She is walking toward me along a rocky beach, in a sheer dress, her supple body limned against the setting sun. Unaware of my presence, she kneels before a tidal pool and for a moment observes the sea life thriving there. She gently stirs the water, rises and continues along the shore. Then she sees me. I smile in a knowing way, she in pleased surprise...

I awoke with a jolt as the bus shuddered and lurched across a monstrous chug-hole. Again, the dream. It had been stalking me for some time, though never with the frequency of the last several weeks, and never so consistently unresolved. I shrugged it off. We must be downtown, I thought; and with the sleeve of my sports coat I wiped the condensation off the window of the bus.

It was the eighteenth of December, 1976—a Saturday evening—and Philadelphia was dressed up for a Bicentennial Christmas. Minuteman mannequins stood mute guard over Christmas displays in the storefront windows; great crepe-paper bells hung from nearly every lamp post. Though the hour was early, few shoppers were out. It was raining hard and rivulets of water ran down the sheetmetal gutters on the brickwork of the old buildings, down the concrete gutters in the streets, down the storefront windows and the windows of the bus. The bus was hot and the acrid smell of sweat hung in the air, overpowering the fragile scents of cologne and deodorant.

11

I asked the driver how much farther we had to go.

"We're here," he answered, and wheeling the charter into a circular drive, he parked before the Philadelphia Liberty Hotel.

"Thank God," someone said, and we all stood and gathered our belongings and began to file off.

Coach, as always, led the way. An impressive figure in greatcoat and fedora, with neatly clipped hair and deeply tanned face, he stepped off the bus and started up the canopied sidewalk, nodding and smiling at the scruffy adolescents with notepads and pens who had gathered in anticipation of our arrival. Coach was lugging a 16-millimeter analyzer projector and several strapped boxes of game film. As he neared the front door of the hotel, he turned and gestured toward me. I reached around him and pulled open the massive door, and out stepped a small, red-faced man in a three-piece suit.

"Where the hell have you been?" he said. "Article nineteen paragraph twelve, you're supposed to be here *at least* forty-eight hours before kick-off." And he crossed his arms and spread wide his legs as if to prevent our passing.

Coach glanced at his watch. "Yes, well, we seem to be a day late." He smiled. "We'll discuss it later."

"But this is a big goddamn game," the man persisted. "What if your plane had gone down? Do you realize the scheduling problems that would have created? And what about the local press? Have you forgotten your obligations to the local press?" The man was angry and bewildered.

"We'll discuss it later," Coach said, and brushing past him, walked inside the hotel.

Phil Tanner, the team's advance man and business manager, was standing in the center of the lobby, smiling nervously as we came in. Coach glowered at him.

"You been holding hands with him, Tanner?"

"I couldn't get rid of him, Coach. I—"

"What's your job? Your job is to get rid of him!"

"But he's from the league office, and he's been screaming at me for two hours. I—"

"Excuses, you're giving me excuses."

"I didn't know what to do, Coach. I mean—"

"Get on with it. Do you know what to do now?"

He did, of course; and as Coach stormed across the lobby for the elevators, Tanner began handing out room keys. A fat, sweaty man, there were perspiration stains in the armpits of his jacket, and I found myself staring at them as he read from an alphabetical list. "Rafferty," he rasped, and when I raised my hand he tossed me the key—room 418. At the newsstand I bought an early edition of the Sunday Philadelphia *Examiner,* then, noting the crowd waiting near the elevators, climbed the stairs to the fourth floor. There I ran into Jan Rutledge and Wayne Law—our quarterback and his favorite receiver. They were headed for a local seafood restaurant and Wayne, my roommate, asked if I wanted to join them.

"Thanks," I said, "but I'm going to try and catch Judy later, maybe eat with her."

"You don't give up, do you."

I gave him a look.

"Suit yourself," Wayne said, and he and Rutledge ambled off down the hall.

In the room I set my attache case on the bureau and the newspaper on the nightstand between the two beds. I took off my coat, tie, and shirt, and hanging everything over the back of a chair, stretched out on the bed nearest the window. I was tired, but it was the kind of tiredness that comes from tension, and I knew it would be difficult to sleep. So, to pass the time, I picked up the *Examiner* sports page and read Mickey Baron's column.

The Las Vegas odds-makers had made us a two-point favorite on the strength of our defense, "but," wrote Baron, "the odds-makers are blind. They have overlooked two insurmountable liabilities..." and he named them: Coach's outrageous play calling, and Rutledge's rag arm. "A disastrous combination," Baron concluded, and picked Philadelphia in a rout.

I turned to the agate columns to check the injury report. Though his observations were valid, I felt Baron could only be right if Wayne Law didn't play—and there was a chance he might not. A game-breaking receiver and our offensive co-captain, Wayne had suffered a mildly pulled hamstring two weeks before, in the

13

fourteenth regular season game, and had not played last week. We didn't really need him then since the opposition was severely outmanned and we won handily. But this game was different. Not only was Philadelphia our match, but we had to win to get into the play-offs. Wayne's presence could mean the difference between winning and losing.

There was nothing to worry about. Wayne was not mentioned in the report: he would play.

After reading the rest of the newspaper I dozed, waking up hungry at eight-fifteen. Judy was due in the hotel at eight-thirty, so I walked down to the lobby to meet her.

The lobby was crowded. Most of the people there were from Washington, team followers, and they all displayed the team colors in one way or another. Their children, similarly bedizened, patrolled the lobby like giggling little Cossacks after autographs. There were about fifteen of them, each clutching pen and paper. As autograph hounds, though, they weren't very discriminating. In fact, any man over six feet was stopped and badgered until he signed his name to every scrap of paper.

Ducking across the lobby, I sat down near the elevators to wait for Judy. Though unnoticed by the kids, I had been spotted by a man in a burgundy hat on the other side of the room. Out of the corner of my eye I could see that he was waving at me. Not wanting to be bothered, I turned away toward the front door of the hotel and continued my watch.

The Cossacks had just finished with the bell captain when Brady Young came in. Brady was Judy's editor at the Washington *Herald*; he carried a suit bag and portable typewriter and was surrounded by kids. "My hands are full," he kept saying, but the kids were persistent and demanded autographs. As Brady put down the typewriter to begin signing, I got up and asked if he'd seen Judy Colton.

Now the Cossacks wanted me.

"I saw her at National Airport," he said. "I don't know—I expect—she's probably stopped somewhere to eat..."

A bell rang, elevator doors opened, and Brady Young disappeared.

After dutifully signing the autographs, I started back across the lobby for the stairs. As I did the man in burgundy stepped forward and doffing his hat, flashed a nervous grin. I knew him after all. He was Charlie Rale, an investment broker from Washington, formerly Jan Rutledge's friend and adviser and once an avuncular member of the team "family"—in fact, the family's self-styled financial coach, and a damned good one at that.

"Are you going to speak to me?" he asked timidly.

"Why, hell yes," I said. "I just didn't recognize you in that ridiculous hat."

"Aw, I bought it in the goddamn gift shop. Tanner's been fucking with me since I got to the hotel."

"They don't give up."

"Harassment, and it's getting worse. This latest thing is nuts."

"I know."

The "latest thing" was Judy's profile of Charlie in her *Herald* column two weeks ago. It was an innocent piece, filler really, intended only as a bit of publicity for Charlie and his failing brokerage business, yet it inspired an incredible response from my employer, Washington club owner Roger Clayton. After reading the article, Mister Clayton had phoned Brady Young at home, delivered a lecture on journalistic improprieties, demanded Judy's resignation. Asked why he'd singled her out, Clayton said: "Treason. She's publicized an individual who tried to destroy the Washington franchise." He was quite serious. But he was also quite drunk, and when Brady, a long-time friend of Clayton's, reminded him of this the following day, Clayton withdrew his request and apologized.

Charlie's problems with Mister Clayton began in April of 1974 and, according to Charlie, stemmed from his association with a California sports attorney who was rounding up talent for the World Football League. Before that an intimate of Mister Clayton, Charlie had served as a liaison for the attorney in his dealings with several Washington players who were interested in the new league. When Mister Clayton found out what was happening he was furious. He had taken good care of Charlie. There had been trips to exotic places, girls, a special seat on the team charter, golf games with important people. For Charlie to help lure Washington players to the other league was treachery. So Mister Clayton expelled Charlie from our midst. But that didn't end it. Using his considerable influence, Clayton began punching holes in Charlie's lifeboat, his brokerage business, and as a result the waves of financial ruin were lapping closer and closer.

"Have you ever tried to talk to him?" I asked. We were walking across the lobby toward the stairwell.

"Who?" he said.

"Mister Clayton. I mean, what the hell."

"You want me to get killed?"

"It's been two years, Charlie. You'd think—"

"There was some other stuff going on there, Brad. I don't want to get into it." He opened the door to the stairwell. "Listen," he said, "I had an appointment with Rutledge tonight and he didn't show. If you see him upstairs, ask him to call me. It's kind of important."

"I think he went out to eat with Wayne."

"Oh."

"Bookbinder's, I think."

"Maybe later then. If you see him. Don't go to any trouble."

"Sure."

"Wayne's leg's all right, I guess?"

I had started up the stairs. "What's up?"

"I mean, he wasn't reported hurt in the paper. He wasn't on the injury report."

"So he's going to play."

"But he's hurt."

"Charlie, if he was hurt he'd be on the report."

"You mean he's playing a hundred percent?"

"I mean if he's not on the report, he's okay."

Charlie shook his head. "Fastest healing hamstring in medical history."

"It wasn't that bad," I said.

"A lot of people'd like to know how hurt he is, you know what I mean?"

"That's not news."

16

"I mean, I thought he was hobbled."

"He's tough, Charlie. You know that. We're all tough."

I knew what he was getting at. More was involved than simply the effect that the presence or absence of a name on the injury report might have on the strategy developed by opposing coaches. Everybody knows about the pink sheets, the football cards, the odds, the big bets. If a key player is injured and unable to play in a particular game, and if this information is withheld, then the handicappers cannot set an accurate point spread and those people with knowledge of the injury have a definite advantage in betting that game. Gamblers would naturally pay a high price for such an edge and that's why the league requires public disclosure of *all* injuries, to minimize if not eliminate the scramble for "inside information." And of course it was this scramble personified that stood sweating before me in a funny hat and disguised as a friend. He was desperate and it angered me.

"You wouldn't be trying to get a little edge, would you, Charlie? You wouldn't be looking to take unfair advantage, would you?"

"Not me, Brad. No way."

"You think I'm stupid?"

"No way."

"No way."

"So what's the story? Gimme a little help here."

"I'm going to bed. Tell that to your friends. Rafferty went to bed early."

I spent the next few hours in my room eating room-service food and watching Saturday-night television. At eleven, just before curfew, Wayne returned. He had been talking with some players in the hall and he came in laughing, his face flushed and his eyes glistening.

"Hey, Brad," he said, "how about Coach this afternoon? He really held back on 'em, didn't he? Can you imagine what that league official would've thought if he'd started in on diurnal rhythms?"

Wayne was laughing and I did too. "He probably would've thought the same thing we thought when we first heard it—that Coach had lost his mind." But of course that was before the team

had been turned over to a group of Georgetown University be-
havioral scientists for three days of intensive study during the last
off-season, at Coach's insistence, and since then we've all become
acutely aware of our bodies' diurnal rhythms and their sensitivity
to change, particularly to the disruptive changes brought about
by travel. That's why we were late arriving in Philadelphia. "The
less time we spend on the road, the better for us," Coach says.
"I'm not gonna bust up the old D-R's any more than I have to.
And if that means stretching a league rule here and there and
heating up Phil Tanner's duodenal ulcer, well, so be it. I'll try
anything to help us win, and for that you will appreciate me."

Wayne was undressing now, carefully hanging and folding his
expensive clothes.

"So how was Bookbinder's," I said.

"You ever eat a bad oyster?"

"Oh, no."

"Rutledge claims he ate a bad oyster. Anyway, he puked all over
himself."

"He's not—"

"No, no. He's fine. He's got a seafood hangover, that's all. And
a helluva laundry bill." Naked now, Wayne rummaged in his suitcase for his playbook.

"After you guys left I ran into Charlie Rale," I said. "We had
a little talk."

"Yeah?—Ah," Wayne said, finding his playbook. "I thought I
left you home, little buddy." And clutching the book—his "little
buddy"—he climbed into bed.

"He was looking for Rutledge," I said. "They've got a deal working or something."

"You mean Charlie's got a deal working and he wants to get
Rutledge involved."

"I don't know, they were supposed to have a meeting—I saw
him in the lobby, that's all."

"Jan won't talk to him, Brad, just like you shouldn't talk to him.
You know how Mister Clayton feels about that." Wayne flipped
through his playbook to the scouting report.

18

"Mister Clayton asks you to shoot Baptists, you gonna shoot Baptists?"

"Did I tell you about Huey Greene? He's a Baptist."

"Goddammit, Wayne, I made some good money with Charlie Rale and I don't understand—"

"He's a Baptist who backpedals, Huey Greene. Unfortunately he has yet to learn when to stop backpedaling and start running and he can't possibly cover me on the post."

"Come on."

"I'm serious," he said. "You remember the Buffalo wide-out who booted the game winner two years ago? That was Huey Greene. Buffalo traded him to Philly, Philly made him a corner and you oughta see the way he plays—all balled up and churning. You can blow right by him on the post, and once you do he overcompensates and that opens up the quick-out. What I'm telling you, this is going to be a piece of cake."

"Can you run the patterns?"

"Hey. The rest was Mister Clayton's idea—rest for the weary, you know. I ran hard on Friday, there was no pain."

"Good."

"Good? That's all?"

"I'm sorry, but it kills me the way he takes care of you, it really does."

"We're a little irritable tonight, aren't we."

"It really does," I said. "I mean, he gives you the week off, he offers you that goddamn job looking after his race horses—it'll never happen either, that job. You wait. It's just a carrot, you know what I mean? A carrot hanging off the top of your helmet so you'll run faster."

"You get left at the gate again or what?"

"I'm not worried."

"She didn't show, did she."

I shrugged.

"Jesus Christ," Wayne muttered, and with a shake of his head got up and went into the bathroom.

He had been in there about twenty minutes and I was just about to fall asleep when the telephone rang. Glancing at my watch, I rolled over and picked up the receiver. It was late, nearly twelve.

"Hello," I said.

"Brad?"

"Judy, hi. I waited in the lobby for you, I was hoping—"

"I'm in New York, Brad." Her voice was flat, indistinct. "I've got a meeting upstate sometime tomorrow, possibly on Monday. I won't be able to make the game."

"What? You're where?"

"I know what you're probably thinking—I don't blame you. But things are going to be different now. Believe me. From now on things are going to be different."

"Judy, for Christ's sake, Brady thinks you're here. In town. I mean, I saw him downstairs—"

"This has nothing to do with Brady."

"But he's your boss—I mean, who's he got to do the game story now? What's-his-name Ed Thomas who's so messed up he can't even write an obituary anymore? You can't stick us with Ed Thomas. Not now. Not this week. We've got Philadelphia this week—"

"Brad, look. I just...I mean, it can't be helped. Okay? I want to be there, you know that. I know what's at stake. It just can't be helped. Okay? I'll be home on Tuesday, I'll fill you in then. Now I've got to go."

"But...I mean...I won't play worth a damn."

"Don't be silly."

"But—"

"I've really got to go, Brad." And she said goodnight, and good luck, then put down the receiver, quickly, before I could get in another word.

New York. Here we go again, I thought, and feeling warm, I got up and opened a window. Outside: the damp, sooty evening. There were oil refineries to the west of the hotel; they were working and had fouled the air. I looked to the northeast, the direction of Manhattan. Not all that far. She could get a cab if she wanted. A train. She could get here, the bitch. And I'm supposed to believe things are going to be different now? From somewhere there arose

20

the neurotic switching wail of a patrol-car siren. I closed the window and went back to bed.

"Wayne," I called toward the bathroom door, "did you see the trainer on your way up?"

Wayne stepped out of the bathroom and tossed me an opaque vial.

"Seconal, huh?"

He nodded.

I swallowed one of the red, bullet-shaped capsules, put two more on the nightstand, and stretched out on the bed. Who was she with this time? Who was she risking her job for this time? I stared at the ceiling. It was white. Rough. Though not that high above my head, it seemed far away and like a wall through which I might smash my way to find the means either to understand Judy or be free of her.

On the nightstand the two remaining Seconals seemed to glow, catching light from somewhere beyond the drapes on the window. I would have to take them soon. I hoped they might put me out like a hammer and stop my longing. I knew that somewhere I still hung onto the notion that by winning football games I could win her.

With that thought, I nearly lunged for the Seconals. They slid down my throat. She wasn't going to see me play tomorrow and that was that and it was too bad. But if I didn't sleep soon I wouldn't be worth seeing by anybody. I needed my sleep. The night was beginning to seem very long. The white ceiling stayed far away.

CHAPTER TWO

Sunday morning I woke up groggy and heavy-headed. The
television set was on, turned to a preacher named Thad Desmond.
The volume was up and the tiny speakers vibrated with Thad
Desmond's message:

"Ladies and gentlemen, when you ask a person 'Are you a Christian?' how does he usually respond? We've all heard it, haven't
we. After searching the very depths of his soul he'll look up and
say, 'Well...I belong to the church.'

"Do you know what I usually say?

"SO DOES THE STEEPLE!"

Thad Desmond grinned. Splendidly dressed, he carried himself
with dignity and self-assurance and I despised him for waking
me.

"Wayne, what time is it," I said.

Wayne didn't answer. Looking wide awake, he was perched on
the end of his bed, watching Desmond, listening intently:

"In the springtime of the year we can see the little blossoms
come out on the apple tree, and the pear tree, and it's a wonderful sight. But what happens to those little blossoms when the
winds begin to blow? Some of them hold on, don't they, ladies

and gentlemen. Some of them hold on and turn into fruit while others—"

Wayne switched the channel to "George of the Jungle." "It's eight-thirty," he said. "Devotional at eight forty-five, pregame and taping at nine."

"So what else is new," I muttered. "Where?"

Wayne handed me the itinerary and went downstairs. Taping and the pregame meal were listed for the Andrew Johnson room, the devotional was to be held in the William Henry Harrison room. Up-and-at-em, I thought; but as I threw back the covers and swung my legs to the floor the room pitched and turned and began to spin. I laid back down for a moment, then tried again, slowly, and this time the room stayed still. It was the pills. I had taken too many damn pills.

When I got downstairs the devotional was already underway. The door to the William Henry Harrison room was shut and I could hear muffled voices coming from within. Cracking the door, I looked inside. Twelve players, Wayne and Rutledge among them, were seated along the back wall of the small room. Coach was standing before the group but off to one side, having just introduced a squat, bespectacled figure—a local representative of the Christian Athletes' Fellowship. He, in turn, was introducing the morning's featured speaker, a quadriplegic Marine captain who had been paralyzed in a helicopter crash in Vietnam.

"He was a lieutenant when it happened," said the CAF representative, smiling beneficently as he touched the captain's capulet on the shoulder of the shriveled victim in the wheelchair beside him, "and for two years afterwards he was a very bitter young man. But then something remarkable happened..."

I wondered if it was the promotion. Certainly being a captain rather than a lieutenant would make up for anything. The prick, I thought. It was the pills and I needed to eat.

But I couldn't eat. Not in the Andrew Johnson room, anyway. The trainer and his assistant were taping ankles near the buffet line and the chemical stench of tape adhesive was overwhelming. The steak, the eggs, the coffee—everything tasted medicinal.

23

Knowing I could get something from Tony, I walked to the lobby and caught a cab to Veteran's Stadium.

My number is 68. I'm thankful for my number because it provides a point of reference in the locker room. It tells me where to go, which Cosby leather-plated shoulder pads to wear, which Adidas shoes belong to me, which Riddell helmet has been expanded to fit my over-sized head. The presence of my number tells me I haven't been traded, cut, released, waived, or otherwise set adrift. It tells me I still belong. I found *68* written in Magic Marker on a piece of adhesive stuck on the facing of the first locker inside the only entrance to the cavernous locker room.

Feeling good, I undressed. After dusting my toes, testicles, and the insides of my thighs with white powdered fungicide, I slipped into a stiff athletic supporter and crossed the uncarpeted concrete floor to the equipment room. Tony, the crotchety equipment manager, was inside. Wearing a club warm-up jacket, he was removing stacks of gray T-shirts from a large black steamer trunk and tossing them on the floor. Behind him, in a corner of the room, a coffee brewer perked and a pot of hot dogs boiled on a hot plate. Food, however, had ceased to be a concern.

"It's *cold* in here, Tony."

Tony did not respond.

"Tony!" I shouted. "It's goddamned *cold* in here."

Nothing. I fiddled with the clear plastic box that encased the thermostat. It was locked. The temperature was 55 degrees.

"What the hell—get away from there," Tony snapped.

"For Christ's sake, it's fifty-five degrees in here." I was shivering.

"Federal regulations, Rafferty. Thermostat's supposed to be at five-five so's we can save some fuel. Where you been anyway?"

"That's the speed limit."

Tony handed me a sweat shirt.

"The *speed limit's* supposed to be fifty-five, not the goddamn temperature. Do you think we're in a car, Tony? This is not a car."

Tony punctured one of the hot dogs with a fork.

24

"I asked you if you thought we were in a car. This is a building, Tony."

"Tube steak?" he asked.

"I...yes. Yes. That's what I'm here for. I also want to explain to you the difference between cars and buildings, you jerk-off."

While we ate Tony said, "You got Dolchik today, huh."

"I haven't even thought about him."

"You better."

"It won't make any difference."

But I knew Tony was right—I wouldn't stand a chance against Dolchik without some mental preparation. So after eating two hot dogs and drinking three cups of coffee I wandered into the training room and stretched out on a cold white wooden table. I folded my hands across my chest, shut my eyes, and tried to conjure up Gary Dolchik, Philadelphia's All-Pro offensive tackle and my opponent for the game. It didn't take long before he came to me, this six-foot-five-inch knot of flesh—and he came as vivid as a night game: his chest hairs curled up around his throat like jungle vines gone wild, his hot stinking meat-breath wafted over my face. To give myself confidence I remembered my latest and only successful encounter with him.

It was in Washington two months ago on a warm and humid Sunday afternoon. It had rained that morning, but by one o'clock the sun had penetrated the overcast and the natural turf of the playing field had become a simmering stew. During the pregame drills I detected the resurgence, particularly in my legs, of a strength and resilience I hadn't known since my first year in the league. I felt responsive, like a sheet of shiny blue steel. I turned and searched downfield for Dolchik, and when I found him mired in slop in the far end zone, struggling like a yak in a rice paddy, I could tell he would wither early, and I knew I would have the game of my life. And I did.

But then the tactic I had used to psych me up suddenly turned and I found myself sinking because I couldn't remember beating Dolchik without also remembering Judy Colton, who had seen me play that day.

My finest performance as a pro coincided with Judy's first important assignment as a sportswriter for the Washington *Herald*. For two years she had been the clean-up correspondent for the *Herald* sports staff. She had answered telephones, edited wire copy and fetched coffee, had covered only the lowest echelon events. Her writing, though restricted to football played in the high schools of suburban Washington, was precise and imaginative, and her approach to the game was unique. Unlike her colleagues, Judy ignored the chessboard strategies and cybernetic aspects of the sport; she responded, instead, to the aesthetics of the game. She experienced football as an aesthetician might experience a ballet, and the quality of her experience surfaced in her columns. She described strikingly the movements of the receiver and the cornerback, and the collisions along the line of scrimmage. She discovered grace and style in a frail flanker from Henry H. Marshall High School in northeast Washington, she uncovered sensitivity in a center from Taft High in Woodbridge, Virginia.

Judy's talents clearly exceeded those of her associates at the *Herald,* yet her column appeared only two days each week squeezed into the fifth page of the sports section between ads for cars and trucks. Brady Young, veteran sports editor for the newspaper, recognized Judy's ability, but he continually frustrated her efforts to expand the scope, location, and frequency of her column.

On Thursday, October fifteenth, three days before my epic performance, Brady had phoned me and asked for my thoughts on the upcoming game. I was surprised to hear from him. I usually spoke to beat man Ed Thomas on such matters, but Thomas was sick (probably hung over) and Brady had been pressed into service. He was uncomfortable. He had not conducted an interview in several years and the conversation, darting from topic to topic like a disoriented homing pigeon, reflected his discomfort. We discussed Dolchik and Philadelphia, the division races, the new collective bargaining agreement.

"You like this interview, Rafferty? I don't. I'm talking in circles... You know why."

"Is this part of the interview?"

"No."

"You're trying to set me up—get me off guard."

"No. No. I don't know what I'm doing. I haven't given an interview in years. That goddamn Ed Thomas."

"He's a drunk, right?"

"No."

"Dump him."

"Dump him? I don't want to just dump him. I can't just dump him. We're old friends."

"Sure."

"You understand that."

"I don't mean to change the subject, but I want—that girl you have on the high school games, she's one helluva writer. What's her name?"

"You know her?"

"Good writer."

"She's a woman, you know what I mean, Rafferty? I can't fire Ed Thomas and move a woman into that slot."

"She'd go over big in the locker room, Brady."

"Judy Colton."

"Yeah."

"That's what I mean, for chrissake."

"I'm serious. The guys are waiting for it. Who's gonna be first?"

"You're the second person this week to tell me I should do this."

"Yeah? Somebody else?"

"I'm between a rock and a hard place with her. She's potentially my best writer, no question. She should be covering the club, but dammit, Ed Thomas is our man and has been for nine years..."

I could tell from his tone that Judy was due for a surprise, and it came the following day when, late that afternoon, Brady summoned her to his office. After informing her that Ed Thomas had become an at-large reporter covering the league as a whole he asked if she would like to fill the vacated position, and on Sunday, October eighteenth, after two days of frantic preparation, she took her place with the other scribes in the pressbox at RFK Stadium. The event: Philadelphia versus Washington, Dolchik versus Rafferty—my finest performance as a pro.

I was excited by Judy's presence. To know that she would attempt to describe the intricacies of my triumph that day was a pleasure. When we met in the catacombs of the stadium after the game Judy greeted me warmly and it occurred to me that Brady had told her something about my part in her promotion. My great day had been her first day in the big time. I liked that. As we walked to the stadium parking lot she slipped her arm through mine—and I liked that, too.

"Thanks for my present," she said softly, holding up the briefcase I'd given her to commemorate the occasion. "And thanks for my day. I'm amazed at the things you do."

"I never had such a day. He was so easy. It was all so easy. I couldn't make a wrong move."

"Is this an interview?"

"Listen, this was my lucky day, too."

"I had fun."

"Shall we go home?" I asked.

"The party?" she said.

"Ah," I said. "I forgot."

We adjourned to JP's, an intimate club in the old section of Alexandria, Virginia, where nearly all our team parties were held. In the relative quiet of the bar Judy climbed up on a high stool and crossed her legs. A slit in her skirt exposed a thin wedge of silken thigh. She smiled, smoothing her skirt, then turned to inspect the crowd. I couldn't take my eyes off her. Tiffany lamps had made fruit salad of the light. She was shining like a polished apple, but at that instant, though at my elbow, no more within my reach than she had ever been.

Judy Colton and I graduated from the Albert Fall High School, Alexandria, Virginia, in the spring of 1966. I'd accepted an athletic scholarship to Stanford and hoped Judy would also go there, but her father, army colonel Sam Colton, had established his family's legal residence in Ohio and insisted that Judy take advantage of the tuition rates made available to Ohio residents by the state's university.

Judy studied drama and dance before settling on journalism as a major. She did straight reporting and occasional features for the school newspaper and she served as the campus correspondent for "The Different Drummer," an underground paper in Columbus. From her letters, and from what I read of the articles she sent along, it was evident that Judy had the gifts of a true reporter, not the least of which was an obsessive dedication to her work.

When I finally got her to attend a homecoming dance and game it was the fall of my sophomore year, and I was amazed to find that she'd switched from investigative reporting to sports reporting. She was "sick of digging through other people's garbage," she said. "You can't find the truth anyway." We were pretty drunk and dancing—it was very late. When I told her I'd help her "find the truth" after we got married, she told me she was confused and that she didn't want to talk about anything serious while she was dancing, she just wanted to keep on dancing. I called her confusion my bad timing and ignored my own confusion. Though our lives took us in and out of several relationships with other people over the next two years I carried with me always the notion of a future time when we would be together, permanently.

Following graduation in June, 1970, we met in Virginia and she was as vibrant, full of life, as she'd ever been. We did June in Mack Sennett time. I'd been selected by Washington in the annual college draft. She would soon be going back to Cleveland to look for newspaper work. After all, she told me, she was an Ohio girl, a Buckeye born and bred. Summer practice would start for me in July and she would leave at that point. We would meet in Cleveland after the season, though of course I planned visits as often as possible. I also planned—and thought she certainly must know it—to propose marriage again on one of those visits. I probably should have tried it right then, or at least attempted to talk her into staying in Washington, but I wanted her to have a chance for her own career. Somehow her desire to write about sports struck me as a personal compliment. I was a sports figure myself, I felt, or was going to be, if I could survive training camp.

So on the day of her first big interview for a Cleveland newspaper job I called her after practice and tried for enthusiasm in spite of a split lip, a sprained wrist and what I was sure was heat exhaustion. What I got for my trouble was the news that she'd gone for a newspaper interview and had ended up making friends with some kind of damn business executive, a man called Keith Thomas Thorley.

"He just came in, Brad. While I was waiting for the sports editor. It was around twelve, you know, and he had come to take the sports editor to lunch, but there was a staff meeting or something—anyway, we sat and talked for a while, and when I came out of my meeting he was waiting for me. 'May I see you for a moment?' he asked. And before I could answer he'd taken my arm and pulled me aside. He gave me his business card. 'Call me,' he said, 'if you can't find what you're looking for in the newspaper business. Will you do that? *Call me?*'"

"Who the hell is he? I thought you wanted to be a sports reporter—"

"Brad, I do. And I'm not going to give up yet. But, these newspaper guys—I mean, it happened again today, more or less, I got the same line I've been getting since I got here, 'The sports section sells the newspaper, it's a man's world and the advertisers, the subscribers, they just won't tolerate a woman in there.' That's what they tell me. 'You wanna write lady's stuff, you wanna write gossip, we'll see what we can do. Sports, though, we're terribly sorry, it's out of the question.' I'm getting tired of it, you know? I'm also getting a little strapped for cash. And maybe that's where Mr. Thorley comes in. I mean if I need a part-time job or something..."

"So this Mr. Thorley, he's waiting for you when you show up for your interview."

"Tell you what," she said, not reacting to my obvious sarcasm...jealousy. "I got off a letter to you this afternoon. Let's wait till you get it. Right now everything sounds kind of complicated and it's really not—okay? Let's wait. I mean, look at us, we're wasting all our time on my stuff when it's your stuff that's really important—how's it going down there? What's it really like? Have you got a shot? *Talk* to me, Brad."

Judy was feeling pretty good, I could tell. I, however, was not feeling good at all, and her letter, when it came, though detailed, did not make me feel any better. Nor did our impromptu meeting in the Cincinnati airport following a Friday night exhibition game at Riverfront Stadium three weeks later. Though preoccupied with the game, I'd've had to have been anesthetized not to be affected by her damned good cheer—she was horrifyingly happy. And it was all on account of her new job—which was *not* part-time.

"It was exciting, Brad," she said as we scooted into a back booth in the airport coffee shop. "I mean, to be assigned to the chief executive officer of any corporation is something, but when you're expecting, you know, the secretarial pool...it was like seven-thirty in the morning and there was nobody around and Mr. Thorley was guiding me back through this maze of offices. 'If you're going to assist me,' he says, and my knees start to wobble. I nearly fall off my heels. He just smiles. 'Now, if you're going to assist me, you must understand a bit about what we do around here. To put it as succinctly as possible, Western Funding, Incorporated'— which is the name of the company—'Western Funding,' he says, 'is an independent and copious source of capital for entrepreneurs who cannot get, or do not want, conventional bank financing.'..."

"Where the hell's our waitress?"

"What?"

"You want coffee? I'm gonna get some coffee."

"Oh, sure. Cream, too. Anyway," she said, nodding her thanks as I returned with a pot of coffee and a pitcher of cream, "the key word here, I think, is copious."

I poured coffee.

"I mean, the amount of money that flows through the company is staggering. And it's interesting. Most of the seed capital comes from Pallas Petroleum, which is this family-owned—"

"Pallas Petroleum."

"That's right. It's the proceeds from Pallas that provide the seed, or working, capital for Western Funding. Or did. I'm not sure of the chronology. At any rate—"

"Judy, I don't give a fuck about Pallas Petroleum. You haven't said one word about the game tonight. Do you realize that? Not one goddamn word."

"I'm sorry, I was just—"

"Judy, for Christ's sake. We've got a huge cut tomorrow and

for you to sit and talk this business shit and not even mention the game—was I that bad? I know I only played the second quarter, and they busted that goddamn trap—but it was a blitz. We had a blitz on. It wasn't my fault. The linebacker was supposed to fill— did it look like my fault? Could you tell from the stands?"

"I didn't see the play, Brad. I'm sorry, I don't know what it looked like."

"It was the sixty-yarder. It was the touchdown, for Christ's sake."

"I didn't get to the game until halftime..."

"Whoa now."

"We had a meeting, I missed the afternoon flight."

"You had a *meeting*."

"Brad, listen to me. Mr. Thorley is no local run-of-the-mill blue-suit investor. Sure, his company's in Cleveland and it's only twenty-two employees, but he's also international, Brad, he loans money world-wide, he's got clients all over the globe. Art dealers in France. Car dealers in California. And his friends, he's got friends in the film industry and television. In business and finance—in pretty high places. Even in fashion. This dress I'm wearing...it's a knock-off of a designer-original, exact in every detail yet retailing for a third the designer price. Mr. Thorley put everybody together— the Hong Kong seamstresses, the American retailers. He's quite something, Brad, and he's going to give me some responsibility in the company. I still care about you...but...well, I can't be running off to football games and parties at the drop of a hat anymore. I've got quite an opportunity here, I don't want to blow it. Okay...?"

Okay, hell...."I only played the second quarter, Judy."

"Brad, did you hear a word I said?"

I muttered something about high rollers in monogrammed silk shirts swirling brandy in fancy French restaurants. "More than anything, I guess, I'm disappointed about you giving up your writing. I liked the idea of you writing about sports, and me, you know, being the kind of person you'd maybe want to write about. Sorry if that sounds dumb but—"

"It could be an option, Brad. The writing. You know, something to go to if this doesn't work out. It's a nice idea," she said. "It's sweet of you to have it. I mean that. Please try to understand, okay...?"

I mumbled something again about high rollers making deals and dropping names. "They're real good at that," I said. "Why, I'll betcha anything Thorley has friends, *close* friends, who know Sammy Davis Junior *personally*." I was only half-kidding. And I hurt. "It's a helluva life, isn't it...nightclubs, gin, brunch with the gold-chain fellows. And what are *you* doing while he's sucking up eggs Benedict with the boys? You're gonna get tired of it, you're gonna get bored." I hoped.

"If I do I'll let you know. I promise. Meanwhile..."

I cut her off, tuned out. I couldn't handle it.

Four months later, on December 24, Washington lost to Minnesota in the first round of the conference play-offs and Judy more than let me know she wasn't bored. The game was played in Minneapolis, in unseasonably warm weather. In spite of the loss I felt good about myself, the game I had played and the season just completed. Because of an injury to the veteran George Andros I'd started five games that year, including the play-offs, and had played well. Wanting nothing more than to be with Judy, I skipped the team charter and caught a commercial flight to Cleveland. In a phone booth in the terminal lobby I dialed her number; she answered on the second ring.

"Merry Christmas," I said. "It's nice to hear your voice."

"Brad? You sound so close. Are you close?"

"At the airport, I need directions."

"But—"

"I'm early, I know. But I couldn't wait. Minneapolis is closer than Washington and I want to see you."

"This is going to sound terrible."

"What?"

"You should've let me know...you should've called me, or something—"

"What are you talking about?"

"I'm leaving for Mexico later tonight...on business and—"

"It's Christmas Eve."

"Yes...but I have to go. I mean I can't get out of it. If it were anyone other than Bobby DeAngelis—he's a client, Brad. West Coast, very important, try to understand—"

"Understand? Judy, I thought we...oh, Jesus fucking Christ."

"What?"

"Good-*by.*"

After that I tried to forget about her. It was hard—impossible, really. I just couldn't shake her. For weeks afterward, at the oddest times, I would find myself thinking about her, wondering just what the hell had happened. I was left to wonder because I couldn't reach her. Phone numbers and addresses had mysteriously changed; once-friendly secretaries had become cold and hostile. Then one day a letter arrived and trying to forget her became a luxury I could no longer afford. Gushing and convoluted, a single dense page, the letter confessed her affair with Keith Thorley. It had been Thorley she'd gone to Mexico with, and not the client DeAngelis. Thorley, old enough to be her father.

I felt as though I'd been punched in the nose. I put the letter down and went outside. I didn't know what to do. The car was there, I had my keys so I got in and drove around for a while, stopping first at a shopping mall to get something to eat (I thought I was hungry) and then at a gas station to buy something to drink (I thought I was thirsty), finally ending up at the club compound for no good reason except I didn't want to go home.

It was after five on a mid-April Tuesday afternoon and the locker room was virtually empty. Most of the guys had already completed their workouts and were gone for the day. I changed into my sweats. Ignoring Tony's protests ("It's too goddamn late to work out. I gotta clean up."), I walked outside. Just beyond the back door, on a vast concrete slab, the weight machines were waiting, neatly arrayed, looking, with their gears and cams and sprockets and straps, like medieval instruments of torture. I let them have their way with me. Because I normally despised working with weights and would usually go to great ends to avoid having to do so (a habit which did not go unnoticed during my rookie year—"You can have all the natural ability in the world," the coaches kept telling me, "but you gotta work to be the best you can possibly be—*you've got to work,*" they told me, and I never listened. I was, as they muttered to themselves many times, "immature")—because I normally detested the weights, my behavior now was a mystery to me, but after the workout everything came clear, so to speak. Because as I stood eyes closed in the hot pummelling shower I found myself, for the first time in my life, enjoying the dead-brain narcotic-like stupor that comes with utter physical exhaustion.

The next day I arrived earlier, stayed longer and worked even harder. I discovered then a group of guys, mostly linemen, who had made the club compound and the off-season weight program the focal point of their lives. Their world was one of musculature and measurements, megavitamins and anabolic steriods in which progress was gauged by inches added to chests and necks and arms—gauged and celebrated; and I couldn't resist joining them, making their world my own—I was a ballplayer, too, after all— why not be the best ballplayer I could possibly be? And so off I went in pursuit of that goal and it was just about the best thing I could've done for myself at the time. As the weeks went by I began to gain the weight and strength required for the assault on greatness I had resolved to make. Finally I was able to forget about Judy Colton. Or so I thought.

Of the days of those weeks, Fridays were always the most important because it was on Fridays that the coaches came by to see how we were doing and to administer the little conditioning test they had devised to confirm the consistently incredible gains recorded on the charts posted inside the locker room. For lack of confidence, I avoided the test for several weeks, but along about the end of the first week in May I felt I was ready and decided to give it a try. What was involved, you had to do twelve repetitions of twelve different exercises, each of which worked a different part of your body, the kicker being that between each exercise you had to run the length of the football field and back—a 220, in other words; and the whole thing was timed, it was run against the clock.

I collapsed at the finish line, drenched in sweat, after hobbling the final 220. I had run the test in 19:45, an excellent time, but it was nearly an hour before I could find the strength to roll over and stand up and drag myself into the locker room; and it was another hour before I could get myself showered and dressed and into my car for the ride home. I'd never felt like this before. My previous experiences with exhaustion were nothing compared to this. My legs and arms quivered uncontrollably at the slightest movement; my eyes fluttered in their sockets and felt as though they might, at any moment, roll back into my skull. Yet there was something very pure about it. It was a feeling very nearly beyond feeling. It was blissful, almost.

As I wheeled into my driveway a spasm shot down my right leg forcing my right foot down on the accelerator. The car leaped forward and with a great clatter and crash, crushed my garbage cans against the garage door. Suddenly sober, more than a little frightened by the loss of control, I backed up, then climbed out of the car to inspect the damage. As I did I became aware of some subtle difference in...something. Something about the house. I couldn't put my finger on it. Screw it. I moved the battered cans out of the way, opened the garage door and started back toward the car. And then, from the shadows of the porch, came a voice, soft and clear and sweet, vaguely familiar, unmistakably feminine—"Hello." I turned and there stood Judy Colton, smiling, hands on hips, four or five pieces of luggage in a row at her feet.

"I got a job with the *Herald*," she said.

I looked at her.

"It's not much, you know, editing wire copy and stuff— Keith...Mr. Thorley...sort of helped with the contact. Kind of a parting gift."

I looked at her. I felt neither anger nor hostility. Just pleasure. I was glad to see her. Relieved.

"I, uh, I was kind of hoping—I mean, I'll need a place to stay until I can find an apartment and I was hoping you might...My God," she said, and suddenly she was stepping over her bags and coming toward me. "You...what..."

"What?"

"Brad, look at you."

"What?" I said. "I've been working out." The expression in her eye was almost the one I had always hoped for. I took off my shirt.

"My God, you're so...I mean..." Gently she began to trace the musculature in my arms and shoulders, neck and chest.

"This is me," I said, shuddering a little at her touch. "This is who I am now. I'm going...to...I..."

She trailed a finger across the flat of my belly.

"God. Come here," I said softly, and she came, unhesitatingly, and the sudden warmth of her body and the gentle heaving of her chest, the feeling of her pressed against me made me shiver.

"Brad...we..."

"Shh..."

In the darkness now, in a corner of the garage, I took her face in my hands and kissed her on the mouth, then knelt in front of her.

"Brad...what...Oh, God," she murmured as my hands began to move slowly, lovingly up the willowy contours of her naked legs. And then, in an urgent whisper: "Wait."

I looked up at her, suddenly afraid—terrified, really—of rejection.

"No, it's all right," she whispered. And in a single, deft, almost elegant movement, she unfastened her skirt.

We ended up in the living room, sprawled naked on the rug, sweat-slick and exhausted, sleep coming over us like a drug. Because everything had happened so fast, I didn't want to go to sleep, I wanted very much to stay awake, to look at her, to hold her and be with her—to be utterly sure of her physical presence. But I was so tired. Maybe if I just closed my eyes for a little while it would be all right, I thought. And I did, and it was...the next thing I knew I was lying in the early evening darkness, watching Judy, listening to the gentle, lilting sounds of her humming as she unpacked groceries in the kitchen. She's here, I thought. Goddammit, she's really *here*. And I guess I was as happy as I'd ever been in my life.

We went out to Mario's, the most expensive restaurant in nearby Reston, Virginia. I wanted the evening to be a kind of celebration, but Judy drank a little more than I remembered her drinking, and as the night wore on she became increasingly distant and introspective. At first I didn't say anything. She had been through a lot since we'd last seen each other and it occurred to me that this might just be her way of relaxing herself, of making what must have been a difficult transition easier. After a while, though, when she still hadn't perked up, I asked her directly if something was wrong.

"No, no. God, no. I'm sorry, I was just thinking about Cleveland and everything, and, well... about how right you were. I got tired of it, you know. Just like you said I would. It was just... I missed the clarity, Brad. Of sports. The hard clean lines... I really did. I've been thinking a lot about it, and... I mean, forgive the high-flown language, but it's the delineations, I think, that make sports so appealing, so attractive to so many people. So... well, so beautiful... I mean, most games are played on fields," she said, "and usually the fields have been marked off out of some larger field, so they always have lines around them. And there's always someone, some nonparticipant who has the job of watching those lines, so there's never any question about in-bounds and out-of-bounds. Do you know what I mean? So if someone's out of bounds, play stops, and you start again from some other point on the field— you always know exactly where the hell you *are*. I mean, there are line markers and hashmarks—you always know *exactly* where you are, and you know because of the lines—the delineations. And it's not just a spatial thing. I mean, you work hard and prepare for a game and then you play and—I mean, it ends. Right? You play for three hours and then it ends and you know right away how you did. It's all up there on the scoreboard and if you won you can feel good and if you lost you got to feel bad, but never for very long because before you know it you're into the next week and there's another game to be played, another challenge... There's something really wonderful about it. Maybe it sounds corny, but what it is is the American dream. Right? People setting goals for themselves, people striving against the odds to reach those goals... I missed it all, Brad. I missed being associated with it. In college, in school, I...well...I knew, and then..."

"Hey," I said.

She looked up, smiling, apologetic.

"Welcome home."

THREE

"Wake up, Rafferty. We got a game today, you know what I mean?" The trainer, lugging his doctorlike bag, walked into the room. "Up, up, up," he said. "We got work to do here."

I groaned and rubbed my eyes.

"Come on, come on," he said, wiping his hands after putting down the bag; as I rolled over and hoisted myself up on the rickety white table, he picked up a small block of plywood. "Get 'er out here," he said; and as I extended my right leg a half-step, he slipped the block under my right heel, a heel-rest to hold the leg in proper taping position. He wiped his hands again and taking up an aerosal can, sprayed my leg with tape adherent. I shuddered; my skin erupted in goose flesh, my testicles retracted, my teeth clattered from the sudden chill of evaporating chemical. The trainer wrapped my leg with a layer of gauze and began applying the strips of adhesive that would anchor the badly stretched ligaments in my right knee.

"We'll get 'er ready, Rafferty, don't you worry about that. You handled Dolchik good last game, this game will be even better..." With a dry rip he tore a strip from the roll, then with a wet slap plaited it to my knee.

"I hope so," I said.

"You're not sure?"

"I...I'm without my inspiration this week."

"We got pills, if that's what you mean."

"No, no. I mean my girl."

"The gal reporter? That's disgusting, Rafferty, girls doin' men's jobs. You should discourage her."

"Sure. Since she started I've been playing the best ball of my career."

"I don't mind her bein' your good luck charm—that's what she oughta be and you should get her to quit pretendin' she's a reporter and be a groupie like she wants to."

"Groupie? She's not even here, I just told you."

"See? Undependable. So who's gonna write about us? And don't tell me Brady Young 'cause all he can write about is Willie Slough. You notice that? Every damn day, Willie Slough. Now I got nothin' against the niggers, Rafferty, I'm just tired of readin' about 'em, that's all. Specially rookie niggers who get more ink than the president when they haven't played a down."

"Tell me about it."

"He ain't comin' out either, Rafferty. Once they get him in there he ain't comin' out, I don't care how bad he is. So don't get hurt, you know what I mean? Stay healthy. Keep them knees up and that head on a swivel." The trainer tore one last strip of adhesive and pressed it horizontally across the top of my knee. "That oughta hold 'er," he said. "Have a good one, huh?"

I hopped off the table and walked around a bit. My knee, packed like a Ming vase bound for shipment, was inflexible; the tape was tight and my right foot tingled and was beginning to swell from the lack of circulation.

"So how's she feel, Rafferty? You're walkin' kinda funny there."

"Same as always," I said; and picking up a pair of scissors and several fresh rolls of tape and gauze, I hobbled into the locker room, where I scissored the tape from the back of my knee to the top of my calf. Relief. As blood rushed into the lower part of my leg, my foot, which had gone blue, returned to color, and the

41

throbbing, which had become acute, subsided. The trainer had the touch of a jackhammer operator, and I had to go through this every week.

As I wound a strip of adhesive around the top of my calf to repair the tape, the double steel doors next to my locker began to rattle. Then they stopped. "Jesus Christ," an angry voice said, and the double steel doors shook violently. "Open up, goddammit." Fists pounding on the steel. "Open *up*."

I stood and pushed on a metal bar, and the doors opened, swinging away from me.

"*You.*" Phil Tanner shook like congealed salad. "You lock these goddamn doors, Rafferty? You fucking guys—where's Tony? These goddamn doors are supposed to be *open*."

"He's in the back, Phil."

"In the back. Why can't anyone do what they're supposed to do around here? Locked out of our own locker room, could've been a goddamn disaster, that's all." Tanner pushed the doors against floor-mounted clasps, then peered down the corridor. "Jesus Christ," he said. A whisper. "They're coming."

All at once I could hear the shuffling of many feet and, over muffled conversations, music—a jazz piece in a minor key—the sound wavering and tinlike, undoubtedly blasting from a portable tape deck.

Backing out of the door, Tanner pressed himself flat against the concrete wall and fixed a theatrical smile to his face. "Good afternoon," he said to Coach, the first of the group to enter the room, and bowed from the waist.

A pregame catatonic, Coach acknowledged neither of us as he passed. Jaw slung forward, eyes fixed to some imaginary playing field, he crossed the locker room and disappeared into his private quarters. Following Coach came the rest of the staff, and though each assistant was as grim as Coach had been, their collective somberness had thus far failed to infect the players, who filed in boisterously, peeling out of the loose line, some sprinting for the crappers (there were only two), others breaking for the training room (to be first in line), most hustling to their lockers to begin the ritual of getting ready.

Tanner slammed the double steel doors behind them.

Across the room Wayne Law sat down and opened his suitcase. After a few minutes of frantic searching he produced his shaving kit, which he quickly unzipped, dumping its contents in his lap. After much further sifting, and some friendly goading from his team mates, he finally uncovered what he was looking for: a clear plastic jar half filled with tiny yellow pills, amphetamines—Benzedrine, Dexedrine, I didn't know which—25 milligrams per tablet.

Wayne had asked Needles, our team physician, for the prescription during training camp. Needles, who was new on the job then, had been uncertain how to handle the request, so he had queried the trainer about it. The trainer, pretending ignorance, had referred him to Mister Clayton.

"If they need the stuff, give it to 'em," Mister Clayton had said. "I don't want to hear about it, that's all."

"Give it to them?"

"Whatever it takes," Mister Clayton told the new Needles.

A crowd of players had gathered 'round Wayne's locker to receive their weekly ration. Grinning, Wayne dispensed the pills. After a while the crowd thinned and Wayne, holding up the jar, looked over at me. I shook my head, no.

"You sure?" he called.

"Goin' it alone," I said.

"What?" He came out of his chair and crossed the room.

"Alone," I said. "Naked. You know."

"Just like that? I mean, on one week, off the next—cold turkey?"

"You're talking like a junkie."

"How many do you want? You can't go out there naked."

"I haven't taken anything since the last Philadelphia game."

"Here," he said, "I'll give you one, you can break it in half. That's fine if you wanna be a pussy. Some of my best friends are pussies—"

"Wayne, I told you—"

"Wait a minute," he said. "Philadelphia? That was eight weeks ago."

"I know."

"You mean I've been giving you pills for eight weeks and you haven't been taking them?"

"I play better without 'em."

He gave me a long, skeptical look.

"I really do."

It was true. The drugs undermined my judgment, made a cinematic blur of my memory; made me play on a purely instinctive level, and I wasn't an instinctive player anymore. I played with my head now—with more finesse than force; my age and the infirmities that went with it precluded any other approach.

But Wayne was not about to abandon our ritual. "Take one," he said...he'd unscrewed the cap to the jar. "I don't give a damn if you stick it up your nose, just take it." And he held out a pill that I took and slipped in my shirt pocket to be disposed of later. Wayne shook two more pills from the jar and tossed them down his throat. "Ignition," he said. "Sorry you won't be joining me..." And making a sound like a rocket, he started back across the room for his locker.

"Don't forget your goggles," I called out, and Wayne turned and smiled and gave me the thumbs-up.

It was time to get dressed. Pulling my gold knit game pants from their hook, I turned the right leg inside out and inserted the foam knee pad, then having reversed the pants leg once again, the fiberglas thigh pad. I repeated the process with the left leg and dropped the pants to the floor. My right knee was taped and ready but I'd been having some problems with the left—some kind of tendonitis—so I pulled on a skidder, a thick rubber sleeve that would warm and support the knee and prevent turf burn. Next I went to work on my socks. Over the thin sanitaries that covered the ankle tape, I pulled on the long burgundy knee socks, and over them, the thick white sweat socks, having first stretched the sweat socks across my thigh to insure equal length. I then carefully wound a strip of half-inch adhesive around the top of each burgundy stocking. The adhesive was functional, preventing the burgundy stockings from slipping down, but it was an aesthetic touch as well. I settled back in my chair, stretched my legs out in front of me and took a few moments to admire my work.

"That's white tape on those socks, Rafferty. There," said Phil Tanner, and he pointed at the adhesive. "That's a violation of the League Uniform Code," he added, and before I could protest he thrust a piece of paper under my nose, a letter from the league office addressed to Mister Clayton:

Dear Roger:
   Your club continues to show very little improvement in its habit of not observing the League Uniform Code. This habit dates back to last season and continues despite ever-increasing concern around the league for player safety.

"Player safety?" I looked up. "What the hell is he talking about?"
"Read," Tanner said.

   In your game last week, Jan Rutledge, William Slough, Jeff Blair, Enrico Monte, and Tommy Norris were reported wearing their pants in such a manner that left portions of their legs bare in the knee area. Slough's case again was the most flagrant. Pete Russell, a violator in the past, seems to have improved, but during the game allowed his jersey to remain out. In addition, Brad Rafferty and Gene Davis had tape of contrasting color across their knees, and John Reese wore a basketball-type knee pad.
   Safety to the player and the appearance of our product make the League Uniform Code important to us all, and I again stress that this office will enforce its observance.
   You club is hereby fined another $2,000 and is directed to forward a club check in this amount to this office. Repeated violations may result in additional, escalated fines.
                              Sincerely,
                     THE COMMISSIONER

"This for me?" My name had been circled in blue ink.
"No," said Tanner, snatching the letter. "This is." And he held out a roll of transparent packing tape. "Come on now," he said. "Off with the white, on with the clear."
"I've already done my socks, Phil."
"Come on, you've seen the letter."
"I play better in white tape."

"That's nuts."

"In five years I've never missed a game and in every one of those games I've worn white tape on my goddamn socks. I'm not gonna change now."

"It's two hundred dollars per infraction, Brad. I'll charge it to your ticket account, how 'bout that."

"I don't care, I'm not gonna change the way I wear my *goddamn socks.*"

Tanner nodded and smiled as he marked the page, then looked up and around the room. "So where's Slough," he said. "I gotta talk to Willie Slough."

"I'd check with the Chamber of Commerce, Phil. He's probably downtown looking at the sights."

"Don't bullshit me, Rafferty. It's twelve o'clock."

"I haven't seen him, Phil."

"You mean he's not here yet?" He stuffed the letter in his coat pocket, hurried off to do whatever it was he did when players weren't where they were supposed to be when they were supposed to be there.

If it was twelve o'clock, then the specialists would be going out in ten minutes, the rest of us in twenty and it would probably take me the full twenty minutes to decide which pair of shoes to wear. There were six in my locker, each representing a different shoe manufacturer, each with different performance characteristics, all brand spanking new, all acquired at no cost. Gratuities. The manufacturers understood the impact for their product of the media coverage of professional football games. Which pair to wear was not just a matter of comfort and performance. There were financial considerations, too. The enticements to wear a particular shoe in a particular game increased with the projected television ratings for that game—from free shoes for a preseason game, to cash, appliances or travel for a World Championship. We were somewhat in between, but rumor had it that Pro-pel, a new manufacturer, would pay two hundred fifty dollars to anyone who would wear their shoes. I usually wear Adidas. But for two hundred fifty dollars...

The double steel doors next to my locker rattled again, this time

like a cage. "HHEEYYAGH!" The prehistoric groan of a masta-
don in distress. Phil Tanner rushed over, and pushing open the
doors found himself face-to-chest with Willie Slough, a six-foot-
nine-inch 335-pound rookie defensive lineman that Mister Clayton had found on the glacier-scraped plains of North Dakota,
presumably frozen in a block of ice. A number one draft choice
(actually a number one, number one: first round, first selection),
Willie was wearing a cranberry and gold pin-striped suit, one of
fourteen identical suits he had brought last spring with his bonus
money. Beneath the suit he wore a bright floral print shirt that,
unbuttoned to his navel, exposed his mountainous chest. I'd never
seen such pectoral muscles. They formed a valley where they
dropped down to connect to his sternum, the valley a kind of
haven for body hair, the hair flourishing there but nowhere else.
Willie was bald. A half dozen gold chains hung around his neck,
four or five rings graced his fingers, a miniature African icon
dangled from his pierced left ear.

Stepping around Tanner, his jewelry tinkling like a wind
chime, Willie ducked into the locker room and began looking
for his locker. Tanner followed, yapping at his heels like a fat
terrier.

"Here, Willie," I said, motioning to the locker next to mine.

"You and me, huh B? Just like always?"

"You need to get dressed, Willie. It's after twelve."

"I'm late, B."

"I know," I said. "You need to get dressed."

As Willie bent to stow his gear I could smell the cologne fumes
rising like weather from his chest. Brut? English Leather? Something. Whatever it was wasn't enough. Willie still smelled like a
gymnasium.

"So where you been, Willie?" Tanner yapping. "You get fucked
this morning?"

"Aw, P...why you wanna say that?"

"You smell like you been fucking, that's all. You been fucking?"

"Naw. Sheeit."

"So where you been?"

Willie looked down at me and blinked slowly. "Who is this dude?"

47

he asked. A joke. He grinned, showing his bad teeth. Then he turned back to Tanner. "Gonna talk to the boss man 'bout you, you hear? I mean it, too."

Tanner was unperturbed. "So where you been, Willie?"

"Missed the bus, P."

"Missed the bus? You stoned or something?"

"Cause I missed the bus?"

"Yeah."

"Aww, man...why you wanna say that?"

"Phil," I said. "We haven't got much time. Will you hurry up?"

Tanner patted his pockets for the letter. "I gotta talk to you about your pants, Willie."

"My pants?"

"Yeah. Last week you were, uh...here it is. Last week you were reported wearing your pants in such a manner that left portions of your legs bare in the knee area. Commissioner says it ain't safe."

Willie looked down. "But I'm okay now, huh?"

"Your *game* pants, Willie."

"Oh."

"They don't fit, you gotta pull 'em down some so your knees don't show. Commissioner says the bare knees look bad on television."

"Oh," Willie said.

"You understand me?"

"Sure."

Tanner seemed relieved, folded the letter and stuck it back in his coat pocket.

"But his ass'll show then, Phil. You ever think about that?"

Tanner gave me a hard look.

"What you say, B?"

"Your ass, Willie. You pull your pants down, your ass'll show."

"Yeah. My ass." Willie seemed to be thinking it over, trying to absorb it.

"Could be a problem, Phil. I mean, we're talking about the tallest man in the league here and his pants don't fit."

"Yeah," Willie said, "and I ain't showin' my ass on no television, neither."

48

"You gonna fine him too, Phil?"

"Will you shut up?"

"You fine me, you gotta fine him, Phil. It's only fair."

"Goddammit, Rafferty—"

"SPECIALISTS," Coach bellowed. "LET'S GO SPECIALISTS."

"Jesus Christ," Tanner said. "I—Willie, you talk to Tony about your pants, okay? Tony'll take care a you. He doesn't, I'll fine him. We all set now? You got me?"

Willie nodded.

"I gotta go," Tanner said, and after a begrudging "good luck," joined the kickers, quarterbacks, and receivers as they filed out of the locker room.

CHAPTER | **FOUR**

I reached up and from the locker shelf removed my Cosby leather-plated shoulder pads. Brushing away the dried mud and bits of grass, the debris from last week's game, I sat down and began adjusting the rawhide laces that held the pads together. They were old, the pads, relics of another era. Purchased new in 1961, they had been worn by George Andros for twelve seasons, then entrusted to me when he retired four or five years ago. I wasn't sure if I wanted the ratty old things, but George had been the club's right defensive end for a long time and it seemed important to him that I, the heir apparent to his position, take his pads and try them, so I did. To my surprise they fit me well, much better than the new plastic models I'd been wearing. Soft and supple and a good two pounds lighter, the Cosbys provided my neck and shoulders a much wider range of motion, and I've been wearing them ever since.

The laces tightened, I slipped the pads over my head. Reaching back for the girths, I pulled them tightly across my armpits and cinched them to the buckles on the breastplates.

Most of the other players were similiarly caparisoned and were now beginning the final stages of preparation. Elbow pads were being fitted in place, hands and fingers were being taped. The

50

offensive linemen, as was their custom, had gathered in a corner of the locker room to complete what they called "The Process," a kind of uniform alteration that, I'm sure, the Commissioner would find disgusting. With disdain for the League Uniform Code they had already pleated their jersey sleeves and taped them tightly to their biceps and were now smearing the pleated sleeves with Vaseline, spraying them with silicone—anything to make the fabric slick, difficult for an opponent to grab. A few feet away defensive tackle Jeff Blair was busy slitting the seams in his game pants so they would accommodate his massive legs. As he worked he was talking to John Reese who was standing nearby, wrapping foam padding around the fiberglass cast on his left wrist. The padding, I was certain, would be discarded as soon as the officials checked the cast during pregame warm-ups.

"FIVE MINUTES," Tony called out. "YOU LUMMOXES GOT FIVE MINUTES."

I pulled my jersey from its hanger, inserted my arms and head, turned my back to Willie, who stood and yanked the jersey over my shoulder pads. As I pulled the tail of the jersey through my legs and fastened it like a diaper to the buttons on the jersey front, Willie slumped glumly back to his chair, the chair legs bending, nearly buckling under his weight. Still naked, he cradled chin in hands and stared dejectedly into his ransacked locker.

"You gonna get dressed?" I asked.

"Can't, B," he mumbled. "I done something stupid."

Afraid of what it might be, I busied myself with the various arm pads.

"You gotta lot a nice shoes, B, you know that?" Willie reached into my locker and sorted through the shoes. "Specially these," he said. "These be real nice..." He picked up a pair of Riddells and weighed them in his hands.

"You forget your game shoes, Willie?"

"Forgot 'em, B." He shook his head.

"You wear Riddells?"

"Sure do."

"You wanna wear mine? Is that it?"

"Could I?" His face brightened.

"I don't know," I said. "What size do you wear?"

"Seventeens."

"Seventeens?"

"Seventeens, yeah."

"I wear a twelve, Willie."

"Oh."

I picked up my helmet. "See you later, huh?"

"But—"

"Talk to Tony about it," I said, and kicking open the double steel doors took an immediate left and walked rapidly down the broad concrete corridor.

Most of the guys get a big charge out of Willie, but sometimes he irritates the hell out of me. Because Willie is a number one draft choice, he'll eventually be given a chance to play and when he does play, however he makes out, it will be reported that he did well. Brady Young will make sure of it. The good plays will be accentuated, enlarged; the missed assignments, the times he's trapped, cut, hooked, suckered will be ignored. Mister Clayton's reputation, as Brady so often puts it, "his genius for personnel," depends on it.

But why does Willie Slough have to play *my* position?

Dodging the vendors, skirting the woodwind section of the Wilkes-Barre High School Band, I made my way down the broad corridor. A few yards past the band a hand-lettered sign proclaimed FIELD, an arrow indicated direction. Turning left again, I entered still another corridor, this one narrower than the last, a tunnel that dropped steeply away from me and ended in a rectangular patch of light some sixty feet off. As I started down the tunnel a sharp, explosive roar erupted from the crowd beyond, then another, a chant of some kind, exactly what I couldn't make out. The sounds were amplified to distortion by the narrow passage. Curious, I hurried down the ramp and looked outside.

It was a cold blustery day, the sky leaden, threatening. The stadium, draped with bunting, plastered with hand-painted signs and banners, was already packed with spectators, some holding brightly colored umbrellas, all bundled against the cold. They had taken an unusual interest in pregame warm-ups and I quickly saw why. On the far end of the field our receivers were running pass patterns, our quarterbacks were throwing—all as usual. On the near end the Philadelphia players were similarly deployed, similarly engaged, but in their midst stood little Hans Stoufer, our Austrian place-kicker. Determined to test the winds at this end of the stadium, ignoring the jeers from the crowd, Hans marked a spot for the holder, backed up two yards, sidled two to his left and nodded his readiness. The holder signaled the center, the football was snapped and positioned, and Hans, taking two quick steps, smacked it with his instep, the ball sailing end-over-end toward the goal posts forty-seven yards away. As it fell wide right the crowd exploded again. "TTHHRREE!" and Hans dropped his head in disgust. Get out of there, I thought, but he didn't. He turned and lined up another attempt. It fell short. FFOOUURR," roared the crowd, and Hans was obviously disturbed. Motioning for the center and holder to follow, he weaved downfield through the sprinting Philadelphia receivers and at the seven-yard line set up to attempt an extra point. The ball was snapped and positioned, and as if to show everyone who was boss Hans drove it into the upper deck. Unfortunately the football did not pass through the uprights on its way, and the crowd became delirious.

By this time the rest of our players had come down the tunnel and spilled out on the field, and when Hans came over to join us one of the latecomers asked him what all the commotion was about.

"You mean this roar?" Hans made a sweeping gesture. "Is for me," he said. "I have them eating from the palm of my hand..."

For a moment I thought he believed it. In his review of our club's liabilities in the Sunday *Examiner,* Mickey Baron neglected to mention the inconsistency of our field goal kicker, Hans Stoufer.

The squad spread out now over the far end of the field for calisthentics. Jan Rutledge and my roomie Wayne Law, our co-captains for the game, put us through a series of stretching exercises, after which the team split up according to position, each position-group having been allotted a particular section of the field to work in. The defensive linemen assembled in the end zone with Hank DeVito, the defensive line coach.

"Let's get some starts," said DeVito, placing a football on the Astroturf, hunkering over it like a center. "Now he's gonna try to pull you off with his cadence, so let's be alert..."

The front four—Reese, Davis, Blair, myself—moved into position, poised and quivering in our stances.

"Shit," said DeVito. Suddenly testy, he stood and hitched his pants. He was looking past us into the end zone, where a short cubic figure in trench coat and rain hat stood observing our drill. On second glance I recognized the chiseled features of Mister Clayton. "Get on with it," he said to DeVito, then turned away as if in disgust. DeVito, muttering, hitching his pants, crouched once more over the football.

"Hut," he called as we settled into our stances, and you could hear the exasperation in his voice. "Hut-hut...HUT—"

Jeff Blair lurched forward, tried to catch himself but fell to his knees.

"God*dammit*, Blair." DeVito was in his face. "That's exactly what I'm talking about. You gotta *concentrate*, for Christ's sake."

"Yes sir," Jeff said.

"You under*stand* me?"

"Yessir."

DeVito moved back over the football, then stood up again. "Where's Slough?" he demanded.

A collective shrug.

"Is he here?"

"Somewhere," I said.

"Jesus Christ," he muttered, and threw another look at Mister Clayton. "The hell with Slough," he said. "Let's go."

Resuming the drill, DeVito snapped the ball on the fifteenth "hut" and we charged upfield. As we turned to go back Blair motioned to me and pointed at DeVito, wrapping his hands around his throat. "He's choking," Blair whispered. "What the hell's gotten into him?"

I directed his attention to Mister Clayton, who was still lurking in the end zone.

"Ah," Jeff said. "The bossman."

Mister Clayton had hired Coach DeVito along with offensive coordinator Red Keane at the conclusion of last off-season for reasons that were unclear until just recently. A conservative man, Mister Clayton believes in conservative football and conservative football coaches, which both Keane and DeVito are, but which Coach has ceased to be. Fed up with the razzledazzle offense and all the blitzing defenses, Clayton dismissed two of Coach's favorite assistants and installed in their places Keane and DeVito, hoping they might temper Coach's wide-open, freewheeling approach. And they might have, had Coach been consulted about the hirings, but he wasn't and so became the immovable object to Clayton's irresistible force, with the new assistants caught in the middle. Keane immediately sided with Clayton, but DeVito wavered, took no position, which was the worst thing he could do...not the brightest of prospects for a fifty-seven-year-old man.

After running a few more starts and working on our stunts for a few minutes the offensive linemen joined us and we ran through plays with them until Coach whistled us up for the team segment. Philadelphia runs a three-man defensive front, so I stepped out of the drill and wandered back by our offensive huddle to watch.

"So how are you feeling?" Wayne sidled over and clapped me on the shoulder.

"Fine," I said. "You?"

"Great, really great."

"The leg all right?"

"Hey," he said, and he flexed his leg and performed a few deep knee bends.

I nodded, watching, relieved.

"You seen him yet?" he asked when he finished.

"Who?" I said.

"The big guy, who else?"

"Willie?"

"No, no. *Their* big guy."

"Only in my dreams," I said.

"He's big," Wayne said. "Holy Christ, I ran a pattern down there—he's bigger than big. I mean, he wins the Ass of the Year

Award hands down. I mean, it's no contest. That big tackle from Chicago—"

"No comparison," I said.

"None."

Searching downfield through the swarm of players, I found 78, Dolchik, leaning into his huddle. The sonofabitch carries three hundred pounds, all in his ass and legs, yet remarkably it is not fat. His haunches are as broad and powerful as a musk ox's.

"Quite a spread on him," I said. "You see him down there?"

"Unbelievable," Wayne replied.

I looked down at my own legs and began to feel slight and wispy, without substance. My legs and arms seemed to be shrinking before my eyes.

"So you're feeling all right?" Wayne asked.

"Fine," I said. "Little tight, though. Stiff. You know. Must be the shit weather."

"Must be," he said.

"Last time we played it was hot. You remember?"

"Hot as hell."

"Second quarter he was done."

"Dolchik?"

"Yeah. They had to pack him in ice afterwards."

"Not today," Wayne said. "He can play all day in this shit. Supposed to get worse, too."

"Don't tell me that."

"It is," he said. "Freezing rain, snow...real Polack weather." Wayne bounced on his toes for a few seconds, like a fighter. "You going with the Jap shoes?" Bouncing, he pointed at my Pro-pels.

"For two-fifty I thought I'd give 'em a shot, yeah."

"Don't know about the Jap shoes," he said. "You gotta be able to dig in today, Brad. I mean, a big Polack like that, he's like a half-track. Slick field won't slow him down a bit."

"So what the hell am I supposed to do? Bring a shovel out here?"

"Get some good shoes. You ever try Converse?"

"You making a pitch?"

"Give 'em a try. I'll get you a couple nice warm-up suits, a travel bag, the works."

I stared at him.

"And some tennis shoes, too. Couple nice pairs of tennis shoes, maybe even a racket—you wanna tennis racket? I'll get you a tennis racket."

"I don't play tennis."

"Yeah? Well after today you might take it up. I mean, look at that big silage-fed son of a bitch..."

Downfield, Dolchik was breaking his huddle. With studied indifference he walked to the line and eased into his stance, strength and power in every movement. At the snap he plowed into the man across from him and, turning him, handling him as if he were a woman, cleared a path for his running back.

I could see Dolchik handling me the same way during the game, with a vengeance. I could see my head snapping back as he hit me, my feet churning and slipping as I tried to fight through his block. He had me now. I could see myself giving ground in an attempt to be rid of him, giving ground but failing, finally going over, backwards, Dolchik's helmet buried in my chest. Dolchik driving me into the ground like a stake...

"Did you know that sonofabitch can stuff a basketball?" Wayne jabbered. "I mean, *stuff it*...two hands behind his back from a standing start. Did you know that?"

"No," I said. I wasn't really listening. Sweat had broken out on my neck and forehead.

"The sonofabitch is a great athlete, Brad, and when guys like us go up against great athletes there's only one thing we can do and that's get into the jar and I mean get into it big. Take a look at me. Do I look worried to you? Do I look like I give a shit about Philadelphia, or Huey Greene, or anything?"

Saliva filled my mouth.

"Hell no," he said, "and that's the difference between you and me right now. You're scared to death and I'm ready to play the game of my life. You're digging yourself a trench and I'm flying those friendly—"

I turned away. Dropping to a knee, I vomited as inconspicuously as possible.

"Jesus Christ," Wayne said.

"I'm all right."

"You sick?"

"No," I said. I stood and wiped my chin with the back of my hand. "I'm all right now."

Soon after, Coach signaled the end of pregame warm-ups. As we jogged off the field Willie Slough emerged from the tunnel, stumbling, juggling his helmet and arm pads, dropping the helmet, picking it up, running a few yards, then dropping the arm pads, bumbling his way out on the field until Coach DeVito could get to him and turn him around and send him back where he came from.

CHAPTER FIVE

The locker room had been cleaned and reorganized in our absence; a space had been cleared in the middle of the room and the folding metal chairs had been arranged there in rows, in two distinct sections, each section facing the slate of a portable two-sided blackboard. Tanner was at the blackboard now, looking over what was written there:

> 12:10 SPECIALISTS
> 12:20 OTHERS
> 12:55 INTRODUCTIONS
> 1:00 WE GO TO WAR!

He erased the first two entries, underscored the last, then wheeled the blackboard off to one side of the room.

Setting my helmet on a back-row chair, I went into the bathroom and washed my face and rinsed my mouth and tried to scrub the upchuck off my uniform. It wouldn't come out. I splashed cologne on my face and emptied a can of Right Guard on the stained portions of my jersey. Then I went back and sat down.

"You got a date or something?" Wayne, sniffing the air, plopped down beside me.

"I—"

"I know," he laughed softly. "Don't worry about it. You need some gum?"

I took two sticks of Juicy Fruit. The room was quiet now. Most of the players were sitting as Wayne was sitting: head down, elbows on knees, feet nervously tapping the concrete. They were waiting now, thinking, going through whatever private rituals necessary to get themselves ready to play. I sat staring at the clock on the far wall, watching as its second hand described continuous circles. In three hours the game would be over. I tried to imagine what this room would be like then, how we would feel. Nothing came.

"Hold it up, men," Tanner said. "Hold it up, please..." As he spoke Coach strode confidently out of his locker room, the assistants following, spreading out in a cordon around the seated players. Moving to the center of the room, Coach reached into the inside pocket of his burgundy blazer and produced a deck of note cards. In his blazer and gray slacks, in his starched white shirt and striped tie, hair fresh-clipped, skin taut and tanned to sunlamp perfection, Coach looked like the chairman of the board of a corporation about to address top management on the challenges of the future. The only concessions to his true profession were the hand-rolled cuffs on his gray slacks, the white sweat socks, and the black ripple-soled shoes he wore in place of his tasseled loafers.

Coach held up the note cards and fanned them like playing cards so that everyone could see them. "Gentlemen," he said, "I've come prepared this afternoon, as you can see. Millie spent two hours typing up these cards and I want you to take a good look at them. Can you see these single-spaced paragraphs, all numbered and lettered so neatly?"

Players nodding.

"Pretty impressive, isn't it."

Players nodding.

"This is an outline, gentlemen. Every number, every letter in this outline represents something we've got to do to win this football game. The staff and I spent a lot of time preparing this outline because we think it's important that when you hit that field you understand precisely what we've got to do to win." He walked over to one side of the room. "But you know something, gentlemen?" He dropped the cards in a trash barrel. "I'm not going to waste your time with it."

We wanted the cards.

"Do you know why?"

Silence.

"Because we *already know* what we've got to do to win. I mean, think about it, men. If we didn't know how to win football games we wouldn't be here, would we?" Coach grinned. "Well, *would we?*"

"NO."

"We wouldn't," he said, moving back to the center of the room. "We already know what we've got to do and we're going to go out there and do it. On offense we're going to move that football, control it, execute. We're going to run wide on them, we're going to get their linebackers pursuing, and when we do—boom—we're going to hit 'em with the counters, the reverses—the misdirection stuff. Now it's wet out there and the ball-handling is going to be difficult. But we don't care about that. When something bad happens we ignore it, we play through it. When something good happens we capitalize. We score. And when we get them down...when we get them down, gentlemen...you'll know what to do, I'm sure. Any questions from you offensive people?"

There were none.

"Okay," Coach said. "Now on defense we've got to do one thing, we've got to stop number thirty-two, Jasmine Jackson. He's a great one, gentlemen, and they're going to get the ball to him any way they can—screens, draws, quick flares, you name it. But what they really want to do is get him running. They get him running and that opens up their precision passing game—the quick slants to the split end, the deep stuff to the flanker, everything we've studied. They get that going and they're a helluva team, men—a *helluva* team. And Jackson's the key to it all. If we can stop him, we've really got us something. If we can't...we're going to, that's all there is to it.

"Now they'll probably have him back there catching punts and kick-offs too, so we're going to kick away from him in those situations. But you special teams men be alert anyway. When Jackson touches that football, he's a threat. He can score from anywhere on the field and no one man can bring him down. So we've got to have everyone covering today, is that clear? *Everyone.*"

Coach left the room for a moment and came back carrying a cup of Gatorade. "We'll introduce our offensive unit," he said quietly, sipping from the cup. "The rest of us will go to our bench and watch the introductions from there. After the introductions we'll line up along our sidelines for the national anthem. The procedure here will be the same as it's been all year. I want you standing at attention, helmets in your left hand, an arm's length between you. As the cameraman pans your faces I want you to sing. If you don't know the words to the song, I want you to sing anyway. I want those lips moving, gentlemen. The nation will be watching." He paused. "Hans?"

"Yes, Coach?"

"I'm talking to you specifically."

Laughter.

"Hold it up, men," Tanner said. "Hold it up, please..."

Coach took another sip of his Gatorade. "Gentlemen," he said, "this football game will be decided by one or two crucial plays. Ironic, isn't it? I mean, we'll be out there for the better part of an afternoon and each team will run off sixty or seventy plays and after all of those plays are run only a few of them will be important. But which few will it be? A short yardage play at mid-field in the first quarter? A fourth quarter punt? A fumble? Tipped pass? We don't know. And I'll tell you something. *We don't care.* Why? Because we're gonna play *every* play with equal intensity. We're not gonna wait. We're not gonna anticipate. We're gonna *go.* And our special teams are gonna set the tempo. If we win the toss, we're going with the wedge-middle return. Everyone got that? Wedge-middle, right up the gut. If we kick-off, we're gonna swarm the bastards, we're gonna gang tackle—we're gonna *make something happen.*" Coach drained his cup and threw it at the trash barrel across the room. "Goddammit, men, this is it." He smiled. "This is our season. Right here. Right now. ARE WE READY?"

"READY."

A moment of silence followed, then the scraping of metal chairs and the rustling of nylon as players stood and made their way toward the exit.

"Have a good one," Wayne said. Yawning, he stood and slapped me on the ass.

"You, too," I said.

Our kick-off coverage team huddled briefly at the 35-yard line, then broke, the players moving back, stringing out along the 30, five yards between each player, five players on either side of Hans Stoufer. Facing the formation, Stoufer counted heads, then turned and bending from the waist, carefully placed the football on the tee. Taking precise steps, he backed up seven yards, sidled two to his left and raised his right hand to signal his readiness. As he did the players tensed in their stances and the spectators stood and filled the stadium with a low, almost musical roar, the beginning of a crescendo that would peak when Stoufer's foot slapped the ball:

"Aaaahhhhh..."

But the official positioned in the far end zone did not acknowledge Stoufer's signal. Instead, he said a few words to the lone Philadelphia safety, then jogged over to the sidelines to speak with a network liaison. The safety, shaking his head, leaned against the padded goal posts, crossed his arms, and gazed up into the crowd.

"Aaaahhhhh..." The crowd still chanting.

"Hans," Coach yelled. "*Hans.*"

Hans turned.

"Single safety, single safety!"

Hans looked downfield, then back at Coach as if for instruction. He hadn't expected a single safety, he'd expected two men deep, the same alignment they'd used all season: on the left, 32, Jasmine Jackson; on the right, 21, Kimberley, a rookie wide receiver. The ball was to have been kicked to the rookie, but now there was no rookie, only Jackson, and Coach gestured emphatically toward the upper deck. Hans nodded. The wind was to his back. He was to kick the ball out of the end zone.

The official moved back into position and blew his whistle. Hans, dropping his arm, approached the football.

A high kick, and short. Drifting upfield to his right, Jackson caught the ball on his six-yard line. He dropped it. The crowd gasped—then cheered as Jackson, finding the handle, scooped up the football and started upfield. "Get him," our players screamed, "GET *HIM*." But Jackson was too slick. Abandoning his wedge at the moment of disintegration, he cut sharply to his right, toward the Philadelphia bench, and no one was there. Enrico Monte, the contain-man on that side, had been drawn in by the fumble, and although it appeared for a moment that he might be able to recapture the flank, as he turned to try he was wiped out by a sprinting 275-pound tackle. Jackson, skirting the tackle's block, rounded the corner, leaped a diving Hans Stoufer, and breezing up the sidelines, pranced into the end zone, unruffled, after a 94-yard jaunt.

"JAS-MINE, JAS-MINE, JAS-MINE." The crowd was chanting as Jackson, fighting off delighted teammates, rifled the football into the stands.

The conversion was good.

Elapsed time: 23 seconds.

Score: Philadelphia 7, Washington 0.

CHAPTER SIX

The referee straddled the football at the 47-yard line.

"We going?" asked Frank Regis, our middle linebacker.

"We're going," said the official; and making a motion like a truck driver yanking the cord on his air horn, he blew his whistle and moved out of the way.

Our offense had done nothing with their first possession. Backed up by a good kick and excellent coverage, they had run three innocuous running plays and then punted, Jackson calling for, and making, a fair catch at the Philadelphia 47. "Stop 'em here," Coach had said before we came out on the field. "We get fourteen down…"

We huddled at the 47. "Philly special," said Regis, and with a sharp clap we broke the huddle and spilled out to our respective positions. Leaving the huddle, I ran vigorously in place for a few seconds, shook out my arms, then whacked myself in the helmet. I felt listless, and sleepy. Scared.

"Come *on*, Brad." Wayne's voice rising above the din. "Let's go, defense."

I looked over at our bench. Our players had spread out along the sidelines, all of them yelling and shouting encouragement. I nodded to Wayne.

"Let's go," he called, raising a clenched fist.

I nodded.

Then the Philadelphia huddle broke and here came Dolchik, jogging to the line of scrimmage, settling into his stance, head down, weight evenly distributed through his legs and arms. Lining up on his outside shoulder, a slight cant to my stance, my legs trembling, I fixed my eyes on Dolchik's helmet, the top and front of which were scraped and scarred, the green paint pounded away.

"*Set*," called the quarterback, looking over our defense. And then he crouched under the center.

My eyes were fixed to Dolchik's helmet because his helmet, his head, would be the first part of his body to move when the ball was snapped, and my reactions were geared to that movement. If his head moved toward me, I would adjust my charge to the outside to prevent his hook block. If his head moved away from me I would slide quickly to the inside to jam the trap or to pursue whatever play happened to be run. If his head moved up, the play was a pass and I would grab him and pull myself upfield as fast as I could.

"Hut," called their quarterback.

But these possibilities, tumbling like dice through my mind, were suddenly supplanted by a more certain bit of information. Contrary to Coach DeVito's instructions, I remembered from our past games that the Philadelphia quarterback had neither the confidence in himself nor his teammates to alter the snap count. Fearing unnecessary penalties, he started nearly every play on the second "hut," changing only during the two minute periods and then always going on the first sound to save time.

Remembering this, I tensed in my stance and listened, and on the next sound leapt across the line of scrimmage. The gamble paid off. Slamming into Dolchik before he could generate any momentum, I quickly shed his block and looked for the football. Jackson had it. He'd been lined up directly behind Dolchik but now he was slanting for an inside hole. I took off after him, scrambling down the line of scrimmage, now diving, my left forearm catching him in the shins, tripping him but not bringing him down, Jackson stumbling forward for five yards before being nailed by Frank Regis.

I got up shaking my left arm, which had gone numb from the blow. Jackson had stumbled forward for five, but if I hadn't tripped him it might have been more—I'd made a good play. Now it was second and five. The staff's breakdown of the Philadelphia offense indicated an equal run-pass tendency in this situation, but with a high incidence of deceptive plays: screens and draws. "Second and five's a dealer's choice," DeVito had said, "and we don't want no dealer's choices. We want to play *our* game, not their's, and to do that *we've got to stop them on the first down.*"

But we hadn't and now the Philadelphia offense was spreading out over the field and Dolchik was settling once more in his stance. Positioning myself on his outside shoulder I again fixed my eyes to his battered helmet. As the quarterback set the team and started his cadence Dolchik began to lean forward in his stance, imperceptibly at first, but then as the quarterback drew nearer the snap count, pronouncedly, his right arm quavering, his knuckles turning white under his weight. *Run,* I thought, and widened my stance, braced for a blow. But it was not a run. At the snap Dolchik fired into me, but quickly recoiled—a bang-block, play-action pass. Recovering, I moved upfield and shot a left jab at Dolchik's chest. I'd intended to follow the left with a roundhouse right to his shoulder but my left hand, palm down, had struck the breastplate of Dolchik's pads and slid into his face, and my index finger had snagged in a nostril. Instinctively Dolchik grabbed my arm and with an angry grunt wrenched my hand from his face. Blood spurted from his nose—then gushed. The sight stunned both of us. We stood frozen for a moment, wondering what the hell had happened. Then I looked down at my hand. Impacted beneath the unclipped fingernail of my left index finger was a ragged hunk of bloody tissue.

"You sonofabitch," Dolchik was screaming, blood spewing. "You rotten sonofabitch..." He was pointing at me. Vengeance was in his eyes.

"It was an accident."

Dolchik snorted a bloody mist.

"It was an accident. I'm sorry."

Dolchik snorted again. His eyes had watered, blood was sluicing from his nose. "I'm gonna get you, you sonofabitch." He pulled his jersey out of his pants, stuffed fabric into his nostril and retreated to his huddle. The pass had been incomplete.

I immediately went to the umpire whose job was to watch the action along the line of scrimmage and to flag infractions—though it was to his credit that he didn't flag every play.

"Excuse me," I said, taking his arm, "but will you watch number seventy-eight for me? He's holding."

"What?" The umpire was a small, wiry man with dark hair and hard eyes.

"Seventy-eight," I said. "He's holding me."

"You guys settle down," he said. "We've only had two plays, for Christ's sake."

"I know, but he's like a goddamn octopus—will you watch him for me, please?"

"Okay, okay."

A moment later the Philadelphia huddle broke and Dolchik walked to the line of scrimmage, a sopping crimson stain across his belly. As he settled into his stance blood trickled from his nose to his face mask, then fell in large coagulating drops to the artificial turf. I could smell it.

All at once the outside linebacker whacked me on the butt and over the cadence of the quarterback called, "Bullet!" Widening, I shifted my attention to Jasmine Jackson, who again was lined up directly behind Dolchik. I couldn't be blocked by Jackson— the linebacker was going to fill inside and his responsibility, containment, had fallen to me.

At the snap I shot upfield, then quickly pulled up as Jackson sidled to the inside. "Draw," someone yelled, and immediately I looked for Dolchik. He made a move toward me, but then, suddenly confused, he wheeled and lunged for the blitzing linebacker. I was free. Knifing inside, I smacked Jackson just as he took the delayed hand-off and dropped him for a four-yard loss, the significance of which I didn't fully realize until my teammates, shouting and banging my helmet, dragged me to my feet—we had held.

"Great job, defense. *Great job.*" Coach was hollering as we trotted off the field.

Accepting congratulations, I shouldered my way through the sideline players and sat down on the bench. I felt good. I had been afraid, but now the adrenaline had taken hold and my fear had dropped away and I was seeing everything with a clarity I hadn't known in a long time. Every detail of this spectacle—the colors, the faces, everything—seemed unnaturally clear and precise, as if time and motion had stopped.

A waterboy stooped in front of me; he was carrying a concessionaire's tray loaded with cups of ice water and strawberry-flavored Gatorade. The Gatorade, as Tony mixes it, is much too strong to take by itself; it laminates your teeth, gums and tongue with a sweet, pink film, and if you drink enough of it you'll taste it for days. Thinking of a postgame steak, I took a cup of each liquid, mixed a half-and-half solution, and rinsed out my mouth.

"You need anything else?" the boy asked. "Wet towel or anything?"

I shook my head, no. As the boy moved on to the next player, Jeff Blair, our right defensive tackle, sat down beside me. "We're moving the ball," he said, indicating the field. "On the ground, too. That wide shit's beginning to work."

"Good," I said. Our view of the field was obstructed by our teammates, but the Philadelphia crowd was quiet, an indication that things were going well for us. "We could use a good drive here," I said. "Maybe get a score, at least turn the field position around..."

Blair nodded. "You made a great play on that draw, Brad. I mean, a great goddamn play. Did you hear me screaming?"

"That you?"

"Yeah. The guard set short, you know, and quick—too quick. I mean, I saw the play right away...and screamed—you heard me, didn't you? I screamed as loud as I could."

"You been in the jar, Jeff?"

"Me?" He smiled. After talking tendencies and technique for a few minutes he left me to see what was happening on the field.

I looked up at the scoreboard. Second and one at the 42; we *were* moving the ball. Time remaining? I didn't know. I had purposely avoided looking at the scoreboard clock. (As a rookie I'd had a recurring dream in which I was playing in my first professional football game. Sometime during the fourth quarter Coach called me to his side and told me to go in for Andros on the next play. "Yes, sir," I said, but I didn't want to go into the game. I wanted to leave. I wanted to walk into the locker room, get dressed and go home. I was scared and sick and when I looked up at the clock to see how long my ordeal would last, it stopped. Forever.)

On the field Rutledge had asked for a measurement. As the referee called for the chain crew, our offensive coordinator Red Keane took off his head phones, left the other coaches and walked back to the offensive bench. On the far end of the bench, as if in a pout, sat a single solemn player. Keane knelt and began to talk to him. I couldn't tell who the player was, only that he was angry and unresponsive. After a few minutes, Keane stood and motioned to Needles, who wandered over and began to examine the player. "Get up," he said to him, and when the player did, Needles lifted his left leg and set his heel on a nearby utility table. Through the pants I could see a wrap around his thigh, the wrap tight, the flesh squeezed out on either end, the folds of flesh destroying the fluid lines of the game uniform. "Bend forward," Needles said, and when the player bent forward Needles pushed down on the man's back until his head touched his knee. "Okay," Needles said, and the player pulled his leg from the table. They spoke quietly for a moment, the three of them, then as Needles and Keane headed back for the sidelines the player slipped behind the bench and after half-heartedly performing a series of stretching exercises, jogged sullenly toward me.

"Wayne," I said.

He jogged by as if he hadn't heard. Apparently following the doctor's orders, he jogged down to the end zone, turned around and jogged back.

"*Wayne,*" I said as he passed.

Nothing.

The Philadelphia crowd had come to life. I couldn't see what was happening on the field, so I picked up my helmet and joined Blair on the sidelines. The scoreboard indicated a third and one from the 19, and I was amazed to see that we had the ball on the Philadelphia 19 and not our own.

"How did we get down there?" I asked Jeff.

"Y reverse," he said. "You didn't see it?"

"No, I—"

"Great goddamn play."

On the field Rutledge had set the team and was calling his cadence.

"Gotta have the first, Brad. Right here. Gotta have it. Come on, baby. Come—"

"*Hut.*" Rutledge took the snap, and pivoting, handed the football to our left halfback who slammed off-tackle and slithered ahead for the necessary yardage.

"All *right,*" Blair called out. "Drive it down their goddamn throats. Drive it down—shit..."

The play had been flagged. We watched as the referee conferred with the umpire, then turned to talk to the Philadelphia captain.

"Fuck," Blair said as the captain nodded affirmatively. "Fuck a goddamn duck."

The referee, having moved away from the football, looked up at the pressbox and grabbed his left wrist with his right hand. Holding. He took a lateral step with his left leg and pointed at our huddle.

"Dumb-ass offensive linemen," Blair muttered. "That was a running play, for Christ's sake..."

A swing pass to the fullback netted six yards, and it was fourth and four from the 23. Coach called for the field goal unit. Kneeling at the 30—it would be a 40-yard attempt—the holder marked a spot on the artificial turf. Stoufer, staring at the spot, backed up his customary three yards, shuffled two to his left and nodded his readiness. The holder turned and extended his hands to receive the snap. It was perfect, as was the hold, but Stoufer hooked the ball, drove it low and wide and to the left of the goal posts, the crowd roaring its approval as the football skidded through the end zone and into the Philadelphia tunnel.

Above the tunnel a fan dressed in a green leprechaun suit leaped up on a railing and began to exhort the cheap-seat spectators. Somehow he was able to focus their random cheers into a thunderous chant that quickly spread throughout the stadium: "FIVE! FIVE! FIVE! FIVE!" Louder and louder it came, and with this display of solidarity the crowd became a factor in the football game.

Earlier they had greeted our good plays with silence and our failures with applause, which had had no effect on us. Now they had an effect, or so it must have seemed to the crowd: as their chant thundered down on us Stoufer dropped to his knees and pounded the turf, one of our coaches tossed a sheaf of papers into the wind and the rest of our team appeared confused and dismayed. The crowd drew strength from our response. As the first half progressed their silences became stark, their cheers raucous and deafening, and we fell apart. It was as though we had decided to appease the crowd rather than to play the game, and during the next sixteen minutes that's exactly what we did, in the only way we could—by making mistakes.

On the next series we stopped Philadelphia on three downs but a fumbled punt led to an easy touchdown and the first quarter ended with the score 14–0, Philadelphia. We returned the following kick-off to our 39-yard line. Staying on the ground, we were able to penetrate Philadelphia territory, but again the drive was stopped by a holding penalty, only this time the penalty took us out of field goal range and we were forced to punt. Deflated by our offensive impotence, our defensive unit then yielded its first sustained drive of the afternoon, Philadelphia moving 80 yards in 12 plays to score their third touchdown with just under two minutes left in the first half.

As if sated by the glut of scoring, the crowd then settled down; many of the people left their seats to go for beer or to the bathroom. Those that stayed seemed distracted, as if the game were about to end and they were all talking about where they should go to celebrate the victory.

Running the wedge-middle return, we brought the kick-off out to midfield, our offense huddling at the 40, Rutledge peering over the huddle at the defensive alignment. Philadelphia had inserted their "pre-vent" personnel—three rushmen, two linebackers, six defensive backs. Rutledge knew that the men in the secondary would line up deep and at the snap would drop even deeper, to "pre-vent" an easy touchdown. He also knew that the "pre-vent" defense would not prevent him from moving the football as long as he stayed on the ground and didn't get impatient. He didn't. It was a textbook two-minute drive. Mixing his plays effectively, using his time-outs judiciously, he marched the club down the field, scoring at the gun on a perfectly executed screen pass.

We were not elated. We were still behind by fourteen.

CHAPTER SEVEN

Wayne had followed Red Keane into the bathroom. They had been there for some time, talking quietly. I was standing in front of a long wooden table looking over the refreshments that had been laid out there: the cans of soft drinks, the quartered oranges, the gum, the Gatorade. The table had been set up just outside the bathroom and I'd seen them going in. As I picked up a section of orange, Wayne's voice shattered the calm.

"Goddammit, *I can play*," he said, and the words echoed off the tiled walls of the bathroom.

"Look—"

"I don't *give a damn* about that! I've got *six months* to heal! If I pop the goddamn hamstring—"

"Take it easy, will you?" Keane was standing in front of a urinal.

"I'm telling you my leg's *all right*." Wayne's back was toward me, he was still wearing his helmet.

"I understand that," Keane said.

"I'm telling you—"

"I under*stand* what you're telling me," Keane said. His head was thrown back and he was staring at the ceiling as he pissed.

"So put me back in the game," Wayne demanded.

Keane shook himself and zipped his pants. "We've got a doctor who decides these things," he said. "It's not up to me." He flushed the urinal. "I'm sorry," but as he turned to leave Wayne stepped in front of him.

"Put me back in the goddamn game. You can't—"

"Talk to the *doctor*." Keane stepped around Wayne, walked out of the bathroom and into the coaches' quarters, slamming the door behind him.

When Wayne came out I tried to stop him and calm him down but he brushed by me saying he had to find Needles. I let him go, turned back to the table, picked up another section of orange and wandered into the locker room.

The room was quiet, as it should have been; it was half-time and we were down 21–7. Sucking at the orange, I sat down with the rest of the defensive players, most of whom were staring at the blackboard. Diagrammed on the board, which had been stationed once more in the center of the room, were the first-half plays we hadn't been able to contain. Before the coaching staff had retreated to their quarters they had drawn up the plays and made some adjustments in our defenses, and those adjustments were what the players were trying to absorb. Most of them were, anyway.

Across the room Willie Slough had positioned a paper cup under a jug of Gatorade. Carefully he pressed the valve on the jug, curiously he watched as the red liquid shot forth. When the cup was filled Willie released the valve and raised the drink to his lips. But suddenly he went stiff; his eyes went wide, his jaw slack. The valve on the jug had broken and red liquid was pouring from the spout, shooting out, soaking his socks and his shoes and splattering the floor. Willie panicked. Calling for help, he set the full cup down and picked up an empty one. Filling that, he reached for another, then another, then another one after that, Gatorade splashing the floor all the while. By the time Tony came over to see what was happening, Willie was standing in a pool of Gatorade, filling still another cup.

"My God," Tony said, and shoving Willie aside, tilted the jug on its back and stopped the flow.

"You got any more shoes?" Willie asked.

75

An official stuck his head inside the double steel doors and flashed his hand at Phil Tanner. "Five minutes," he said. Tanner nodded. As the official left, Tanner walked over to the blackboard and wheeled it out of the way. A moment later Coach emerged from his locker room, assistants following, spreading out around the seated players as before. The room became silent.

"Everyone here?" Coach said.

"Everyone's here," Tanner told him.

Coach, shaking his head, began to pace the floor. "I don't know what to say, men. I guess...I guess I'm just embarrassed for us." He spoke softly. "We've had a tremendous season until now and I've been proud of you. We've worked hard, we've played hard, and we've won a lot of football games. But now I don't know. I'm not so proud now." He stopped pacing and faced the team; his eyes were actually moist. "Gentlemen, we went out on that field today and in the biggest game we've ever been in played the worst half of football we've ever played. We embarrassed ourselves, gentlemen. We embarrassed ourselves, our families, our friends, our fans—I want to know why. I want to know what's happened to us. Where's our pride? Our poise? Our self-respect? Can anyone tell me?"

Silence.

"What is it, men? I mean, is it *our* fault?" He motioned to the staff. "Have we taught you to play like this? Like a bunch of goddamn kiddie-leaguers? Have we failed you as coaches? Is that it?"

Silence.

"Or have you failed yourselves as ballplayers. As professionals. Think about it, men. Think about the fumbles and the penalties, the missed tackles. Have you played your very best today? Ask yourselves. Have you given this game *everything you've got?* If the answer is no, then you'd better make that commitment *now,* before it's too late. This is a good life, gentlemen, a privileged life, but like everything else it has its price. Some of you aren't paying that price."

Coach left the room.

When we took the field for the second half we were a different ball club; we had been shamed and now we were angry—at Philadelphia for humiliating us, at ourselves for letting it happen. But something else had taken place as well. As we filed down the tunnel to the field, word had spread that Wayne Law would be reinserted in the lineup. Wayne was an important player for us and he hadn't been able to play, but now he was and the whole team seemed to take some new confidence from that. Suddenly we were bound for redemption—and on our first possession of the second half we struck a blow. Following another excellent kick-off return, and with Wayne making three crucial third-down receptions, we drove 63 yards in nine plays to score our second touchdown with 7:48 remaining in the third quarter.

Pumping hands and clapping backs, Coach greeted the offensive players as they came off the field. Then, as the kick-off coverage team deployed, he thrust his hands in his pockets and began to pace. "We need a break now," he muttered, glancing up at the scoreboard, "we need a goddamn *break...*"

Stoufer, dropping his arm, approached the football and whacked another high, short kick that Jackson fielded against the far sidelines near the ten yard marker. He dropped it. It appeared to be an intentional fumble, an attempt to duplicate his previous return, but this time Enrico Monte wasn't fooled. Maintaining leverage as he slipped his blocker, Monte collared Jackson just as he was picking up the football and hurled him out of bounds at the nine. Three plays lost four yards and Philadelphia was faced with a fourth and fourteen from the five. Coach called for a punt block middle—a ten-man rush. As the punter, waiting for the snap, stood fidgeting near his own end line, our players darted back and forth across the line of scrimmage to confuse the coverage men, to draw one of them offsides. They held firm in their stances and calmly pointed out to one another whom they were going to block. Then, all at once, our men shifted. Yelling, pointing, the coverage men tried to solve the shift, but in the confusion the ball was snapped and our men surged for the punter, two of them— Blair from the inside, Monte from the outside—breaking clear of the blocking. Caught in a double bind, the deep back blocked Blair and Monte was free.

Sprinting for a spot five yards in front of the punter, for the spot where, under normal circumstances, the punter's foot would smack the ball, Monte coiled and lunged, twisting as he did, extending his arms, throwing as much of his body as he could into the projected path of the football. Except these weren't normal circumstances. The punter had sensed the danger, took only one quick step before he kicked and Monte went sailing by, missing the block by a good three yards. Disgusted with himself for having blown the play, Monte got up kicking and thrashing, but Jeff Blair was quickly at his side and to show Monte what he *had* done, Blair spun him around and pointed downfield. At the Philadelphia 27 an official stood toeing the spot where the hurried punt had squibbed out of bounds.

It was the break we needed. With the good field position, our offense bounded onto the pitch and five plays later tied the game, the score coming on a Rutledge pass, a ten-yard quick-out to Wayne Law. The third quarter ended then and it started to rain, but the changes in direction and weather did nothing to dampen our momentum. On the next series we stopped Philadelphia on three downs, then staying on the ground, taking no unnecessary risks, we moved downfield to the Philadelphia 32. There the drive faltered, but Hans Stoufer came on and calmly drilled a 48-yard field goal, which, with 9:27 left to play, gave us the lead for the first time. The score: Washington 24, Philadelphia 21.

The referee straddled the football at the Philadelphia 25-yard line. It was raining and the ball had been draped with a clean white towel to keep it dry.

"We going?" asked Frank Regis, our middle linebacker.

"We're not," said the referee. "We have a television time-out."

Pulling an index card from his hip pocket, the referee walked over and joined the other officials, who were standing nearby examining their own cards, apparently discussing what was written there: the infractions that had been called, the names of the offenders, the number of time-outs remaining, the names of the players who could call those time-outs. The cards were wrinkled, the ink smeared from the damp.

"Listen up,"said Regis, stepping into the huddle. "You guys see that?" He jerked his thumb at the scoreboard. "We're up three," he said. "They don't score, they don't win—it's as simple as that. Everyone understand?"

Players nodded.

"Then let's get 'em in here," he said. We made a pile of our hands and broke the huddle.

The referee marked the ball for play. Philadelphia broke their huddle, and at a dead trot here came Dolchik, shoes squishing, pads clattering, face blank as a fresh-plastered wall.

"Hello in there," I said.

Nothing. Dolchik settled into his stance. He had me worried.

I had played a good game against Dolchik—nothing spectacular, just a good, solid football game—but I'd gotten no confirmation from him, no "nice rush" or "good hit," none of the usual compliments exchanged by opposing players. In fact Dolchik had said nothing to me since the incident in the first quarter. He had not acknowledged my repeated apologies, nor retaliated, something I thought he would have done by now. Had he seen me talking to the umpire, complaining about his "holding"? If he had, if he'd been watching me between plays he surely would have noticed that the umpire had quickly gotten tired of my complaints and had refused (rather demonstratively) to discuss the matter with me any further. All of that had happened in the second quarter and now it was the fourth and still Dolchik had done nothing. What was he waiting for? Had he forgotten the incident? Not very damn likely...his jersey was smeared with blood, his nose was packed with cotton...so what the hell was he waiting for?

The tight end had lined up in the backfield. As the quarterback barked his signals the tight end shifted to the line of scrimmage and dropped down next to Dolchik. He was lined up too tight for a pass—foot-to-foot—and out of the corner of my eye I could see him sizing me up. Anticipating a run, a down-block, I moved back off the ball and widened my stance. At the snap I took a lateral step with my right foot and slammed my forearm into the tight end's chest. As I did Dolchik pulled behind his block, to the outside. Beyond Dolchik I could see Jackson, who had been lined up behind the opposite tackle, taking the hand-off, swinging wide and in my direction. I held my ground until Jackson crossed my face, then, controlling the tight end, I worked laterally down the line of scrimmage. When the linebacker, who had been working Dolchik's outside shoulder, shot upfield to force the play, Jackson cut back to the inside, right into me, and I wrestled him down at the 27. A two-yard gain.

The next play was an incompleted pass. Now it was third and eight from the 27, a crucial down. If we could stop Philadelphia here, then any kind of drive by our offense would wrap up the game and send us to the play-offs. A fact not lost on our coaches, who before we could even huddle started hollering instructions from the sidelines. Frank Regis, unable to hear over the roar of the crowd, ran over to see what they wanted.

"Watch the bullshit," he said on his return. "Coach says *watch the bullshit.* Jeff, you're supposed to hold for screens and draws. The rest of you guys can take off, but for Christ's sake *be alert.*"

Dolchik was in his stance now, and I couldn't believe what I was seeing. A huge gap separated him from the right guard...he was nearly a yard off the ball. A *yard.* Talk about bullshit, the sonofabitch was in the backfield. I glanced over at the line judge to see if he'd noticed. He hadn't. As there was still plenty of time before the snap—the quarterback had yet to move under the center—I stood and gestured at the official.

"Look at this," I shouted, pointing at Dolchik. "He's in the goddamn backfield."

The line judge shrugged.

"Look at this!" I shouted. *"That's a goddamn penalty!"*

The line judge shrugged.

"Blue, forty-eight!" the quarterback called out, and as he crouched under the center I dropped back in my stance.

Still, I could not get over Dolchik. It was an obvious passing down, but there was no reason for him to be so far off the ball—

he'd never had any trouble getting back to protect and he'd never tipped a play in his life. And the split—an offensive lineman *never* takes this kind of split. Unless the play is a run. A run? On third and eight? Couldn't be. Not in this situation. *They've got to throw.*

At the snap Dolchik took a drop-step with his outside leg as if setting for a pass. Charging upfield, I reached for the shredded jersey sleeve that hung off his left shoulder, a fistful of which, with a mighty pull, would launch me toward the quarterback. It vanished. The sleeve, the arm, Dolchik himself. I pulled up, confused. Jasmine Jackson, who had been positioned directly behind Dolchik, was now squaring up in front of me as if *he* were going to do the blocking. A scat-back pass-blocking a defensive end? What kind of play was this? I shot a glance at the quarterback, and when I saw him backing away from the center and looking downfield, I got excited; the play *was* a pass, Jackson couldn't block me—I was gonna sack this bastard...

But Jackson had no intention of blocking me. As I bore down on him he pivoted away and bolted across the backfield. As he passed, the quarterback, still looking downfield, had cocked his arm as if to throw. Jackson snatched the ball from his hand and sprinted for the corner. I was right on his ass. The play was forced quickly from the outside and Jackson, cutting back, was skewered by the strongside linebacker. It was a vicious tackle. Head buried in Jackson's stomach, arms wrapped around his thighs, the linebacker raised up and dropped Jackson on his head. The ball popped loose. "FUMBLE," players screamed as it dribbled crazily toward our sidelines. "*FUMBLE.*" I'd come hard in pursuit and now, hurdling Jackson and the linebacker, I began to stalk the tumbling football. I was alone, I could sense it. In the background I could see our sideline players yelling and pointing and jumping up and down—*concentrate,* I told myself, get the high-hop and—

Suddenly an official materialized from the periphery and blocked my path to the ball. It was the head linesman. I didn't know what he was doing. I swept him aside with my left arm and scooping up the football, started up the sidelines for the end zone. A whistle blasted, then another—then a whole chorus of them. What the hell...? I pulled up, stopped and turned around. Our bench was in a frenzy. Our players and coaches were shouting and pointing at the head linesman, the head linesman was shouting and pointing at me, a yellow penalty flag was drifting across my face.

"What the hell's going on here!" I was screaming.

The referee had called the penalty. "You punched the head linesman," he said as he walked over to pick up his flag. "You're lucky to be in the ball game."

"*YOU* CALLED THE PENALTY? FOR—*WHAT?*" I lunged for the referee but was restrained by my teammates. "ARE YOU BLIND? THE LINESMAN WAS STANDING ON THE GOD-DAMN FOOTBALL."

The referee picked up his flag and stuffed it in his back pocket. "The ball was blown dead when Jackson hit the ground," he said calmly. "There was no fumble." Then he turned and trotted to midfield. He was a large man, strong-legged, his movements were crisp and athletic. He faced the pressbox and raised his arms perpendicular to his body.

"Tell the world," I shouted.

The referee did exactly that. He was wired with a transistorized microphone that broadcast his explanations through the stadium's public-address system and across the nationwide television hook-up.

"UNSPORTSMANLIKE CONDUCT," he boomed out. "ON WASHINGTON. NUMBER SIXTY-EIGHT." Then he stepped off fifteen yards, placed the football on the 42-yard line and signaled a Philadelphia first down. When he finished I was in his face, arguing with him, beefing like Billy Martin with an umpire.

"*B.*" Willie Slough grabbed my arm and pulled me away. "I got ya, B—take a blow." He pushed me toward the sidelines.

"But—"

"I got ya til ya calm down. Coach DeVito says."

The referee had marked the ball for play. I left the field, slowly.

By the time I got to the sidelines Philadelphia had broken their huddle and deployed and the Philadelphia quarterback was sliding under the center. Ignoring the turmoil around me—players and coaches were still demanding explanations of the head lines-man—I watched as the quarterback, with an emphatic jerk of his

82

head, called, "Set." As the offensive linemen dropped into their stances Frank Regis, pointing at the quarterback, turned to the umpire.

"He can't do that!" Regis screamed over the roar of the crowd. "He can't move his head while he's calling cadence!"

"*Hut.*" The quarterback called it with the same emphatic shrug— and Willie Slough lurched into the neutral zone.

"That's a goddamn procedure penalty," wailed Jeff Blair, unaware of Willie as he stood to join the protest. "He can't—"

"*Hut,*" called the quarterback, and taking the snap, pivoted and handed the football to his short-haul fullback, who before our players knew what was happening had slammed off-tackle and exploded into the secondary, the beginnings of an uncontested 58-yard touchdown run—by far the longest and easiest touchdown run of that fullback's career.

When the play was over yellow penalty flags littered the playing field. But they were not for the procedure penalty our players had demanded.

"OFFSIDES, DEFENSE," the referee announced following a meeting of the officials. "The touchdown," he said, "will stand."

CHAPTER | EIGHT

The rain fell harder now. Water trickled off my face mask and ran in rivulets down my rain cape; the cape absorbed the water like a cheap tent. Beneath the cape my saturated uniform was as heavy as chain mail and my legs had begun to ache from carrying the extra weight. Shivering, I watched as our offense huddled at the Philadelphia 10-yard line. They had driven 76 yards through the splash and spray, from our 20 to the Philadelphia four, and the drive had taken a full eight minutes. I didn't much care. I'd gotten cold and stiff from standing on the sidelines and didn't want to go back in the game. I was tired, I didn't want to face Dolchik again. I looked up at the scoreboard. Though down 28–24, we were threatening, but only 11 seconds remained on the scoreboard clock and the clock was moving. This would be the final play.

"DEE-FENSE! DEE-FENSE!" The crowd chanted as with a sharp, wet clap our offense broke their huddle.

Seven seconds, six seconds...

We could win, I knew, but fatigue had dulled the edge of anticipation I might otherwise have felt.

Five seconds...

Fatigue, and a vague sense of foreboding.

84

"DEE-FENSE."

Rutledge crouched under the center.

Three seconds...

"*Set,*" he called out, taking the snap, and the two teams sprang to action.

As Rutledge, dropping three quick steps, cocked his arm for rapid fire, Wayne Law drove off the line of scrimmage for Philly's left corner, Huey Greene. Greene backpedaled, feet churning like pistons. Three yards deep in the end zone Wayne feinted right and broke crisply for the goal posts, and Huey Greene slipped down. "Now," players screamed, "*throw* it." Rutledge hesitated. "*Throw it.*" And he did, he lofted a fluttering, butterfly-pass toward Wayne, who, climbing into the air, snagged the wobbling football with his outstretched right hand.

"TOUCHDOWN. TOUCH—"

The field judge, signaling that Wayne was beyond the end line when he made the reception, nullified the play.

"WHAT?" Coach was outraged. "WHAT THE GODDAMN—?" He charged out on the field, ranting and screaming for the referee. As he reached him, the line judge ended the game by firing a blank cartridge from a starter's pistol, and both the gunshot and Coach's arguments were absorbed in the swollen roar of the Philadelphia crowd.

Players spilled and sloshed into the locker room like so many keelhauled sailors; water-logged uniforms were deposited in laundry baskets, bloated kangaroo-skin football shoes were tossed into trash barrels. While Jan Rutledge, red-eyed and crying, sat down in front of his locker and buried his face in a clean white towel, Wayne Law picked up a section of orange and wandered into the equipment room. Coach and Phil Tanner were waiting inside. They talked quietly for a while, Wayne and Coach, while Tanner stood nearby mechanically slapping his thigh with a rolled-up game program. Then Coach nodded to Tanner and Tanner waddled into the locker room.

"Hold it up, men," he said. "Hold it up, please. Coach has a few words..."

Coach, his hands clasped behind his back, his squishing shoes leaving ripple-soled prints on the concrete floor, walked the length of the room without speaking. Heeling smartly in front of my locker, he retraced his steps to the center of the room, there stopped and braced himself on the corner of a laundry basket. He shook his head slowly.

"I'm proud of you, gentlemen," he said. "I'm proud of every man-jack of you. I'm proud of the way you played, I'm proud of the way you fought and clawed and came back when it would have been so easy to quit. I remember what Bobby Layne used to say. Do any of you remember Bobby Layne?"

Coach straightened up as the older players nodded.

"Bobby Layne used to say that he never lost a football game. Can you imagine that? The man played on one of the worst football teams of all time and he had the *audacity* to say that he *never lost a game.* And he didn't. He only ran out of time.

"Gentlemen, *we* did not run out of time. Space, gentlemen, that was our problem: the field was too goddamn short. Jan hesitated on his throw when he saw Greene slip and the ball got to Wayne a little bit late. Wayne made a circus catch, but he...where are you, Wayne?"

Wayne raised his hand; he was leaning against the wall next to the equipment-room door.

"Were you out, Wayne?" Coach asked.

"I was," he answered. "It was a good call by the official."

"The only one," Coach muttered. "Men, we should never have been in that position in the first place, trying to play catch-up in the final seconds of the game. No," he said. "In my opinion the play that killed us came nine minutes earlier...."

Across the room Rutledge lifted his head and rubbed his eyes with the towel. He breathed deeply and seemed relieved but puzzled, as though he could not quite believe that the responsibility for the loss had been so easily shifted. He gave me a sympathetic glance, then began to undress.

"I've never seen anything like it, men. Not in twenty years of professional football." Coach was pacing now. "First of all, Jackson fumbled. I saw it, we all saw it. It was our football. But no. The referee claimed he had blown the ball dead. So what. It's fourth down, they have to punt and we get the ball back anyway. But then the son of a bitch calls Rafferty here for slugging the head linesman. Now if Rafferty had slugged the head linesman, he'd've been immediately ejected, probably suspended and certainly fined. Brad, were you ejected? Anything?

"No."

"What's his name, Phil? Gimme the name of the referee."

Tanner rifled his frayed game program.

"Whoever he is—"

"Farrell," Tanner blurted. "No...referee, uh..."

"Whoever—"

"Pasco, Coach. His name's Al Pasco. It says here he's a lawyer from Levittown, Pennsylvania."

"Yes, well, the son of a bitch has a peculiar sense of justice, doesn't he. I say this to all of you. Al Pasco will never officiate another one of our games and this one will be protested. *Protested,* Phil. Do you understand? I want you on it first thing tomorrow morning."

"Excuse me, Coach," Tanner put in, "but the supervisor of officials was here today and he's already stated that a judgment call can't *be* protested..."

Coach glowered at him.

"I'm sorry, Coach, but that's what he said."

"Then find out what *can* be done, Phil. Goddammit. We've got a responsibility to these guys and we can't just...I mean, we played too goddamn hard to..." Coach sighed. "Rest assured, gentlemen, that something will be done. And *soon,* I promise you. Now let's spend some time with the man upstairs."

Coach leaned against the laundry basket and closed his eyes; players slid off their folding metal chairs and knelt on the floor. The prayer was silent and lasted for thirty seconds.

"One more thing before we go," Coach said. "We haven't talked much about this because quite frankly we thought we could control our own destiny. But Phil tells me Dallas lost today. Now what that means, I think, is that if New York can beat Los Angeles tomorrow night, then we're in this thing—maybe—as a wildcard. Who'll we play, Phil? New Orleans?"

Tanner nodded.

"Now I know it's a long shot, but if it should come off, I want you back for practice Tuesday morning. We'll watch a little film, get loosened up, the usual. If New York loses, I...well, I guess that's it. But we had a fine season and no matter what happens from here on out they can't take that away from us." Coach smiled a sick smile. "Okay, Phil," he said. "Bring on the press."

As Coach disappeared into the staff locker room I reached up on the facing of my locker and tore off the strip of tape that bore my number. I was not particularly excited about rehashing this one with the press and without the identifying label on my locker they would have trouble finding me.

"It's not as bad as you think, Brad," Tanner said, pausing on his way out the door. "The supervisor of officials has at least admitted you didn't slug the head linesman."

I mashed the tape into a ball and dropped it in a garbage can.

"Brushing, he's saying now. You were guilty of brushing an official."

"Brushing? What?"

"You won't get fined or anything."

"Brushing an official?"

"It's all taken care of," Tanner said. And before I could ask him what was taken care of and where in the rule book one found an infraction called "brushing an official," he walked out the door and down the hall, where, behind a police barricade, the reporters were impatiently waiting to be taken to the locker room for their interviews.

Brushing an official?

I rummaged in the garbage can for the balled-up tape, found it, smoothed it out and fixed it once more to the facing of my locker. Then I undressed and took a quick shower. When I got back they were waiting for me, six or seven sportswriters, all in rumpled suits and ties with overcoats slung over their arms and notebooks in hand.

"Excuse me, gentlemen," I said as I slipped through, dropped the towel from my waist and stepped into my undershorts.

"Brad?" The oldest writer, a gaunt, silver-headed man, edged forward and extended his hand. "I'm Mickey Baron from the Philadelphia *Examiner.*"

"Oh, yes," I said as we shook hands. "You had this one pegged pretty good."

"Well, thank you, thank you very much," he said. "Big games are tough to pick, of course, but as you must've read I had some serious doubts about young Rutledge..." He flipped open his notebook and pulled a pen from his shirt pocket. "Brad, you were involved in a controversial play in the fourth quarter that could well have been the turning point of the ball game..."

I looked at him.

"What, exactly, did you say to the official to draw that penalty?"

"What?"

Baron consulted his notes. "As I understand it the call was unsportsmanlike conduct for verbal abuse, and I was wondering—"

"Verbal abuse?"

"Yes."

"Where did you get that?"

"From the league's publicity director," Baron said. "He had an explanation of the call printed up and distributed not five minutes after it happened." Baron reached into the breastpocket of his jacket and produced the mimeographed sheet. "Here," he said. "Following the fumble there was a heated discussion and Brad Rafferty, Washington's right defensive end, was penalized fifteen yards for verbally abusing an official..."

"Jesus Christ—the league's—what about the TV guys? Did they—"

"Same thing," Baron said. "Made all the wire services, too."

"Christ, this is all wrong—did you get to the referee on this thing?"

"No reason to, until now. I doubt if we could've done anything there anyway, Brad. You know the way the league protects the officials from having to talk to us or anybody else. They're gone.

They shower and they're gone. I'd love to talk to one of them bastards."

"Coach? Did he—"

"Not a thing," Baron said. "He locked himself in the staff locker room and went out the back way..."

I explained the play and the controversial call to the reporters. When I finished Baron shook his head. "That beats all I've ever heard," he said. "From the pressbox all we could see was the aftermath—the yelling and screaming...verbal abuse seemed an appropriate call. But this thing—what was it again?"

"Brushing an official," I said.

"Well," said Baron, "this is getting very interesting."

"I don't know if that's what I'd call it."

"Oh, it is. Mister Clayton visited with some of us in the hall after the game—he was very upset—and I have an interesting quote here." Baron fumbled through his notebook. "Here we are. 'An incompetent call by an incapable official' is what he said, but he never specified—"

"You're gonna print that, I hope."

"I don't know, Brad. We'll have to see. But I wanted you to hear the off-the-record stuff. Where the hell—here. The referee, Clayton went on to say, should not only be dismissed from the job but—get this—banned from the playing fields of America..."

"Amen," I said, and knew I shouldn't.

Baron smiled.

"On the record or off, that's pretty strong stuff, isn't it?"

Baron just smiled.

"About the only thing stronger," put in one of the other reporters, "was his breath."

They all laughed and flipped shut their notebooks, thanked me for my time and wandered off to finish their postgame interviews. I slumped to my chair. My equipment lay in front of me, a damp mess. I had to clean and stow it before I could leave. I didn't know if I could do it. I was exhausted and angry. It was just so god-damned unfair. Everything. The publicity director writes an out-rageous version of a play he knows nothing about and I end up taking the heat. Clayton tries to deflect the heat but he's drunk and everybody has a good laugh. If only the holding penalties hadn't come when they did. It could drive you nuts. We worked so hard to get into scoring position and twice some guard or tackle fucked up and it was their fuck-ups that made my play so crucial, because if we'd put some points on the board it just wouldn't have mattered, it would have been one of those curious but inconsequential plays that sometimes happen. But now, instead of a freak, it was a fuck-up, and it was *my* fuck-up, and everybody was talking about it...

I picked up my helmet. Burgundy, striped in gold and white, it was actually dented, the face mask loosened from the day's repeated impacts. I wiped it off with a damp towel and stuffed it in the equipment bag.

And Wayne. If only Wayne had played the whole game. The stats he would've had in the first half—they were just so goddamn careful with him. Him screaming he was ready and them telling him he wasn't. Sure they had to save him a little for next week. But now there might not be a next week...

As I reached for my shoulder pads a sharp stabbing pain descended from my left knee into my lower leg. It curled my toes. More than anything the pain surprised me because my left knee was my good knee, and until a moment ago it had felt fine. And if surprise was what I experienced at the pain, shock was what I registered when I saw that the source of the pain was a massive contusion rising blue and hard on the outside of my left thigh just above the joint. Shock, because I was not only unaware of it, I had no idea how I'd gotten it. None. It was a mystery my muddy mind refused even to begin to think on.

"Uh, excuse me, Brad. I know you've already been through this, but I didn't get down here until a few minutes ago and—well..." The writer extended his hand. "I'm Jim Smith of the Delaware *Times*."

"Good."

"Is it—"

"No."

"What?"

"Go fuck yourself, Jim," I said. I didn't even raise my voice.

CHAPTER | **NINE**

6:15 P.M.

From my window seat in the coach section of the United Airlines charter I watched the ground crew transfer steamer trunks and equipment bags from a rented truck to the baggage compartment of the 727. The men worked quickly. It had stopped raining but the temperature had dropped and the day-long drizzle had become a thick icy fog that cut visibility and threatened to close the airport. When the final piece of luggage was stowed the baggage compartment was sealed and a member of the ground crew signaled the pilot. Jet engines whined as the aircraft lurched from its mooring near the air freight terminal and taxied toward the main runway.

"Roomie? You wanna say fuck to this season," Wayne said as he hoisted a foaming can of Schlitz.

"I do," I said. "Fuck football."

Wayne threw back his head and took a gulp from the can, beer trickling down his chin, spotting his tie and the lapels of his sports jacket. We had been drinking steadily since we boarded the plane, taking refreshment from the seat pockets before us where we'd stashed our allotment of beer. Crushed cans and sandwich wrappers littered the vacant chair between us; peanut husks covered the floor. The warm beer bubbled in my throat.

"Nassau, Brad. Next weekend. I can get us comped at the Island Princess, all we gotta do is let 'em know."

"We're going to be playing next weekend."

"Bullshit," he said, "New York hasn't won a game since October. Let's at least make some airline reservations."

"I got to see Jack. I promised I'd be out the first week after the end of the season."

"So tell him you changed your mind. You're gonna fool around with your uncle when you could be romping with the boys in the Bahamas? Come on."

"I'm thinking about taking Judy this trip."

"Boring."

"I'm going to ask her Tuesday, I think. When she gets back from wherever she is. Things are going to be different now. Like they were before. We had a little talk last night."

"Oh," Wayne said. He took another long sloppy pull at his beer. "Good. Great."

The 727 accelerated down the pitted runway, and in a few minutes we were airborne and above the overcast. I felt kind of sick. I was tired and sore from the game and couldn't get comfortable. My leg hurt.

"Brad, the trainer asked me to give you these," a stewardess said, and leaned over and handed me a packet of pills, an Ace bandage and, carefully, a dripping plastic bag filled with ice.

"Thanks," I said, pocketing the pills. "If I beg would you mind bringing me a cold beer when you get a chance?"

"Not at all." She smiled.

As she wandered off toward the front of the plane I rolled my left pants leg to mid-thigh, placed the ice bag over the outside of my swollen knee, wrapped the damp package with the Ace bandage, then collapsed the seat back in front of me and propped up my throbbing leg.

"That's a truly great bruise."

"Looks like someone bit me. A bear. I don't know for sure when or how or by whom, but I got dinged pretty good. You see any bears on the field?"

Wayne nodded. "Fucking bears."

93

"You okay?"

"Disappointed, is all." He shifted in the chair, sliding his legs into the empty space between us. His face was flushed from all the Benzedrine he'd taken and his forehead was beaded with perspiration. "They're gonna get a basketball player to do the Chantilly Cadillac deal. I heard what's-his-name the dealer talking on the bus from the stadium."

"That's too bad," I said. I'd thought he meant disappointed that we lost. He was talking commerce.

"Fucking Rutledge," he muttered. "He throws me a decent ball instead of that wounded duck... I mean, one play and we're there, Brad. One play. And Rutledge chokes it off."

"He got surprised when Greene fell. It threw off the timing."

"You're saying I faked Greene too good. That's my job. I faked him out of his shoes. The poor fuck tripped over his own feet. He was a pretzel. That's my job. I did my job. And then Rutledge puts up this bubble ball. Fucking pussy. He throws like a girl."

"You're being too hard on him."

"Yeah? I'll remember that when I see Wesley Unseld doing my goddamn commercial. And when my pay check's five grand light from not making the goddamn Pro Bowl. It's in Hawaii this year, too. A week in Hawaii, and there's a big junket to the Far East after that. Fucking Rutledge. I'll be in Oklahoma watching the goddamn wind blow."

"One play, huh? One play and we're there? Come on," I said. "Look at that call on me. That goddamn Pasco."

"You shouldn't have cursed him, Brad."

"I *didn't*."

"I heard the call."

"I didn't curse the son of a bitch."

"You're cursing him now. See?"

"He's not here now."

"That's good. He'd penalize us off the bus."

"Plane."

"Plane. Right. We're on a plane. Fucking plane. You can't worry about the refs, Brad. They're different."

"Different? First half. Two scoring drives stopped cold. You

94

remember? Holding penalties, for Christ's sake."

"Listen, Brad, listen to me. The officials are like part of the field. You step out of bounds, you run into the goal posts, it's one of those things. You know what I mean? You get a bad call, it's one of those things. I mean, we play sixteen games and the refs have fucked up how many? Tell me how many."

"I don't know. Two."

"Two. And two ain't that bad. Especially when you think about all the calls they have to make—did you see the thing in the paper on that? Somebody figured it out with a computer. There's thousands of calls, it turns out—thousands of 'em—and they end up accurate ninety-seven, ninety-eight percent of the time."

"If you could have played more...you play the first half, we win."

"Maybe. Blake thought I was favoring the leg."

"Yeah."

"I don't know. Needles took a look at it—they were just watching out for me, Brad. I talked to 'em, I got back in the game."

"Yelling is not talking. You were yelling."

"So I lost my temper. You know how it is. The shit's in the barn. I got carried away, that's all. Quit trying to make something out of nothing."

"I'm not, I just...I mean, I'm the goddamn goat, not you or Rutledge. I don't know. They had it all so fucked up."

"Who had it all fucked up?"

"The media guys. I mean, I straightened out the reporters—"

"What are you talking about?"

"They had me—they thought the call was for verbal abuse. Even you did, for Christ's sake. I straightened out the reporters, but the TV guys, they had it wrong too and there's no way to get to them. I mean, they just say what they say and that's it. It's done. Yesterday I was a decent ballplayer, today I'm the asshole who cost his team a shot at the play-offs."

"But they'll forget about it, Brad. The fans, I mean. They're just sort of out there—you know. They like to yell. You need a commercial."

"I need something."

"Maybe we should do like they do for Phyllis. Only for ourselves."

"What?"

"They don't love Phyllis, you know."

"Who?"

"The fans."

"All those 'We Love Phyllis' signs. The fans put 'em up."

"Maybe we should put up some 'We Love Wayne Law' and 'We Love Brad' posters."

"Are you saying the fans don't love Phyllis George?"

"The technicians put 'em up. I caught 'em when I went out to check the field this morning. There were three or four of 'em and they were taping up 'We Love Phyllis' posters, one in front of every camera so that no matter which camera was operating one poster would always be in the picture. I asked 'em what they were doing and they laughed. We could put some up for us, make it part of our pregame."

"Sure."

"You knew the technicians were doing that?"

"Well, no, but—wait a minute."

The stewardess reappeared and tossed me my beer. Wedging the can between my legs I plucked the packet of pills from my shirt pocket and emptied it in the palm of my hand. The pills were round and flat, yellowish, each with a dividing line running across its middle. Beneath the line, written in cursive, was the word *Endo,* followed by a number, 122.

"Percodan," Wayne said almost immediately. "Endo's the name of the manufacturer. The great Mr. Endo."

"And the number? What's the number mean?"

"That's how many of these little bastards you'd like to have."

I swallowed two of the pills, chasing them with cold beer.

Wayne shook his head. "I don't get it, Brad. I mean, you won't eat the speed any more, yet you eat this stuff like it's candy." He returned the pill. "That's morphine, for Christ's sake."

"I can't eat the speed because I can't think on it. Okay? I gotta know what I'm doing when I'm doing it but I don't want to feel it when I'm done. I can't make it any clearer than that. I *hurt.*"

Wayne finished his beer.

"So where were we?" I said.

"What? Oh. CBS," he said, fishing for another in the seat pocket before him. "The signs."

"Yes, well, it's no big surprise if you think about it," I said. "I mean, the league and the networks, they're both interested in presenting *exciting* football games, as a media thing, as a program, and broadcasting personalities, hype—like the signs—that's all a part of it. Good football means good ratings, the advertisers jump in and that's where the money comes from. And it's a lot of money."

"Millions," Wayne said. "Hundreds of millions."

"Right. So what I'm wondering now is who's in charge. Is it the guy who gives or the guy who gets? I mean, if it were you and me and you had the money, I guess you'd be in charge. But being a classy guy with all this money, you wouldn't make me *feel* like you were in charge. You'd sort of make suggestions. And being a smart guy who likes money, I'd sort of carry 'em out, if they weren't too outrageous. Right?"

"Sure."

"Right. Like if I were a network guy and you were a league guy and I said it would be nice if certain games started at certain times so we could pull some prime-time viewers, you'd probably agree. And if I said we had to have so many commercials per game to make the money we're paying you, you'd probably find a way to work 'em in. And if I wanted artificial turf in all the stadiums so we could eliminate the problem of mud and smeared jerseys and bad pictures, you'd probably agree to that too, even though you knew the turf screwed up your players—after all, you could always get more players—"

"Wait a minute, Brad. Hey, are you ripped? You're ripped."

"I'm talking about the relationship between the league and the networks."

"No. You're *speculating* about the relationship—"

"It's not unreasonable, what I'm saying."

"Not yet, but it's getting that way."

"Wayne, you know what I mean."

"Why do I get the feeling we're going to argue?"

"I don't know, let's find out."

"Just so long as it's clear we're speculating. I mean, let's be sure and make that distinction."

"Absolutely."

"Let's call it pretending."

"Okay."

"We're just pretending."

"Bullshitting," I said.

"Right, we're bullshitting."

"Speculationing..." The pills had hit me like a load of bricks. "I..." My mind was beginning to swim.

I fumbled for the button on the inside of my armrest.

"You're ripped, you're ripped right out of your skull."

Nodding, I found the button and pressed it and leaned back in my chair.

"All right, speculation on *what?*"

"I...can't..."

"What? You can't what?"

"Re-mem-ber," I said. And I could hold open my eyes no longer. Something beside the pain-killers was also getting to me, but I didn't know what it was.

When I woke up the Fasten Seat Belt signs were on and a stewardess was announcing the beginning of our descent into Washington's Dulles International Airport. I was cold and stiff and water was trickling down my left leg. For a moment I thought I had had the kind of accident you sometimes have when you take too many pills, but of course it was just the leaking ice pack. I unwrapped it and dropped it to the floor, then tore the napkin from the headrest of the middle seat and tried to soak up some of the moisture. I'd dreamt of Dolchik and the sonofabitch was still strutting around in my mind.

"Here," Wayne said, handing me a sogged paper cup as he sat down in his chair. "It's whiskey. Keane sends his regards."

"Thanks," I said, and took a sip from the cup.

"You're looking a little glum."

"Oh, I was just thinking some more about the game. I mean,

maybe...maybe I could've done something myself—"

"It's over, Brad."

"I know, but if I get a sack on one of those drives, if I make some kind of play—anything...screw it, they keep changing the goddamn rules and I'm not gonna worry about it. And I'm not gonna let 'em get to me, either."

"Who?"

"The league. They keep changing the goddamn rules."

"You keep saying that."

"And they keep doing it. Every year they do it. Every year they change the goddamn rules and every change is directed at the defense. Don't tell me you haven't noticed. They hate us, they hate defense."

"Sure, but—"

"It's driving me nuts. Your statistics keep getting better, don't they. I mean, every year you catch more passes for more yardage—you think that happens because you're such a great fucking receiver?"

"Part of it."

"Part of it, that's right. The rest of it's because of these damn rules changes. They keep shackling the defense. They've got the secondary in leg irons, the linemen in manacles—you can't make a play anymore. I mean, Dolchik, you know, he used to be a sucker for a head slap. George Andros—you remember George—George used to put him on rollerskates with the damn thing. So I watched George. I watched him for three years and when I finally learned the move, when I was finally ready to play, they changed the damn rules, they said you could only use the head slap if you hit the tackle on your first step. That lasted a year, then they took it away altogether and at the same time they redefined what constituted holding, they legalized holding, and I had to learn the damn game all over again."

"They don't want you guys mauling the quarterbacks, that's all. They're just trying to protect 'em, you can't blame 'em for that—"

"So protect 'em with *players,* not with rules changes. I mean, why penalize me for doing my job? Why take away my skills with

99

a rules change when all they've really got to do is reallocate their resources?"

"Go back to sleep."

"Who are the highest paid players in the league?"

"Quarterbacks."

"Followed by?"

"Running backs."

"And then?"

"Receivers? I'm not sure."

"It's defensive linemen because a good big man is hard to find, and when they do find one they stick him on defense. Now if there's a premium on quarterbacks and running backs, there should also be a premium on the guys who protect 'em, but there's not— the offensive linemen aren't of our calibre but the league helps them out by making these rules changes, by fixing the level of competition so that an average offensive lineman can handle a good defensive lineman, and that's not right. They're handicapping us like horses and the same thing's happening in the secondary with the one-chuck rule and and the five-yard limit—if the league's going to do this, Wayne, if they're going to open up the game by shackling the defense, if they're going to go for the ratings and the TV bucks, then by God they ought to do it *right*. They ought to get some talent in there, someone who understands what the hell they're trying to do. I'm saying hire Red Klotz, is what they ought to do, they ought to make Red Klotz the Commissioner."

"Red Klotz?"

"He's the man for the job."

"Red Klotz?"

"How could you forget a name like Red Klotz? Forget it, I'm sorry I brought it up." Unfastening my seat belt, I leaned forward, pulled up my socks and tied my shoes.

"So who is he?" Wayne said impatiently.

"He's a basketball coach," I said. "A very successful one. A defensive genius, matter of fact."

"A basketball coach?"

"I'm sure he could make the transition. Of course, the money would have to be right, the perks—"

100

"Pro? College? What?"

"Pro," I said. "Very successful. He's coached the same team for twenty-eight years and during that time he's compiled an incredible record, something like four wins against three thousand five hundred and twenty some-odd defeats. And his owners are very proud of him, particularly of his losing streak, which runs somewhere around eight hundred and eighty consecutive games."

"You mean winning streak."

"I mean losing streak. Red coaches the opposition for the Harlem Globetrotters. He's supposed to lose and he does it very well. In fact he does it better than any other coach in the history of sport. He's a real winner, this Red Klotz."

"He's a loser!"

"But he's *successful,* and the league ought to hire him, make him Commissioner of Defense. I mean, this is a situation Red Klotz would understand perfectly, he's been jerking off you glory-guys for years."

"Fuck you."

"Or they could give us a better game plan. We're on television all the time. If they really want to control it they could bring in the television people—they could give us scripts. Right? For every game. Have Brent Musberger write out these scripts so we would know what to do and we wouldn't have to get the shit beat out of us and feel this way. We could have stunt men. We could be like a really great adventure series. Right? Scripts. That's what they ought to do. For every game."

"You're nuts, Brad. Have another pill. You're not the only one who lost today, you know. Stop feeling sorry for yourself."

"All you're pissed about losing is your commercial, pretty boy. Don't kid me."

"Up yours."

The 727 touched down, brakes squealing, engines whining in reverse. As a stewardess asked that we please remain seated until the aircraft came to a complete stop, Wayne stood up, gathered his belongings and without so much as a good-by bolted for the front of the plane.

TEN

I woke up groggy. I reached for the telephone. A rigid ache toward the rear of my neck descended suddenly into my left arm. I fell back to the bed, unable to complete the simple task. Now more alert, I laughed at myself—it was all right, it was only the dream. She wouldn't have been home anyway, not until tomorrow.

Before trying to move again I took a moment to assess the damage to my body from the game. Again the toll was heaviest on my left side. There was the fiery, shooting pain in my neck and shoulder, which was not new but which seemed to grow in intensity every week in spite of diligent application of the treatment prescribed by Needles some three months ago.

"It hurts," I'd said one morning in the training room, "when I do this." Carefully I raised my left arm. Slowly, wincing, I extended my elbow.

"Don't do that." Needles smiled. "Until you take some of these." And he pressed a packet of pills in my palm.

"What are they?"

"Empirin compound," he said, "codeine and aspirin, mostly codeine."

"Will they help my injury?"

"You won't miss a practice."

"But will they help my *injury?*"

"You won't feel a thing," he'd said.

But I was feeling it now. My neck, shoulder and elbow were throbbing. My fingers were inflamed and had bled where the unclipped nails had been torn from the flesh. My appendix was sore, so were my abdomen, groin, and testicles. There was an acute twinge in my lower back and a strange snag in my left hip. My left knee was swollen like a big fruit and my left ankle cracked rhythmically when rotated. I reached for what was left of last night's Percodan.

After a while, when my body began to feel like it belonged to someone else, I got up, struggled into my bathrobe and hobbled to the kitchen. Because I hadn't really eaten anything since hotdogs with Tony, I was very hungry. Hot cakes and hash browns, cold milk and sausage...I opened the door of the refrigerator. Inside were two bottles of mineral water, three eggs, a jar of instant coffee and a rotting pineapple. So much for a complete breakfast. As I did every morning I took out the eggs and coffee and set them on the kitchen counter, then filled a pan with water, put the eggs in the pan and the pan on the stove, turned on a burner. From the cupboard I took out a plate and cup and spooned some coffee into the cup. As the water began to boil I went into the livingroom and looked through a stack of records for some music. I had a particular album in mind—it was already on the turntable. I switched on the stereo amplifier and turned up the volume. By then the water was boiling and the eggs were cooked and after making coffee I carried the food into the livingroom, where I sat down and ate breakfast with Gustav Holst, a German composer whose soaring "Jupiter, Bringer of Jollity" now rattled the walls and windows of my apartment.

Not that I was a connoisseur of classical music. Far from it. In fact Holst was about the only composer I really knew and I wouldn't have known him had my college roommate been anyone other than Larry (Lawrence III) Roblaine. Larry's mother was a patron of the musical arts, and while we were in school she weighed down the mails with boxes that contained, along with back issues of the quarterly newsletter from the Juilliard School of Music and patron applications to various Bay area symphonies, an assortment of her favorite classical recordings, among which the works of Holst were always well represented. Larry, who had taken up the study of law, which would eventually land him a high paying (and in the eyes of his mother, ignominious) job with the Los Angeles County District Attorney's office. Larry, who hated music even more than he hated his mother, would collect these boxes at the post office and lug them to our room, cursing all the while, and there, having quickly discarded the printed material, he would sort through the albums, bequeathing to me the ones with the most attractive covers, using the others as disposable Frisbees.

"The bitch," he would say. "This shit is absolutely incomprehensible..."

And the albums would sail out of our third-floor window.

I laughed now, remembering, and glanced at my watch, thinking I might give him a call. But in Los Angeles, where Larry worked, it was still much too early. Maybe later, I thought, walked outside and picked up the morning paper and the mail.

Along with a postcard from my uncle Jack ("See you soon?") and a check from the Pro-pel shoe manufacturers, there was a snotty letter from the Stanford Annual Fund demanding money. "You are a G," it began. "You didn't know that, did you. But that's how you're classified by the Stanford Annual Fund. It works like this..." A G was a nondonor, which I was and would forever be.

I wasn't particularly pleased with my education. It was my faculty adviser...as a liaison for the athletic department, whose interests, I see now, he was bound to promote, my adviser had encouraged me to pursue a program of "Interdisciplinary Studies" so that I wouldn't be too "distracted" during football season. Which I did. I took a spectrum of engineering courses, because that's where my interests were, but when I graduated I found that I was neither a civil, mechanical, aeronautical, biomedical, or electrical engineer, and being none of the above I was eminently unemployable. After playing professional football for five years I still am, only more so, if that's possible, because now it would take me four years of additional school, instead of two, to complete one of the degrees.

I put the letter aside and reached for the newspaper. I had

saved the newspaper until last because for the first time in several weeks my name would be in all the stories about the game. I'd affected the outcome of an important event, had been martyred in our bid to make the conference play-offs. I was sure the papers would justify my actions. No need to hurry, though, I thought, and unfolding the paper on the kitchen table, I casually looked over the front page.

A teaser caught my attention. It ran across the top of the page above the *Herald* logo. "Washington Blows Big One," it said. "See Sports, D–1." That was not exactly the vindicating tone I'd anticipated. I turned to the sports section.

PHILLY RUINS WASHINGTON'S HOPES

The black print squirmed before me.

CONTROVERSIAL CALL STIFLES COMEBACK

A passage in Ed Thomas' play-by-play account leaped off the page:

> Pasco and his cohorts ruled that there was no fumble. Coach led a vehement show of outrage at his bench, near where the key play occurred. Defensive end Brad Rafferty had to be restrained from going after an official. He was eventually assessed with a fifteen-yard penalty for verbal abuse, and Philly, instead of being on defense at their own 27, had a first and ten at the 42.

I hadn't spoken with Ed Thomas after the game, he'd written his story from the league publicity director's press release. But I wasn't going to worry about Ed Thomas. Ed Thomas was a degenerate and nobody read the play-by-play anyway. No. What was important here was what Brady Young had to say in his column. It was important because Brady's column was the showpiece of the sports section. Set in 10-point type on an 11-point slug, 24 picas wide, it ran down the left-hand side of the first page of the section, top to bottom, and was read by more people than any other feature in the newspaper. Brady wrote:

In the marvelous world of professional sports, emotional folks are certainly more entertaining than those who are not. They are more entertaining because they wear their humanity on their sleeves. Brad Rafferty is one of those people and I admire his humanness. But I wish for his sake, and for the sake of our gallant Washington team, that he would have controlled his emotions Sunday afternoon in Veteran's Stadium.

But Rafferty didn't.

He blew his top over what appeared to be a bad call by the officials, and Washington, despite the heroic efforts of Wayne Law, was blown right out of the football game.

It was a costly display of emotion.

Too costly.

Too bad.

Sweat had broken out on the back of my neck and trickled down my spine and into the crack of my ass. What the hell was going on here? It seemed that Brady, too, had written his story straight from the league publicity director's press release. Had he run short of time? Maybe. I had no idea what kind of deadline he was working against. Or maybe he was just a lazy bastard as the trainer had intimated in the locker room before the game. I didn't know and it didn't really matter...the damage had been done and it was more extensive than I could have imagined, and I was going to have to do something to fix it.

Shifting in the uncomfortable kitchen chair I turned to the back pages of the section and glanced at the related stories:

GAME DRAWS LARGE TV AUDIENCE
IRATE FANS FLOOD HERALD PHONES
"INCOMPETENT" CALL BEAT US, OWNER RAGES
GAME OFFICIALS CAN MAKE, BREAK SEASON
PASCO UNAVAILABLE FOR COMMENT

And I paused to read these sidebars:

DEKO TO PAY PART OF FINE

(AP/UPI) Cleveland owner Arthur Deko has offered to pay part of the $10,000 fine incurred by Washington club owner Roger Clayton in the wake of Sunday's controversial game. "I will pay half," said Deko from his fashionable home in Cleveland. "I feel for Roger and the fans of the Washington team. They were (obscenity)."

WILL REPLAYS REMEDY OFFICIATING PROBLEMS?

(AP/UPI) "If there's a practical way, if the mechanics can be worked out, we are not opposed to the idea," the Commissioner said today. "I will ask the Rules Committee to evaluate the feasibility of instant replay use and report to the league at the annual meeting this March in Rancho La Costa, California."

I closed the newspaper and sipped at the cold coffee. He's said this before, the Commissioner. He has assured us that he is not opposed to the idea and he has told us that he will refer it to the Rules Committee for evaluation. But nothing ever happens. Maybe this year was the year. I hoped so. It was clear to me that if the league had adopted some use of the replay technology to help its officials, then all of this might have been avoided...

I was sitting in a pool of sweat. I slipped out of my flannel bathrobe and took a shower. I was beginning to smell like the goat Brady Young had made me out to be.

CHAPTER ELEVEN

At the end of a long dimly lit corridor, behind a mahogany desk in a sparsely furnished anteroom, sat Millie, the staff receptionist. She was working diligently on her fingernails, her bowed figure in silhouette against the massive flood-lit door behind her.

"Millie?"

She looked up. "Oh, Brad. Hi. I was just..." She hurriedly cleared her desk. "Did you want to see Coach? He's with Mister Lacewell from Chantilly Cadillac, but he said if anything came up—"

"I wouldn't want to disturb him, Millie. I'd just like to take a look at the Philadelphia game film."

"Sure," she said, and smoothing her skirt as she stood, she walked back to the door, opened it quietly and slipped into the room.

Shot from high up in the stadium, game films provide a unique perspective on the action, and I wanted the advantage of that perspective before I spoke to anyone about the game. I wanted to be sure that what had happened Sunday was what I thought had happened. In a moment Millie came back with the film.

"This is still a little confusing to me," she said, spreading five

variously colored canisters out on her desk, "so you just take whatever you need..."

Millie was relatively new on the job, so her confusion was un-
derstandable. Film of a football game is shot sequentially, as the
game happens, but is then edited for ease of evaluation; the offensive, defensive and kicking game plays are culled, wound on
separate reels and put in an appropriately colored canister: red
for defense, gold for offense, black for the kicking game. The
colors and the illegible labels, most of them marked in Red Keane's
curious third-grade scrawl, could easily be confusing to an un-
initiate.

Looking over the film I immediately picked up the red canister
marked "Second Half Defense" and after a moment's hesitation,
the gold canister marked "First Half Offense." While the film in
the red canister would show me the controversial fourth-quarter
play, the film in the gold canister would show me the first-half
holding penalties and, I hoped, Wayne's first series, when he was
supposedly favoring his leg. Neither the holding penalties nor
Wayne's first-half absence had, as I remembered, been mentioned
in the newspaper.

"Is anyone in the conference room, Millie?"

"No, Brad, help yourself."

Down the hall in the conference room, door closed behind me,
I sat down at a long rectangular table and emptied the red canister.
I snapped the reel of film on the upper arm of a 16-millimeter
analyzer projector, attached the film leader to the take-up reel
and ran off three-quarters of the film before threading the machine. I set the film speed to normal, turned off the lights and
proceeded to watch the last defensive plays of the football game.

The emotional pitch of the game was not, of course, translated
onto the screen. There was no sound. It was eerie. The grunting
of the players, the cracking of pads were lost; the screaming fans
were silent. And because the film had been shot from so high in
the stadium, the fierce action had a quiet, detached, almost civi-
lized quality, as if the players were merely preprogrammed pieces
in a game of human chess.

I was a rook. On the crucial play I hesitated for an instant as first Dolchik, then Jackson squared up in front of me; then as Jackson skittered across the backfield I recognized the play and came hard in its pursuit. My angle was good. I hadn't realized it until now, but if our linebacker hadn't upended Jackson, I would have. I was in the right position. I watched myself slowing down, controlling my speed, then coiling in anticipation of the hit. But suddenly Gary Dolchik reappeared, a massive blindside blur. He'd been tracking me as I flowed with the play. I watched in surprise as the nub of his helmet smashed the flesh of my left thigh, as my left knee buckled and my ligaments stretched to the point of snapping. Then, as suddenly as it had happened, it ended. Dolchik had overextended himself and couldn't maintain contact. As he fell with a splash to the wet turf I somehow freed my leg from his crushing mass and regained my balance. There'd been a fumble and now, oblivious to all that had happened, I was stalking the bouncing ball.

I shut off the projector. Dolchik had tried to cripple me and I hadn't even realized it. The sonofabitch. He'd waited the whole game for that play, knowing it would provide a perfect opportunity to do what he did. He had stalked me as if I were an animal, and then when I was most vulnerable he'd hit me with a blindside peelback block. And he'd hit me low. He could've hit me high but he hadn't, he hit me low—the bastard had tried to end my career. I reached down and massaged my swollen, aching knee. Maybe he'd succeeded. If he had, I would get a gun and shoot the sonofabitch.

I restarted the film. The ball had popped loose and was dribbling crazily toward our sidelines. The camera angle was such that I couldn't tell whether Jackson fumbled before or after he hit the ground. Apparently a whistle had sounded, because the head linesman was moving out on the field to mark Jackson's forward progress. As he crossed my path I put my left hand on his shoulder and pushed him aside. It was obviously not a malicious act—I was fixed on the football—yet as I picked it up and started up the sidelines he stood there yelling and pointing, and then the referee ran over and threw his flag.

"Did you hear a whistle, Brad?"

"What?" I turned, startled.

Coach was leaning against the back wall of the room. "A whistle," he said, pulling up a chair. "Did you hear a whistle?"

"No. Nothing."

"Neither did I," Coach said. "But the way the officials were acting, there must have been one."

"It was a horseshit call either way."

"Yes. Absolutely. But I think that whistle helps explain why Pasco made the call he made. Run it back and I'll show you what I mean."

I reversed the projector, and the film ran backward to the beginning of the play. Pasco, the referee, was positioned behind and to the right of the offensive backfield, ten yards from the line of scrimmage. I set a switch to forward and slowed the film speed. Coach spoke as the play unfolded.

"On a running play the referee's job is to observe the quarterback during and after the hand-off, right? See, he's doing that. And then to trail the play, checking the runner as he goes. Pasco is doing that too. When the runner's downed the referee is supposed to look to the head linesman for forward progress so he can mark the ball for the next play. But watch. Pasco has blown the play dead, he looks for the head linesman but the head linesman's not where he's supposed to be. He's almost on his butt. Your left arm is extended—it looks to Pasco like you deliberately belted the head linesman, *and* that you did it after the whistle. He runs over and throws his flag."

I stopped the projector. "But I barely touched the linesman—"

"Pasco made a mistake, Brad." Coach leaned back and turned on the light. "We all make 'em, don't we."

"But—"

"I know how you feel," he said. "I felt the same way until this morning when I found out Al Pasco is one of the best referees in the league, if not *the* best. That's straight from one of my old coaching buddies who works for the supervisor of officials. One of his jobs is to grade these guys and he told me Pasco has consistently rated in the top two or three percent in everything they look at—mechanics, accuracy, everything. He's first rate, Brad. Twelve years experience, five years running in the play-offs, twice selected to work the World Championship, and you know what an honor that is for an official. We've been too hard on him."

I nodded, almost convinced.

"But all that aside," he said, "we've got to remember this was only one play. It was an important play, sure, and Pasco missed it, but before we start dumping blame on him we've got to accept our share, and in this game, with the way we played, our share is the lion's share. I mean, we made mistakes all over the place. In the kicking game we had a breakdown in coverage that cost us a touchdown. On offense we couldn't get the damn ball in the end zone—"

"Hell no, we couldn't," I said, reaching for and opening the gold canister. "Every time we got close we had all those holding penalties."

The canister was empty.

"Mistakes. Guys were holding."

I showed him the empty canister. "I was thinking about those first-half holding penalties."

"That's not your responsibility, Brad. What could you learn from looking at guards and tackles holding?"

"I know, but I was thinking—I mean, in relation to my play, if the holding penalties hadn't come when they did, always in such crucial situations—"

"Tell them. Tell those players they let you down. And *every* situation is crucial, Brad. To tell you the truth, we were damned lucky with those calls. Damned lucky. I mean, Farrell—"

"Farrell?"

"Richard Farrell, the umpire. I mean, the way the rules are structured now the umpire can call holding on every play if he feels like it. He doesn't, of course, but once in a while he'll flag one to keep the offense honest, and that's what Farrell did to us."

"Twice."

"Exactly. What's twice? I mean, that's two under our average, Brad. It could've been worse, believe me. Both calls were on Lee

112

Fair, but with the way he was hooking and reaching and grabbing out there...you know how desperate he gets when he's playing someone like Rabbit Earle."

"I guess I just—"

"It's no problem if you want to take a look, Brad. Coach Keane has that reel, I think. We've got a staff meeting in a few minutes and he's just trying to finish up his grading."

"No. I...It's just—"

"Listen," he said, "you're doing a little second-guessing here, that's all. Hell, anybody who's any kind of competitor—it's a perfectly natural thing to do. I do it all the time myself. In this game it would be what we did with Wayne. We hold him out the first half thinking he might be hurt, the second half he runs Huey Greene out of the stadium. You don't think I thought about that last night? The difference, of course, is that when I woke up this morning I found some support for the decision in the medical report. Doctor Morris, you know, he made it very clear how slow traumatic fibromyocitis is to heal and how easily the injury can be aggravated if proper precautions aren't taken. You, on the other hand, woke up and found yourself crucified in the newspapers."

"Yeah, I couldn't believe it."

"Neither could I, and I've taken the liberty—Tanner's already been in touch with Brady's office, Brad. I hope you don't mind. A retraction and apology have been demanded and we'll see what happens when Brady gets in, although I don't anticipate any problems. The whole thing should be resolved by Wednesday latest."

"You're sure."

"Positive."

"Jesus, I had this whole scenario worked out in my mind—going down to the paper, storming into Brady's office—" I broke off. Someone was rapping at the conference-room door.

"Coach?" It was Millie.

"Okay," he called.

"It's time for the meeting."

"Yeah—you headed for the parking lot?"

I nodded.

"I'll walk you out," he said. "I want to be sure you understand

113

how important it is that we put this game behind us and start thinking about the play-offs. Do you have any idea how poorly Los Angeles has played in late season games in cold weather cities?"

"No."

"Well," he began...and as we made our way out of the conference room and down the hall Coach rattled off five years worth of Los Angeles won-lost statistics that so proved his point that by the time I got to the car I was not only convinced we were going to be in the play-offs, I was already feeling the subtle shift in body juices that meant I was getting ready to play.

It felt good. The only thing that still bothered me about the Philadelphia game was Wayne, and how we'd left things on the plane. I'd talked crazy to him and he'd left in a huff—I'll take him to lunch, I thought, as I cranked up the car. We'll go to JP's and have a couple of beers and everything will be fine.

Sure.

CHAPTER | **TWELVE**

Three miles north of the club compound a narrow, winding, two-lane road broadened and turned straight as it entered the red brick and wrought-iron world of Pleasant Glen. Lurching over speed bumps I drove slowly past a clubhouse with its empty swimming pool and vacant, netless tennis courts, through a section of detached housing and into what the development's promotional brochure described as "A Little Bit of Olde England"—a small shopping center with a fish-and-chips shop followed by two blocks of "traditional English country cottage townhouses." Wayne lived at the end of the second block in the last house on the right. I wheeled into his driveway and parked behind his burgundy Mercedes.

A sudden chill rocked me as I got out of the car. It was clear and very cold and in my anger that morning I'd left the house without a coat. Hurrying to the front porch I rapped the bronze knocker, and without waiting for an answer unlatched the door and walked inside.

"Roomie?"

The house was dark and smelled bad. In the unfurnished livingroom, newspapers were spread and stained, the carpet too, and from somewhere—the garage, perhaps—I could hear the

115

scratching and yelping of an exiled pup. I wandered back to the den and found Wayne sitting on the floor, his back propped against the rented sofa, an empty bottle of wine wedged between his legs. He was staring at the television set, a game show. There was no sound.

"Hey, Speed."

He looked up. The room was dark and in the circle of gray-blue light his face looked swollen, as if he'd been asleep. "Where you been," he asked thickly. "I'm upset."

"With Coach," I said. "We've been talking. I was pretty pissed myself."

"It's terrible, Brad."

"I know." I sat down in an armchair across from him. "It helped to talk, though."

Wayne nodded as if in understanding, but there was something heavy, somber in the gesture.

"Poor Judy," he said.

"Judy?"

Wayne stared at me. For a long time he stared at me. "Didn't Sam tell you?"

"Sam? Colton?"

He nodded slowly.

"No. Wha—"

"Why didn't he tell you? What the hell's the matter with him?"

"What the hell are you talking about?"

"He's been trying to reach you all morning."

"Sam?"

"Judy's dead, Brad. She was in a car accident in New York. Jesus, I'm sorry, I thought you knew..."

PART **TWO**

CHAPTER THIRTEEN

A Mexican woman in a faded kimono stepped out on the front porch of the white frame house and moved to an old schoolhouse bell on the south porch railing. She pulled twice at the clapper of the old bell, then turned and walked back inside the house, the screen door banging behind her. Fifty yards away a wide corrugated-tin gate swung open and Jack emerged from the wrecking yard, striding briskly through dust toward the white frame house, where, no doubt, dinner was being served. At his heels, snorting, struggling to keep up, came Toby, Jack's ancient pit-bulldog, and a few yards behind Toby came the chickens, maybe thirty of them, spilling into the yard, heads bobbing curiously, intent more on escape, it seemed, than a meal.

Hearing the clucking, Jack stopped and turned. "Goddammit," he muttered. "Camillio!" And he ran back toward the chickens, waving his thick arms in the air, sliding back and forth in the now billowing dust, hollering at the squawking birds as he tried to herd them back through the open gate, a task soon accomplished with the arrival of Camillio and his two boys.

When they were finished Jack took off his ragged Stetson, mopped a handkerchief over his sunburned, heavy-jowled face, spat some rapid Spanish at Camillio, who, pretending not to understand, turned and fastened the gate.

119

"They're your goddamn chickens," Jack said in English, "and I ain't gonna be responsible for 'em." He pushed the soaked wad of his handkerchief into the breast pocket of his dungarees and pulled the Stetson tightly over his head. "No more," he added, and began beating the dust out of his dungarees with his big hairy hands.

"Jack, hello," I called as I picked up my suitcase and stepped from the shade of a mulberry tree. Jack turned, scowled and squinted into the failing sun.

"Well, I'll be," he said. "What the hell you doin'? You shoulda called me. I can't believe you didn't call."

"I should've, but I didn't know I was coming. I mean, not until I got here..."

He grinned. "You ain't makin' no sense," he said. "As usual." He cupped his hands around his mouth and called for Camillio's boys.

As we climbed the stairs to the front porch Camillio, apparently unable to find the boys, hurried over himself and took my suitcase and carried it off across the driveway toward another smaller white frame house.

"Sleep at Ada's, huh? Like always?" Jack jerked his thumb at the smaller house.

"Fine," I said.

"You eat?"

"On the plane."

"That ain't eatin', Brad. You wanna eat, mama-san's cookin' up some rice and beans and enchiladas..." Mama-san is what Jack calls Pasquela, Camillio's wife. Japanese Mexican. "You wanna eat, we got plenty," he said.

"I'm not very hungry, Jack. You go ahead." I sat down on an old sofa Jack had converted into a porch swing.

"You feel all right?"

"Rough flight."

"Yeah, you look a little rough. I'll be right back." Jack beat more dust out of his dungarees, then walked inside the house and called for mama-san.

I lay down in the swing. The Thursday afternoon sun was low

120

over the Coastal Range. Dim orange light filtered through dust and mulberry trees into the porch. Jack came back carrying an unopened bottle of expensive bourbon and two dirty glasses. Setting the glasses on a metal utility table, he sat down in a high-backed wooden chair and cracked the seal on the bottle.

"You need a little something to take the edge off," he said, and filled the bottoms of the dirty glasses and handed one to me.

I raised the glass to my lips and threw down the whiskey.

"More?"

"A little."

He refilled the bottom of my glass, then his. I could feel the whiskey beginning to work.

"So what the hell you doin' here, Brad? I mean, Dallas and Los Angeles, they both lost—you're still in the thing, aren't you?"

"Wildcard."

"So when do you play?"

"Sunday. In New Orleans."

"You AWOL? Or aren't you boys practicing for this one."

"No, no. I needed a break, is all. Coach gave me a little break."

"Oh."

"You know how it is."

"Oh, yeah...sure. There must be a lot of pressure. Sometimes I could almost see it, you know, rising off the field like heat. That last game...hell, you know what I mean."

"Sure."

"I'm talking too much, aren't I."

"No, Christ."

"I always worry about that. Talkin' too much, askin' too many questions. You must get this all the time."

"Jack, listen—"

"You hungry? I'm gonna eat."

"I'll get something later, you go ahead."

"You sure?"

"I'm fine, Jack. Really. Really."

It was dark, getting cold. Jack had eaten, I'd napped for a while and now we were sitting on the porch watching Camillio push the

121

corrugated-tin gate across the entrance to the wrecking yard.

"He's a good man, Camillio," Jack was saying. "I never could've done it without him, you know. I mean, when Kathleen...you know."

I nodded. Jack's wife Kathleen had died three years earlier after a long fight with cancer.

Camillio now walked over to the yard office, where a police radio sat chattering and spitting. Nearby, within earshot of the radio, the night drivers had assembled. They were standing around a fire they had built in an empty oil drum, warming themselves as they awaited the first call. Camillio turned down the volume on the radio and talked to the men in urgent, rapid Spanish.

"What's that all about?" I asked Jack.

"Oh, there's been some thievin'. Camillio's just asking 'em to keep their eyes open. The kids around here are car-crazy and we got all our tools back there, and all the parts, and some damn valuable cars..."

"You got anything we can work on? I was thinking I'd like to work on an old car. Maybe get one running or something."

"You got problems you ain't telling me about?"

"I guess I do," I said, and asked Jack if he remembered Judy Colton. She'd never been out here, but I'd talked enough about her that I thought he'd remember her, and of course he did. And then I told him what Wayne had told me three days before...that Judy had been killed in a traffic accident somewhere in upstate New York, that she had fallen asleep at the wheel and slammed into a bridge abutment.

"That's all I know," I said. "The funeral's on Friday in Arlington and I'm supposed to be a pallbearer. I can't do it. I just..."

"I'm damn sorry," Jack said.

"I haven't been able to practice either."

He nodded.

"I haven't been able to do much of anything."

We sat for a while in silence. Then Jack got up and clapped his ample belly and said, "An old car, you say? Well, let me think about that." And he began pacing the porch and pulling at his stubbled jowls and said, "Matter of fact, there's a forty-seven Packard back there somewhere, a Custom Super Clipper at that. We brought 'er in four or five years ago and she was in pretty good shape, too. Then," he said. "Now, I'm not so sure."

"Sounds like just what the doctor ordered," I said.

CHAPTER | **FOURTEEN**

On Friday morning Jack and I walked back into the wrecking yard to look for the Packard. Jack's a beefy man, round and stout, with a thick neck and massive arms that hang from his shoulders like oars from a skiff. He favors the ragged Stetson, a pair of hand-tooled, round-toed boots, and any of a closetful of worn-out dungarees. He looks sort of like a successful rancher or farmer, and in a way I suppose he is. Jack's the owner-operator of Rafferty's 24 Hour Wrecker Service, a thriving enterprise situated on fifty acres of prime dirt six miles north of Wasco in the heart of California's Kern County...Jack harvests the county's highways.

Old Jack grew up in Wasco. A restless boy, he was the youngest son of Ada Rafferty, a proud woman who had migrated to California to escape her drunken husband and the Oklahoma dust bowl. Ada ran a small truckfarm on the outskirts of town, sold her produce at a roadside stand and took in sewing and did domestic work. Ada tried to instill in young Jack at least the spiritual rewards of their farming life, but Jack was more interested in automobiles. When Ada died he turned the barn into a garage, bought a truck on credit, and as the fields went to weed, he got started in the wrecking business.

We followed a narrow dirt road that began at the entrance to the yard and wound deep into the property through an endless canyon of automobiles stripped to their frames and stacked five high on either side of the road. The wrecking yard was organized like an archeologist's dig, and now as we came to the Mesozoic age of cars we found the Packard.

It was an enormous automobile—over eighteen feet long, weighing in excess of 4,000 pounds, sitting all by itself in the northeast corner of the yard. It had been parked there for six years and the tires, electrical wiring and upholstery had rotted. Much of the chrome trim had been dismantled and sold, but the original hub caps, inlaid with intricate hexagonal designs, were still intact. The engine and body were in remarkable condition.

Jack wasn't surprised. "It's the air, no humidity. The San Joaquin's really a desert, desert air is dry and don't corrode." He walked around the car. "It's the dust too," he said. "Look here." The car was covered with a thick layer of dust. Taking a penknife from his pocket, Jack chipped some of it off the hood. "Baked on," he said, "keeps out the sun..."

We walked back to the garage and Jack asked Camillio to bring in the Packard.

"We'll take a look at the engine first," Jack said.

The 356-cubic-inch Packard straight eight fit snugly in its housing, and we had to remove the hood, front fenders and grillwork to get at it. I enjoyed the work, it was a good anesthetic and the day passed quickly.

After dinner, a brochette of chihuahua garnished with raisins and shredded carrots that Pasquela served promptly at six in the garage, Jack and I went to the front porch for whiskey and conversation.

"Good idea, Brad, digging up that old Packard," Jack said as he sat down in his high-backed chair and poured himself a drink. "I'd forgotten, but when I was a kid I'd always wanted a Packard. It was a symbol, you know, like a Cadillac or a Lincoln is now. I mean, if you had a Packard, then by God you'd made it. Everything about the car was first class, even the ads. I collected some of them...there was one, I had it tacked up on the wall in my room, it showed a picture of this touring Packard dusting along a country lane past a little boy with a bicycle. 'Maybe you were that boy,' the caption said, and hell, I was." Jack freshened his drink. "So how you doin'?"

"Fine," I said. I was sitting on the porch railing.

"You want a drink or something?"

"Maybe later, I've got some things to do. You going to be out here for a while?"

"For an hour or so."

"I won't be that long," I said, and walked down the porch steps and across the driveway to Ada's old frame house.

It had been a warm brilliant afternoon, but the night had come blue and hard and it was cold again. Inside I fired the gas heaters, sat down at a small desk in the living room. I'd been thinking of Judy, aching for her, and I wanted to share my feelings with Sam Colton because he must've been feeling the same way...he had buried her that morning.

I started to write. There were some things I wanted to tell Sam, little things, about his daughter. Like the time in school in English class. I was new at Albert Fall High School, had transferred the previous week. I was called on to recite something. Lumbering to the front of the room, dread in my chest, I stood in front of the group and began to read something by John Donne, and the words didn't come out of my mouth right. I paused for a moment clearing my throat and, to the amusement of my classmates, continued reading a stanza before sensing the incongruity of a behemoth speaking such delicate words. I stopped reading and went back to my desk and they all turned and looked and laughed, until Judy, who was seated near the front of the room, stood up and told them to shut up. That she would do such a thing, that she would risk her standing with the class, her own acceptance, seemed amazing to me then. It still does, especially since we'd never really met...I wanted to tell Sam about that, and I wanted to describe for him the night years later at JP's how stunningly beautiful she was as she sat in the fractured light—but I couldn't. When I read what I'd written I found that those special moments had become in the telling stiff and turgid, nothing more than biographical anecdotes.

I tore up the letter and dropped it in a wastebasket. Questions, that's all I could offer Sam, and it wouldn't be right to burden him with those. Not now. I dialed Wayne Law.

"Hullo." He yawned into the receiver.

"You awake?"

"Roomie?"

"Yeah."

"What time is it?"

"It's early," I said. "You should be out."

"I'm beat and we've got an early practice in the morning. You comin' back for the game?"

"I don't know."

"Slough's lookin' pretty good, Brad. They're all excited."

"You mean Roger Clayton's excited."

"Yeah, well—"

"Did you see Sam Colton today?"

"Sam? Yeah. I spent the morning with him."

"Was he sore I wasn't there? I should've been there."

"I don't know, Brad. He was disappointed at first, but I told him how you were feeling and I think he understood. He didn't exactly want to go himself, you know. It was tough on him."

"I can imagine."

"There were a lot of people there I'd never seen before. Sam either."

"Who were they?"

"Oh, newspaper people, people from the league—people you never see. She had a lot of friends...Do you want to hear this?"

"Why was she in New York? Anybody say?"

"Not that I know."

"Did you hear any more about the accident?"

"Well, some, yeah. It happened around eleven-thirty Sunday night. She was driving a Hertz car. A Pinto. Somebody said north on the Palisades Interstate Parkway, and she went off out in Rockland County near a little town called Orangeburg. She hit this

127

bridge abutment. The park police figure she fell asleep at the wheel. It was a one-car accident, late at night and the medical examiner found traces of a barbiturate in her blood. Sam wanted me to ask you about that. He didn't know she was taking them."

"Neither did I. But she could get wound up pretty tight sometimes. Maybe this was one of those times."

"Maybe so," Wayne said. "I'll tell Sam."

"So she hit a bridge abutment?"

"That's what they said, yeah."

"It must've been an old road."

"I guess so."

"I don't know that area."

"Me neither."

"So where was she going?"

"I don't know. Sam said she was on assignment for the paper."

"Yeah."

"She wasn't?"

"No, she was running around, doing something on her own."

"A story?"

"Something...I think she was seeing somebody...some guy...I don't know, it doesn't really matter. I mean how could she hit a fucking bridge abutment?"

"It's getting late, Brad."

"You explain that to me. How could she? You get tired, you stop, right? You get sleepy, you either find a motel or pull off the highway—"

"It's getting late, Brad. I've got to get some sleep—"

"Was this a new highway or what?"

"Coach'll be asking about you in the morning...do you want me to tell him anything?"

"New highways don't have bridges with abutments. Must've been an old road..."

"I'll tell him we haven't talked. Take care, Brad. I'll, uh, see you when I see you..."

"Wayne—"

He racked the phone.

CHAPTER FIFTEEN

In front of Ada's house a streetlight leaned out over the dusty, unpaved road. In the feeble light of its single bulb hung a weathered sign proclaiming Rafferty's to be the largest wrecker service in all of the San Joaquin Valley. The sign swayed and creaked in the cool evening breeze.

I pulled on a sweater and crossed the driveway that led back to the wrecking yard. As I started up the stairs to the porch a tow truck rumbled out of the yard and down the drive, its yellow cab-light flashing. Camillio was at the wheel, a radio microphone pressed to his mouth. He turned left and passed beneath the sign, dust billowing as he roared off toward town.

"Head-on," Jack said from the darkness of the porch. "Truck, maybe. Camillio don't go out for no fender-benders."

I nodded and sat down on the stairs. "People and cars, why don't they learn to drive."

"I used to be the same way, you know. Wouldn't climb into a cab unless it was something special. Truck. Head-on..."

I took a big drink. "She ran into a bridge abutment."

"Who?"

"Judy."

"Oh? How'd she do that, Brad?"

"Nobody knows."

"Drunk?"

"No."

"No witnesses, huh?"

"You mind if I get ripped? I'll replace what I drink."

"You do and I'll break your arm."

"I'm a professional athlete. Can't afford that."

"So we'll do some serious drinking and watch the moon."

"Dumb," I said.

"Nobody saw it, huh?"

"No."

"Too bad it's not around here."

"What?"

"The scene of the accident. We could go take a look at it. It's like a blueprint sometimes. You know what you're lookin at, you can tell what happened."

"Yeh."

"It's amazing sometimes. It's just common sense, of course, like the time Bobby Masengale got killed. I ever tell you about that?"

"No."

"That was a sonofabitch, a head-on collision, two cars, both drivers killed, both cars spun off the road, no witnesses. One of the drivers was a rich old coot everybody thought controlled gambling and prostitution in the county, the other was Bobby Masengale, a young fella, diesel mechanic, married, kids, from right here in Wasco. The townfolks wanted to take this racketeer to the cleaners so they talked Betty Masengale into filing a great big lawsuit against the racketeer's estate. But there was a little problem. The evidence collected at the scene indicated the wreck happened in the eastbound lane, but there was no way of telling which car was traveling east. I mean, it could've been the racketeer's, you see what I mean?"

"So then what happened."

"Betty's attorney went over to Bakersfield and hired old B.F. Fenton to investigate. B.F.'s about the best accident reconstruction investigator anybody ever saw, and he came over to take a look. He snapped a lot of pictures, made a lot of measurements, but

130

he couldn't come up with any conclusions. The wrecks were back there in the yard—I'd hauled 'em in, me and B.F. Every day after work we'd talk, and he'd tell me how he wasn't gettin' anywhere and he'd show me the pictures and the measurements and gradually he pulled me into the thing.

"One night after B.F. had gone home I was sittin' out here on the porch and all of a sudden I had like this thunderbolt of an idea and it excited the crap out of me. That day B.F. had shown me all the pictures again, pictures of both cars from every angle— front, side, rear—from every angle 'cept one. There was no pictures from above. So I called B.F. and he came back out and we rigged up some lights and took the pictures. Next day he had 'em enlarged and once he had the enlargements he cut out the outlines of the cars and started fiddlin' with 'em to see if they'd fit together somehow and they did—together they made a great big wide V, something like this here." Jack formed the shape with his hands. "Now the road at the scene was gently curved, with the eastbound lane on the outside. When the cutouts were positioned on a diagram of the road the angle of that V fit the curve of the road only when Bobby Masengale's car was eastbound." Jack smiled. "How about that, huh?...So what I'm sayin' is if it was around here we could look it over ourselves. Might put your mind to rest to know exactly what happened."

"Where's this B.F. now? You still know him?"

"I know him, but he's retired."

"I'm just going to get drunk," I said.

"Nothin' wrong with that."

"You know, every time I see it, it's a different kind of crash."

"Imagination knows how to torture a man."

"How do you think it happened? She falls asleep, she drifts, that's it. Bang."

"Must've been an old road."

"That's what I said. Wayne didn't know."

"You'd damn near have to aim to hit a bridge abutment on a new road."

"Aim?"

"They're a long ways off to the side."

"You could tell those things from looking?"

"I was to see it, I could."

"Okay, what else am I going to do? I got money, Jack. I'm in the play-offs. We could go."

"You wanna? I never been to New York."

"I want to know."

"I ain't no B.F. Fenton, but I've been around long enough to know how these fellas work. You just cover expenses."

"I mean, if I know what happened...maybe then I can put it to rest."

"Well, tomorrow we'd lose in the details...I'd have to run over to Bakersfield and talk to B.F. Fenton and maybe borrow some of his tools. You'd have to get on the horn and find out where we can get a copy of the police accident report and where they've stored the wreck. So I'd say Sunday, we ought to leave Sunday at the latest."

"I'll miss the game. You think I ought to miss the game?"

"Now that's something you're gonna have to think on, Brad. But we wait around too long and instead of a car we'll find one of them bales of metal, smelter-bound..."

That night I waited until I was roaring drunk and then I phoned Coach to ask for permission to miss the game. I told him my girl was dead and I was going to stay drunk for a week. I was going to stay drunk for the rest of my life. He said he'd cover for me as long as he could. He said he knew I'd be able to contribute again and that I should think of him as a friend as well as a coach and business associate. I told him I was drunk and my girl was dead. He said he was sorry and then I pretended I was crying and when I realized I was no longer pretending I hung up.

CHAPTER | **SIXTEEN**

Monday, 11 A.M.

Judy's car had been demolished in the accident, and Hertz had transferred title to the Dunson Ford dealership in Orangeburg, New York; the car was supposedly stored on the premises. As I pulled into the dealership Jack reached into the back seat for the fat black attache case he had borrowed from B.F. Fenton. Setting the case in his lap, he quickly worked the combination lock and the case popped open. Inside, tucked into small compartments cut from foam rubber, were the tools of the trade: a pocket transit-compass used to record the angles of intersections, a Rola-tape used for measuring distances across pavement, a stop watch, a carpenter's tape measure, a folding tripod, a 35-millimeter camera and lenses. Jack removed the camera and mounted a 50-millimeter lens, then adjusted the film settings and opened the car door.

"You ready?" he asked.

I nodded. "What did you think about the accident report?"

"B.F. don't put much stock in accident reports."

"But—"

"You ready?" he asked.

"I guess so," I said.

We had just come from Bear Mountain, New York, the head-quarters of the Palisades Interstate Park Police. While I tried to

133

locate the officer who had investigated Judy's accident, Jack had picked up a copy of the police accident report.

"I read the damn thing, Brad. She had sixty-seven milligrams of some shit in her I'd never heard of. So I called the county coroner's office and talked to a deputy medical examiner. He tells me it's pentobarbi-something, and I tell him I know that, gimme the goddamn brand name. Nembutal, he says, which is good because I know something about Nembutal; I took it for a couple months when Kathleen passed on. So I test the guy. Sixty-seven milligrams, I say, is that enough to induce sleep? And he says, Under the circumstances. Now I know he's fulla shit and I'm not gonna let it go by. I put the needle in him. You sure? I say, and I can hear him start to worry. Under the circumstances, *yes,* he says. But that's less than one pill! I say. And there's a long silence. He's thinkin' how to get out of this? Finally it comes. Are you a doctor? he asks. I laugh. Are *you?* And that does it, he hangs up the phone..."

In the calm, crisp morning, the cars on the lot were still encrusted with the previous evening's frost, but the sun was bright and the day seemed warm. I shed my topcoat and unlimbered my stiff legs.

"What are you saying, Jack?"

"B.F. don't put much stock in accident reports."

"I know."

"And he's right," Jack said. "I gotta feeling that cop—you didn't find him, did you?"

"No," I said.

"I gotta feeling that cop tied his whole investigation to the coroner's report. Now if the coroner's report is wrong, like I think it is, then the accident report ain't gonna mean much either. You follow me? So we'll just check it later, if that's all right with you."

Since the accident report was tucked away in Jack's left hip pocket I couldn't do much else but agree.

"Anyway," Jack said, "B.F. tells me we should just look around, see what there is to see and draw our own conclusions."

"Well, there's not much to see so far."

"Have some patience," Jack said. "No self-respecting car dealer's

134

gonna display a junked automobile. No sir, he's probably got 'er stored back there in one of them garages." And he pointed beyond the service area, where there were two long, corrugated metal buildings.

As we approached the buildings we were intercepted by a short, swarthy man who had come from the salesmen's office on the used car lot.

"Morning, gentlemen," he said, brushing lint from his knit suit. "Can I help you with something?"

"You the manager?" Jack asked.

"Yessir. Jasper Sims at your service." He extended his hand, which Jack shook. "In the market for a used car this morning?"

"No, sir—"

"Ah, a new car then?"

"No, sir."

"Just browsing?"

"Lookin' for a Pinto," Jack said.

"A fine automobile indeed," said Sims, smiling and nodding. "Any particular color?"

"Blue and white," Jack said. "A girl was killed in this one last week. The car's supposed to be stored here and I'd like to take a look." Jack handed Jasper Sims one of B.F. Fenton's business cards.

Sims' smile soured. "This is getting to be a regular goddamn circus," he muttered, handing the card back to Jack. "Look, I'm real busy—"

"Have the police examined the vehicle?" Jack asked.

"No. Now like I was saying, I'm real busy. If I spend time with you I might lose a customer, you know what I mean? Besides that, the insurance people have already been here, the Hertz people have already been here—that ought to be enough."

"I understand," Jack said, "but all the same, I'd sure appreciate having a look. We'll only be a few minutes and...well, you don't want to get involved in this lawsuit, do you?"

"There's a lawsuit?"

Jack nodded solemnly. "You wanna get involved?"

"No, no. Come on, I guess it's all right."

We followed Sims back to one of the corrugated metal buildings, where Sims unlocked and rolled back a large sliding door. In the darkness at the far end of the long empty warehouse I could see a dim outline of the mangled Pinto. Sims turned on the overhead lights and Jack readjusted his camera settings.

The back half of the car was generally undamaged; there was a small dent in the right rear fender and a smaller related dent in the right rear bumper, but that was all. The front half did not exist. It had been crushed, the framework and sheet metal compressed like an accordian on the down-stroke. On the driver's side a maze of twisted steel jutted into the front seat. The steering wheel, its sides bent drastically forward, enveloped the blunt steering post like a tortilla. The steering grips, the dashboard, the shredded seat covers were stained with blood.

Jack took several pictures while we were still ten yards from the car, then walked quickly around it at close range, knelt behind it and snapped still another picture, this one a close-up of the license plate. To complete the identification process he walked to the front of the car, where after a careful search he located and recorded the engine serial numbers. Just above the crushed engine housing, on a piece of unbroken windshield, someone had placed a crudely lettered sticker:

NOTICE: PICTURES OF THIS ACCIDENT
WERE TAKEN WHERE IT HAPPENED.
IF YOU WANT PICTURES CALL:
914–651–6551

Jack noted this number too.

"He should be along in a little while," Sims said. "You won't have to call him."

"Who's that?" Jack asked.

"Slade," Sims said. "The guy who took the pictures. He'll probably want to sell you some. Does portraits too."

"Terrific," Jack said, and then told me to fetch a dolly from a corner of the warehouse. I did. Stretching out on the dolly, Jack scooted under the car, observed the damage to the underpinnings and checked for parts that might have left gouge marks in the highway. Apparently finding nothing of interest, he slid out from under the car, stood and dusted himself off, then lifted the hatchback and surveyed the storage compartment.

"Her personal belongings, they've been shipped to next of kin?"

"Yup," said Sims, "her father, I believe. Somewhere in Virginia."

Jack slammed the lid shut, then walked once more around the car, slowly this time, paying particular attention to the dents in the right rear fender and bumper.

"Well, that oughta do 'er," he said. "Sure do appreciate it, Mister Sims."

We walked back to our car, where we were met by Slade, the accident photographer. Tall and gangling, Slade wore an ill-fitting topcoat over a white shirt and brown slacks, the shirt frayed at the collar, the slacks threadbare and shining in the sun. He carried two dog-eared manila envelopes, one of which he offered to Jack.

"You might be interested in my pictures," he said, showing a gap-toothed smile. "You're the investigator, aren't you?"

"Yes," Jack said. He accepted the envelope and removed a stack of pictures. "Real good," Jack said as he shuffled through the pack, "you do real good work..."

He was lying. The pictures were underexposed. Worthless.

"So how'd the accident happen?" Jack asked, still shuffling. "You hear anything?"

"Oh, yeah," said Slade. "Sure. Girl on dope, you know, just fell asleep and, uh, drifted off into the bridge there. Weren't no skid marks or nothin'. That's about it. Happened two miles south here."

"Girl on dope, huh?"

"That's what they say, yeah."

"I see. Well, I don't think we can use these." He handed the envelope back to Slade. "But they tell me you do portraits, that right?"

"Sure do. Things been kind of slow, you know. Got my best work right here, though. Maybe you'll like it."

Slade unwound the string on the second envelope and produced

137

yet another photograph of the wreck, this one a tight shot of the driver's side, this one clear and properly exposed, this one a portrait of Judy, her head resting face down on the dashboard, her limbs twisted, her body crumpled.

She was impaled on the steering post.

CHAPTER | **SEVENTEEN**

I'd seen enough. I wanted to go home. But Jack, having examined the vehicle, intimated that he doubted more than ever the official version of what happened in the accident. He insisted we proceed to the scene, which, after a brief argument, we did.

Judy had been traveling north up the west bank of the Hudson River on the Palisades Interstate Parkway—a four-lane, limited access, divided highway. She had hit a granite bridge abutment at the 640 overpass two miles south of Orangeburg. The road curves to the west at that point, cutting through thick forest and gently rolling hills, and it is from the crest of one hill to the crest of another that the bridge spans, an extended arch of block granite with piers rooted perilously close to the road's surface. I parked on the left shoulder in front of the abutment that bore scars.

"Coming?" Jack asked.

I shook my head, no.

Jack nodded. Retrieving the attache case from the back seat, he climbed out of the car, set the case on the hood and removed the camera. After snapping pictures of the scene he returned to the case and picked up the tape measure and Rola-tape. Then, the camera slung over his shoulder, he crossed the highway and walked south, eventually disappearing around the bend in the road.

Twenty minutes later he reappeared on the opposite side of the road, walking slowly toward the car, kneeling occasionally to examine what appeared to be tire tracks in the grass shoulder. I watched him in the rearview mirror, walking and kneeling, and in a few more minutes he reached the car. After repacking the case and returning it to the back seat Jack opened the front door and sat down, heavily, the car swaying as it absorbed his weight.

"The lazy bastards," he muttered. "They've worked their magic, Brad." He unbuttoned his topcoat, took an unfiltered cigarette from his shirt pocket and packed it against the dash.

"Who?" I said.

"All of 'em, seems like." Jack lit the cigarette and inhaled deeply. "The coroner, he screwed it up for sure. I mean, I ain't a doctor or nothin', but I know damn good and well sixty-seven milligrams of Nembutal won't drop a baby. Hell, I used to take the stuff myself. Each pill is a hundred milligrams and you gotta swallow a fistful just to get a nap."

"But that's for you, Jack. I mean, you're a pretty good-sized man. Judy, she—"

"You find me a doctor who's an expert—what do they call 'em? Toxi-something."

"Yeah."

"You find me a good one and I'll guaran-damn-tee you he'll confirm what I've said."

"You're that sure?"

"Mark my words," he said, and spat out a fleck of tobacco. "Now the way I figure it, for the coroner to make that conclusion he had to assume that the effect of the drug was compounded by something else. But what? You mix Nembutal with alcohol you got big problems—even I know that—but there was no alcohol, no anything. Fatigue maybe, but I doubt it. I bet she was a hard worker with her career and all, and with the way newspapers run those presses and the goddamn deadlines they keep, I bet she was up all night bangin' out copy and sluggin' down stir—that was her routine probably, stayin' up late, and the chances of her falling asleep then—when was it? Eleven? Eleven-thirty?"

"Yeah."

"Pretty goddamn slim, I'd say, because I can prove she was awake when she hit that bridge."

"What?"

"At least I think I can. But I'm getting ahead of myself here. First I want you to see how these people sometimes work." He crushed out his cigarette and from his left hip pocket produced our copy of the police accident report. Folding back the cover page, a mimeographed sheet printed with the key to the number codes used in the report, he spread the second page, the report itself, out on his lap.

"The cop—what's his name? I can't read this."

"Padgett."

"You couldn't locate him, that right?"

"No, I couldn't. The desk sergeant said he was on duty somewhere."

"But he didn't say where."

"No."

"Did you tell the desk sergeant why you wanted to see Padgett?"

"I told him."

"He tipped him off then. The sonofabitch was probably hiding."

"Why?"

"Because Officer Padgett didn't investigate a goddamn thing, that's why. He just fabricated his report to fit the coroner's findings. You can tell by the filing date, and...look here." Jack pointed to the report, then to the code sheet, back and forth, translating:

LOCATION OF MOST SEVERE PHYSICAL COMPLAINT	Chest
TYPE OF PHYSICAL COMPLAINT	Puncture
VICTIM'S EMOTIONAL AND PHYSICAL STATUS	Apparent death
CONTRIBUTING FACTORS, HUMAN	Drugs; sleep

"What the hell is going on here?"

"This Padgett's dumber than dirt," Jack said. "I mean, the clincher is his schematic of the wreck. See here? He's got your friend driving north in the right-hand lane. That's all right—but he's got her drifting off to the left and into the bridge abutment,

141

and that just ain't hardly possible. I mean, all these roads, if they're built proper, are peaked in the middle for drainage. Now if her car was *drifting*, it would *not* have gone off to the left, it would've gone off to the *right* and up a goddamn embankment—common sense, right?"

"But the road isn't peaked that much, Jack." In the rearview mirror I'd caught the reflection of the road and it seemed flat.

"Maybe so," Jack said, having checked it again himself. "Truth is it don't really matter. If Padgett had examined the wreck he'd of known that."

"You're telling me she wasn't drifting?"

"Absolutely not."

"And you could tell from the wreck?"

"You got to know what you're lookin at, Brad. Did you notice the steering wheel, the way the sides of the steering wheel were bent forward?"

I had.

"Well, think about that for a minute. If she'd been unconscious at impact, asleep, would the sides of the steering wheel have been bent forward like that? If she'd been asleep...her body would've been the first thing to hit the wheel with any force. If she'd been asleep, the top and bottom of the wheel would've been bent."

"They weren't."

"No, they weren't."

"The sides were."

I was beginning to understand.

"When she hit that damn bridge, Brad, she was not only awake, she was holding the wheel and she'd locked her elbows against the crash. Here's how I see it,"—he fired another cigarette—"she was driving north in the right-hand lane like Padgett said. But suddenly she skidded across the highway and off the left—"

"Where's the bridge abutment in relation to all of this?"

"Hell, she's nowhere near the bridge abutment. This is back up the road about two hundred yards. There's rubber all over the highway."

"Skid marks?"

"Skid marks, right."

"But Slade—"

"He missed 'em," Jack said. "Padgett too. It was late, dark— the lazy bastards probably didn't even look. Anyway," he said, "she straightened the wheel and drove along the shoulder for nearly a hundred yards. The tracks are there, clear as day. She came around the bend and, well—"

"She didn't try to get back on the road?"

"I don't think so. It was like something was there, keeping her off. You remember those dents in the right rear fender and bumper? They were fresh. No road film. I think somebody slammed her good before she hit that bridge. Now, I don't know if they were trying to..." Jack glanced at the accident report. "Padgett here says it was foggy. Maybe someone was just trying to pull her over."

"She could've stopped then. I mean, the bridge abutment, it just came up on her...she could've stopped."

Jack cracked his wind-wing and flipped his cigarette into the road. "But she didn't," he said. "And I'm wondering now what she had that was so goddamned important. Did she carry a lotta cash with her? Jewelry? Anything like that?"

"We've got to get this investigation reopened, Jack."

"So what the hell was she working on?"

"Does it matter? We're talking homicide here, Jack."

He shook his head.

"What the hell else could it be?"

"I don't know, Brad. I don't know how they'd handle it. Truth is, I don't think they'll handle it at all."

"Jack—"

"You don't know what she was working on?"

"No, but goddammit, she was a sports reporter, Jack. So she was working on bullshit. What could it be? So important that...?"

"So look at what we've got here. If I'm right about this stuff then the coroner's office, the department, particularly this Padgett, they don't look too good right now. We've caught 'em with their pants down and the first thing they're gonna do is cover their ass. Now if we go to the right people and show 'em what we've got we can probably get Padgett busted and we can probably get a review of the coroner's report, but that's about it and that ain't enough. On the other hand if you knew what Judy was up to, who she was involved with—stuff like that—why, we maybe could get these guys to forget their asses a minute and get interested in the case. The way things are, though, we're gonna have problems with 'em, sure as hell. I mean, it ain't clear what's going on. I mean, maybe—maybe it was just some crazy bastard harassin' her or something."

"You're still talking homicide, Jack. We're talking about somebody killed her. That's what we're doing, Jack. We're sitting here, for Christ's sake, we're talking about somebody killed Judy. Jesus Christ!"

"Now don't misunderstand me," he said. "We'll pursue this thing if you want. We'll go through channels—hell, we'll have to go through channels—just don't expect no help from these guys, that's all. No help at all. Is that clear?"

"What are we really talking about?"

"Let's get me to a telephone," he said. "I got to talk to B.F. Fenton."

"Let's go."

When traffic cleared I wheeled out onto the parkway and drove back to Orangeburg, exiting there, driving again past Dunson Ford. Across the street from the dealership, at a filling station, there was a telephone booth. Jack made his call there. Fifteen minutes later he returned.

"Find us a motel," he said. "Looks like we're gonna be here for a while."

There was a Ramada Inn down the street. As I drove to the motel Jack filled me in on his phone conversation. It turned out B.F. agreed with Jack's analysis of the accident, and his anticipation of problems with the police. B.F. suggested Jack seek independent confirmation of his theories before making any formal presentation. According to B.F. this would take a week, maybe two. Jack would have to get his film developed, he would have to find and interview two or three reputable toxicologists, he would have to dismantle the Pinto's right rear fender and bumper and send the parts to a laboratory for analysis. After that, assuming

144

confirming results from both the interviews and lab analysis, he should be ready to confront the appropriate officials.

"And if they won't reopen the investigation," Jack said, "why, the facts'll keep. But let me tell you something, nobody else is gonna touch this thing either, not without more information. You gotta lay it out for 'em, Brad. That's what B.F. says. There's gotta be a motive here. If it was just some crazy bastard—"

"They're not going to try and hunt down some crazy sonofabitch?"

"They don't seem to want to hunt anybody. I'm just saying we could have more leverage. I mean, she was a reporter, wasn't she? Couldn't she have been on to something? Couldn't she have had some sonofabitch cornered?"

"She covered football, Jack. She was a *sports* reporter..."

"Well, you said she was involved with some other man, right? So maybe she wanted to be done with him. Or he with her. Or the guy's wife found out. People get crazy in certain situations. Or he could have been involved in something shady, she finds out. She's a reporter on top of everything. We need more information, is what I'm trying to tell you, Brad. We can drop this thing or come up with more information before we accuse these local folks here of fouling up."

"Her father might know something."

"You know him?"

"Sure."

"Maybe she had to be here. Maybe it was more important to be here. Find out what the hell she was doing. If you gotta go home to do it, then go. It ain't gonna hurt none to leave me up here. Matter a fact it might be the best thing. While you're home I can get this stuff nailed down. If I'm right and you find something strange going on, then you'll know you're operating on solid ground. If nothin's going on, then you've still seen what you wanted to see and that's why we came up here in the first place. Am I right or am I right?"

Later that afternoon Jack dropped me off on a Manhattan street corner. I caught a cab to La Guardia and boarded a commuter flight to Washington. On the flight I sat in the midst of a group of businessmen who couldn't stop talking about the Washington-New Orleans play-off game. One of the men had been to the game and mentioned the outstanding play of Jan Rutledge and Wayne Law, and "a giant rookie" whose name he couldn't recall. Willie Slough? I asked for the score. He told me. "Thanks," I said, turned away and looked out the window and tried to figure out how I felt.

It was 28–7, Washington. Without defensive right end Brad Rafferty...

CHAPTER EIGHTEEN

Sam Colton climbed up the steep, muddy sidewalk that led to his house. He had studied the path carefully before setting out, and now he was picking his way up the hill, side-stepping puddles, tiptoeing through mud, trying to preserve the shine on his military shoes. Except for the shoes Sam was in mufti—rumpled suit, white shirt and dark tie, bucket-topped Irish tweed hat. In his right hand he carried a sheaf of government papers, in his left an umbrella unfurled against a light drizzle, the drizzle becoming rain as he climbed. When Sam reached the top of the hill he paused for a moment, chest heaving, to catch his breath.

"Colonel, is that you?"

Backing up a step as if in fear, Sam raised his eyes to the porch, where I stood huddled against the weather. "Brad?"

"You should be arrested for impersonating a civilian," I replied. "I hardly recognized you."

"Boy, you startled me."

"I'm sorry, Sam. I—"

"Well, don't be," he said. "It's good to see you."

Moving toward the porch, Sam shifted the papers to his left hand, juggled them for a moment, then extended his right.

"I've never seen you in civvies before."

"You mean the suit? A little experiment," he said. "I've been

147

working with some systems analysts at TRW. I wanted them to be comfortable with me so I didn't wear my uniform. As it turned out I was the one who was uncomfortable and I couldn't do a thing all day." He laughed. "It's going to be hell when I retire, Brad. Well, come on in, we'll have a drink."

While Sam fixed drinks in the kitchen I wandered into the livingroom and sat down. The room was strewn with the daily debris—unopened mail, yesterday's papers—but its musk and mood, its furnishings, even the arrangement of its furnishings hadn't changed in ten years. It could have been 1966, and I did nothing to disturb the setting. In fact I'd unwittingly completed it. I was sitting exactly where I used to sit when I came to see Judy—on the worn cerulean sofa, within reach of the stereo console—and I was feeling the same flutter of anticipation in my stomach.

"Refreshments," Sam announced, wheeling a stainless-steel serving cart into the living room. "Bourbon for you? Is that all right?"

"Fine."

Sam wiped his hands on a dishtowel, then handed me a tall glass filled with ice, bourbon and mineral water. "Of course the wife usually handles the hospitality," he said, "but she's off visiting our eldest for a few weeks..."

"You're doing fine, Sam."

"Is the drink all right?"

"Perfect," I said.

Sam poured a martini for himself, set out a can of mixed nuts and settled into an overstuffed armchair.

"Your eldest," I said, "you mean Dan?"

"Yes, did you know him well?"

"Well, no, not really. Being older, you know, and off at college most of the time, he wasn't around much. Except for the night we wrote the alma mater for Albert Fall."

"The night you what?"

"The night we wrote the alma mater for Albert Fall. He was home on vacation, I guess."

"The real alma mater?"

"Yeah, the one they use."

"You guys did that?"

"It was pretty funny," I said. "Albert Fall was a new school then with no song and there was a contest or something. Anyway, Judy and I were up the night before the deadline trying to write the damn thing. We wanted to get away from the Hail-to-Thee kind of stuff but weren't having much luck—in fact we were about to give it up when Dan came in and asked what we were doing. We told him and Dan said, 'Hell, that oughta be easy—do you know who Albert Fall is?' We didn't, of course, but Danny told us and an hour later we had the lyrics, and an hour after that the melody, and the next day we entered the song and I'll be damned if we didn't win the contest. The song really had nothing to do with the school, it was a kind of glowing tribute to this guy named Albert Fall, the real joke being that a man less deserving of celebration never ever existed."

"So who the hell was he?" Sam asked.

"He was Secretary of Interior under President Harding. He resigned in disgrace during the Teapot Dome scandal."

"That's funny?"

"In response to the resignation Harding offered him an appointment to the Supreme Court."

"What?"

"It's true."

"And the song, it was tribute to the character of this man? To Albert Fall?"

"Yes, and to the jerks on the schoolboard who named our school after him. They're still using the damn song."

Sam smiled and shook his head.

"Judy wrote most of the lyrics," I said, reaching for my glass. "I wish I could remember them. She really nailed the bastards, Sam."

Sam's smile had melted like hot wax.

"You okay, Sam?"

"Judy was a great kid, wasn't she?"

"Yes," I said, "she was."

"Excuse me," he said.

When Sam returned he'd composed himself and was smiling apologetically. I'd decided to leave, but now, as Sam freshened the drinks, I could see he was anxious for me to stay.

"So how was California?" he asked, settling once more in the overstuffed chair. "Did you have a good trip?"

"Fine, Sam. I just—I should've been here," I said. "I kept thinking the whole time I should've been here. I hope Wayne explained why I wasn't."

"Yes. Don't worry about it."

"I tried to write you, I wanted to explain myself, but I also wanted...that's where I ran into trouble. I sat down to write but she...there were little stories, you know, but I just couldn't..."

Sam nodded and drained his glass. "The dead are hard to be with." He refilled his glass.

"But in time—"

"Sure," he said. "Time takes care of everything, doesn't it."

"So they say."

"There were other men in her life, Brad."

"I know that. Why was she in New York?"

The question was abrupt, Sam didn't answer right away. He reached for the can of mixed nuts. After a while he said, "I guess I don't really know. I spoke to her Saturday morning before she left and from everything she said I assumed she was going to Philadelphia. When she ended up in New York I just chalked it up to the paper."

"Did she call you?"

"Yes," he said. "Seeking some fatherly advice. She was excited about the game but at the same time she was dreading the flight up. She was supposed to travel with Brady Young and Ed Thomas, but she didn't want to. Apparently Thomas had propositioned her recently—she hadn't liked that—and Brady, he was still upset with her about an article she'd written a few weeks ago. She was feeling a little vulnerable, we talked about it and everything seemed fine."

"Brady was upset with her?"

"It was a political thing. She'd written a feature for the Sunday

150

paper on somebody—I can't remember the guy's name. An investment broker or something, friend of the players—I'm sure you know him."

"Charlie Rale?"

"Right. The article didn't sit well with the local football establishment. First your owner, then your coach, then somebody else, they all said Brady was pissed off one way or another about the piece. I think Mister Clayton even demanded Judy resign. I'm sure you've heard all this—"

"Judy was doing her job. And Charlie Rale would never try to hurt the Washington franchise. Where does this crap come from?"

"But to get them all so mad at him they resent an article about him..."

"Listen, Sam, Charlie's been hanging around the team for years. At first he was just Jan Rutledge's running partner but he kept hanging around and after a while Tanner and those guys got to know him and like him, and they introduced him to Mister Clayton, who got to like him too, and pretty soon Charlie was doing little favors for Mister Clayton and in return Clayton was steering Charlie a little business. So Charlie involved a few players in these deals, the deals worked out reasonably well, and pretty soon Charlie was representing quite a few players. This went on until the World Football League came along. So some of the players Charlie represented approached him about the new league. So naturally Charlie researched the situation and put those players in touch with a California sports attorney and a few players signed. That's his job. Anyway, by the following year the league had folded and everything was back to normal. Everything except Charlie's business, which by that time was in the process of being destroyed by Mister Clayton. All of this happened two years ago. To think that after all that time they're still carrying a grudge against Charlie Rale...who the hell do these people think they are—"

"But I can see Clayton's view of it, Brad. I mean, what you're telling me is that Charlie was sort of a member of the team family and he—"

"There's no family, Sam."

151

"Your owner apparently sees things differently," he said. "Coach too, from what I've read. Even some of the players. Judy got caught in the middle, but in their minds that really didn't matter. By publicizing Charlie Rale she'd let them down, betrayed the family trust, so to speak."

"You're probably right," I said, "but do you...could this explain her being in New York? Her problem with Brady over this? Was she running from the damn thing?"

"No, no, this was a trivial incident. I think Brady was probably irritated with her, and he might even have replaced her had it been up to him, but it wasn't. Judy was hired by Mrs. Neuberg, the publisher of the newspaper. She loved Judy's work and Judy knew it...What is it, Brad? I mean, all these questions—you're asking a lot of questions here."

"I've seen the wreck, Sam."

"You've seen the wreck?"

"This morning. There were irregularities in both the coroner's report and the police accident report. I'm in the process of having them checked out."

"Irregularities? What are you talking about?"

"She didn't fall asleep at the wheel, Sam."

"What?"

"She was forced off the road."

"But—"

"Listen to me, I'm speculating here. None of this is nailed down. I want you to understand that before I say another word—"

"You can't leave her alone, can you, Brad?" He looked me square in the eye. "You can't, can you? You never really could. You were always around here, odd hours of the day and night. Throwing rocks at the windows, sniffing around like some goddamn..." Sam sighed and drained his glass. "So what do you want?" he said.

"I think she was working on something, Sam. I'd like to go through her personal belongings, the things that were shipped down from New York. If nothing's there, I'll need her keys. Car keys. Apartment keys. Keys to her desk."

Sam mumbled something into the glass, his breath condensing in a circle of moisture.

"I didn't hear you, Sam."

"Everything's here," he said without turning. "In her bedroom."

CHAPTER NINETEEN

Judy's room had been sealed off from the rest of the house. The furnace dampers had been drawn shut and the carpet and draperies had been removed along with most of the furniture. Three pieces remained: a twin bed, its mattress sagging under the weight of two bulging cardboard boxes; an antique French dresser with drawers exposed and empty; a taboret. A garment bag had been placed on the taboret, a set of matching luggage on the floor nearby, among other boxes, these larger and more carefully packed than those that were on the bed. BEKINS was written on these boxes; and in Sam's uneven printing: APARTMENT.

After slitting the masking tape that sealed the apartment cartons I sifted quickly through the contents of each box, shucking the newspaper packing, examining each item and discarding it for the next. Finding nothing of interest I ransacked the luggage, two pieces of which she had taken with her to New York. In those suitcases were a skirt and some blouses, several pairs of jeans and shoes and other travel incidentals—make-up kit, a hairdryer, magazines—nothing important. Wiping sweat from my face, I sat down on the bed and after pausing for a moment to catch my breath, turned to the two remaining boxes marked: OFFICE.

I set the nearest box against my left hip, slit the top and began.

154

There were ten years of league record manuals, twelve years of Washington press books, a copy of the league media directory, Hall of Fame updates, propaganda from the league management council, counterpropaganda from the players' association, reference material on the upcoming college draft, game programs from the previous season. I repacked the box, moved it to the floor, slid the next one into position. More garbage.

There was a copy of the club's petition for a temporary restraining order and injunction against the World Football League, dated May 10, 1974. It said that the WFL defendants

> ...have embarked upon and are actively engaged in a concerted program and course of conduct to obtain players for the WFL by directly, intentionally, and tortiously interfering with the contractual relationships existing between the club and its players...

and that

> ...Unless the defendants are immediately restrained and enjoined from continuing said activities, the club will suffer irreparable injury for which it cannot be adequately compensated in monetary damages.

As I read the twenty-page document and remembered how fast the new league had disappeared, not only from the playing fields but from the courts, not to mention the disdain the owners and fans showed toward the new league—a disdain not shown among our players, who stood to benefit financially from the league's existence—I began to agree with Sam and his notion that Charlie Rale must have done something then to provoke the prolonged embarrassment he'd suffered ever since at the hands of Mister Clayton. But what? After reading the document I could only conclude that it had little to do with Charlie's rather meager involvement with the World Football League.

Because Judy was not the club correspondent in May, 1974, I assumed she'd dredged up the petition in her research for the Rale article. I rescanned the pages of the petition, looking for

155

pencil marks or underlinings, for some indication that she'd read the document in preparation for the article. There was nothing there, so I rifled the remaining contents of the second box, searching for her notes on that story, or a rough draft—anything. Nothing. But there had to be more...

"Everything's here, Brad."

It was Sam. Now dressed in fatigues, ragged but clean, knife-edged creases in the trousers, wearing an army cap with his outfit's insignia stitched into the crown. He was leaning casually against the door frame, martini cupped in his left palm.

"I don't think so," I said.

He shrugged, surveyed the room. "Quite a mess here, Brad. And you can think what you want, everything's here." His words were beginning to slur.

Everything, I thought, but her work. Where is her work? The spiral notebooks, the current files...Suddenly I knew what was missing.

"Her briefcase, Sam," I said. "I gave her a briefcase two months ago. Heavy combination lock. It had a sort of needlepoint facing. Where is it?"

"I don't know," he said. I followed him back into the livingroom. He said again he had no recollection of the briefcase, but did remember that along with the luggage that had been shipped from New York there'd also been an inventory form and after a brief search he was able to locate it. After he'd handed me the form he weaved unsteadily to his overstuffed chair and collapsed.

I read the inventory form and found, as I'd suspected, the briefcase unlisted. Feeling sure now that the briefcase, or whatever was in it—her work—had been the object of the assault, I began rethinking the events of the past few weeks, searching for inconsistencies, for some clue to her work, to her death. It was no use. I didn't know a goddamn thing about her work. She'd never mentioned it to me or Sam, the people she was closest to, and not to Brady Young or Ed Thomas, the people she worked with. If she had, Brady would have known where she was when I asked after her that Saturday night in Philadelphia. He would have told me she was on assignment in New York.

I wandered into the diningroom, stared at the fruit and flowers that flanked a thin leather book. Printed across the top of the first page were the words THOSE WHO ATTENDED SERVICES, and in a column beneath the heading, scratched over a dim drawing of Christ on the cross, were the signatures, twenty to a page, for seven pages. It was the funeral register. As I began to read through the names I remembered how Wayne had been impressed with the service but surprised at the number of mourners he hadn't known, and I saw why. The names on the first several pages were of Judy's school friends, people from Albert Fall and Ohio State. The names on the next few pages were of Sam's friends, army officers and their families. And at the bottom of the sixth page and stretching over to the seventh were the names of her colleagues at the paper, and following them, the league functionaries—all people Wayne wouldn't have known. The names were beginning to blur until I got to the twelfth name on the seventh page.

Obliterating the knees of Christ was the signature of Judy's ex-employer, the Cleveland financier, Keith Thomas Thorley.

TWENTY

Thorley. I'd gotten a jolt when I saw the name. Why? Judy had liked the man, he'd helped her, and maybe my reaction had something to do with that—him being the one and not me. Back home now, I headed straight for the bedroom, fell into bed and instant sleep...

I wanted to wake up, I knew I wanted to wake up. It was that dream again. She was walking toward me along a rocky beach. Unaware of my presence, she knelt at a tidal pool and for a moment watched the sea life thriving there. Then, having gently stirred the water, she rose and continued along the shore, still unaware of me though coming near. At last she saw me. I smiled in a knowing way; she looked. Fidgeted. I was confused. I said something to calm her—she was turning away. She was clambering over the rocks. I ran in the other direction and—

I sat up in the dark and walked to the louvered closet doors. I pulled open the doors and began feeling along the top shelf for the shoebox I knew was there.

While Judy was in Cleveland we'd kept our relationship going through letters. There'd been sporadic visits too, of course, and occasional telephone calls, but Judy felt the telephone was a superficial kind of communication and had insisted we write. I don't know what became of my letters but I'd filed hers chronologically and stored them in the shoebox.

I lay down on the bed and began to read through the first packet of letters, dated July-December. As I read the first few— a note hastily scribbled on the plane that brought back our farewell at the airport gate, another written in an empty Cleveland apartment that described something of the apprehension she was feeling then—as I read these first letters from Judy the memories came flooding back.

July 7

...I had my first job interview this morning. It was with Jim Keaton, the sports editor at the Cleveland *Sentinel.* James Rollin—do you remember? He worked on the paper with me at school—he's now a community affairs reporter at the *Sentinel* and he set up the interview. He said I wouldn't have any problem, that Keaton was keen on the idea. All of this was said last week over lunch and preceded what I now see was a proposition. I wish I'd seen it then but I didn't so I showed up at the *Sentinel* this morning thinking Keaton was expecting me. When I announced my presence to Keaton's secretary she looked at me as if I'd just stepped off the moon. "He's in a meeting," she said. Like an idiot I just stood there until she told me to wait in the lounge down the hall.

So I trudged down the hall and into the lounge and waited and waited and I'd about decided that I'd been had, that Keaton had no idea who I was or what I wanted much less any intention of seeing me, when the secretary appeared again, with a tall, distinguished-looking man who, it seemed, had come to see Keaton, too. "He'll just be a few more minutes," the secretary told him, then asked if he'd like some coffee. "No," the man snapped, then, frowning, sat down. By now I'd taken a good look at him, at his elegant clothes and manicured nails and well, if Jim Keaton would keep *him* waiting he'd keep anybody waiting, and so I decided to wait around and see what would happen.

It wasn't long before Mr. Thorley and I were talking. That's his name. Thorley. He's a Cleveland businessman, about fifty years old, married, established, a pillar of the community—or so I gathered from the conversation. He was here because the president of the Parks Commission had asked him to talk to Keaton about a plan to refurbish Municipal Stadium, apparently a sensitive issue. Thorley had agreed, but, he said, had he known Keaton was such a bore he would've refused the request. Thorley then asked why I was there and I told him and the subject must have interested him, because he asked more questions, and pretty soon I was babbling away about my plans, and just about the time I realized I was talking too much, Keaton arrived. Ignoring me completely, he went straight to Mr. Thorley and after apologizing for being late, took his arm and would have had him out of the door and down the hall if Mr. Thorley hadn't said, "I believe Miss Colton was here before me." "Ah," said Keaton, "of course." As it turned out Rollin had spoken to Keaton after all, but had lied to me about Keaton's wanting a woman sportswriter on his staff. The interview lasted all of three minutes and ended with Keaton suggesting I might have better luck over at the *News-Sun,* which, I found out later, is a political weekly.

Male Chauvinist Pig.

And so I left. Discouraged, of course, but not down. Tomorrow I'll try the *Plain Dealer,* and if I fail there I'll try every one of the small-town newspapers nearby, and if I strike out there I'll probably still have a job because as I left the *Sentinel* Mr. Thorley stopped me and handed me his business card, told me if I had any problems finding work to give him a call...

And she did have problems finding work. The next several letters detailed similar experiences at the Cleveland *Plain Dealer,* the Akron *Beacon-Journal,* the Ashtabula *Star-Beacon* and the Lorain *Journal.* On August 12, now thoroughly discouraged, her money running out, she wrote about her intention to call Keith Thorley and ask for a job. On the 16th she reported the result:

...*Hired.* Just like that. Aspiring journalist becomes assistant to executive secretary to president of little-known but exceedingly powerful finance company. The company, called Western Funding, Incorporated, occupies a suite of furnished offices atop the prestigious Lakeway Towers in downtown Cleveland, Ohio. From her desk the new secretary has a glorious view of Lake Erie and its principal tributary, the Cuyahoga River, which, I am sad to report, is so thick with sludge and oil slick that one night last week she just burst into flame, spontaneously, like an oily rag in an old garage. Disgusting, isn't it? But I digress. I wanted to tell you something of the company. It's such an exciting, fascinating surprise...

The final pages of the letter described in general terms how Western Funding worked: where the money came from, whom it was loaned to and at what exorbitant price, all of which I found sort of upsetting. In my reply letter I compared Thorley to Shylock, which must have offended her because in subsequent letters she never again mentioned company activities. Instead she wrote about Thorley (she now called him "Keith"), as if trying to convince me about his good character. The letters had the opposite effect. They were so damn full of "Keith" that I came to see him not as the dynamic, Renaissance character that she described but as a rich middle-aged lech who was in the process of seducing my still surprisingly naive Judy. I stupidly said as much and she said that I was nuts, off the wall, etc. Finally I believed her...mostly because I wanted to, partly because in her November-December correspondence she stopped mentioning him, as she'd stopped mentioning the subject of Western Funding. Now she wrote about the city, her experiences there—where she went, what she did. And I wrote about football—the characters on the team, the excitement of the season (I was playing some, we were winning)— and although we were physically apart I began to sense a certain strength in our relationship. I began to feel we were sort of meant to be together on a permanent basis. It was with these feelings in mind that I reminded her about the plans we'd made that summer and suggested a visit, our first. In a letter dated December 19 she wrote: "Come! By all means! We'll have a wonderful time!" And so it was agreed...the club had made the play-offs, we'd meet the weekend following our elimination, when and if it came.

It came sooner than I'd have liked...after all, I was a professional football player. We played Minnesota in the first round and lost. I skipped the team charter and flew directly to Cleveland without calling. I'd surprise her, she'd help drown my loser's sorrows. When I called to tell her I was there...she told me she couldn't see me. She'd be traveling that night to Mexico with a client, DeAngelis. I was stunned, even though I was there early and unannounced, so in a way it was my own damn fault—or so I tried to convince myself on the flight home.

But then I didn't hear from her for an unusually long time. Six weeks?...I reached for a second pack of letters, withdrew the first envelope and examined its postmark. January 27, 1971. So yes, it had been six weeks. Six weeks of misery. During that time she wouldn't even answer my letters, wouldn't return my phone calls. What the hell had happened? At some point I'd checked with Sam, who told me he'd heard from her two days before, that as far as he knew she was "great." I suspected then that she'd found someone else. Which was confirmed ten days later when I came back from a visit with Jack and found her letter of the 27th in my mailbox. I was looking at that letter now. On a single page of sky-blue stationery, on one close-packed page, she'd managed to explain...I've lied to you, Brad, she began, and she had. But as I put the letter back in its envelope (I'd read it a hundred times), I realized she could've done worse—she could've told me the truth. If she had, if she'd told me that night in Cleveland that she was traveling to Mexico not with DeAngelis but with Thorley, if she'd admitted then that she was having an affair with Keith Thorley...I'd have broken it off with her for good. As it happened, she waited six weeks to tell me, and by then I was so relieved just to hear from her that the affair, a fling, didn't matter so much. What really mattered, I realized, was that it had ended and now that it had she was telling me she was sorry and wanted things back the way they were. Great. Three months later she was standing on my doorstep, suitcase in hand. Through a lead provided by Thorley—a parting gift, she said he'd called it—she'd gotten a job with the Washington *Herald* and was looking for a place to stay. She could've gone home to Sam but she hadn't. She'd come to me. As I lay back on my bed now and remembered that day, and the days and weeks that followed it, the thoughts and images somehow seemed to merge, melt into each other...I began to smile, it was like she'd come to me again, I could sense her presence in the room...

It passed. The moment I acknowledged the feeling it passed, and its passing left me empty—filled with the details of her death, empty of her.

I got up, returned the letters to the shoebox and the box to the closet shelf. I searched my pants pockets for the copy of the inventory form I'd taken from Sam, and when I found it I tore it up and dropped the scraps in a waste basket. If I'd had copies of the coroner's report and the police accident report I'd have done the same with them. This whole goddamn thing was crazy. All these reports and forms and documents. I couldn't leave her alone, but I had to. I was ruining it...whatever it was we had, I was ruining it with all this bullshit. And why? Because Jack said the coroner and the investigating police officer had screwed up. Because Jack said this and Jack said that—what the hell difference did it make what Jack said? I'd been listening to an old man who ran a junk yard.

No more. I tried to call Jack to tell him to forget it, but he was out. I'd tell him tomorrow night. Next stop, back where I came from. Where I belonged.

CHAPTER TWENTY-ONE

Tuesday, 8:15 A.M.

Turning left off Highway 137, I wheeled into Clayton Lane and drove slowly toward the club compound's security gate, careful to obey the series of signs staked out along the right side of the road:

SPEED LIMIT
10 MPH

ALL TRAFFIC STOP
100 FEET

DIM LIGHTS

STOP HERE

Sarge, the club's gendarme, slid open the side door of his tiny booth and stepped outside. He was scowling.

"Wasn't speeding, was I?"

"No," Sarge said. Behind him, in the side window of his booth, hung a large clock, to which he now turned. "You see this?" He rapped the glass. "You're early."

I nodded.

"That'll cost ya," he said.

I nodded.

Sarge grinned. Stepping back inside, he noted my name on the schedule, then pressed a button on his panel. The tollgate rose and Sarge waved me through.

I parked in my assigned space, walked to the back door of the club headquarters building. I took out a plastic identification card, inserted it into the slot in the doorframe, waited for the buzz that would unlock the door. Nothing happened. Next to the slot, built into the cinderblock wall, was an intercom speaker with a red button. Though a sign indicated the intercom was to be used only in emergencies, I pressed the button anyway.

"State your business," said a garbled, disembodied voice.

"For Christ's sake—"

"*State your business.*"

"Subversion."

Sarge laughed. "If you'da come fifteen minutes later you wouldna had to go through this bullshit—you know that, don't you? It wouldna cost you twenty-five big ones either."

"Unlock the goddamn door, Sarge. I'm hungry."

"Tryin' to get a jump on the boys, huh?"

"Yes, now will you unlock the door. Please?"

The door buzzed.

"*Thanks,*" I said.

Hiring Sarge was Mister Clayton's idea—also installing the card security system, getting the guard dogs and putting up the ten-foot-high hurricane fence sheeted with canvas and charged with a paralyzing electrical current that now surrounded the compound.

Measures taken, in Mister Clayton's words, "to eliminate distractions," "to improve concentration." They'd accomplished that, but they'd also given the compound the look and feel of a damned prison. Some guys felt the atmosphere had something to do with the fact that we seemed to play with less spontaneity than we once did.

To recapture that feeling and soften the impression that we're working in a correctional institute, Coach, while Mister Clayton was away last spring on vacation, revamped the locker room area of the club compound. On the floor, expensive deep-pile shag carpeting replaced the indoor Astroturf specified by Clayton when the compound was constructed. Couches, endtables, lamps were bought for those open areas previously furnished with wooden benches; action photographs were hung on the bare walls; and the ceiling was dropped three feet to cover the plumbing pipes and the heating and air-conditioning ducts that had been naked. All welcome changes, but none so welcome as the introduction of the hospitality table. Set up each morning just inside the back door and intended as a way for the club's bachelor players to supplement their junk food diets, the table is loaded with trays of low calorie pastries, bowls of fruit, jars of vitamins, urns of tea and coffee and coolers of ice and various kinds of fruit juice.

Grabbing an apple, a donut and a cup of coffee, I went to my locker, set the food on a lower shelf, drew up a chair and sat down to enjoy the feast. It felt good to be back. I hadn't realized it until now, but I'd missed this life, missed it badly. The drama of the games, the feeling of belonging, of doing something people cared about, the recognition, even esteem—I missed all of it. Even its mindless reliance on body, on the thought-killing routines required to train that body—even that, and maybe that most of all...to live this life you didn't have to think, and I was tired of thinking.

At eight-thirty a bell rang signaling the shutdown of the security system. A few moments later the back door swung open and in walked Jan Rutledge and Wayne Law, faces animated, voices charged with excitement. Following them came Jeff Blair, smiling and whistling and with a copy of the Wall Street *Journal* tucked under his arm. And following him came a whole stream of players, filing by the hospitality table, taking up great handfuls of food and then heading for their lockers, everyone talking now, and laughing. Oh yes...it was good to be back.

"Brad!" Wayne called out when he spotted me. He stepped over the defensive backs sprawled on the floor between us munching donuts and beginning a game of tonk. "Brad," he said again but broke off—one of the card players had taken hold of his leg and wouldn't let go.

I extended my hand, and Wayne grabbed it to pull himself free.

"Damned oxes," he muttered. "If they'd spend as much time studying the game plan as they do playing cards..." He shut up for a moment, then grinned. "So how you doin'?" He clapped my shoulder. "Everything all right? Hey," he said before I could answer, "you'll never guess what happened this morning."

"Tell me."

"We got the Chantilly Cadillac account."

"No," I said, and forced a smile.

"Me and Rutledge. I mean, the guy saw the New Orleans game and got all excited—listen to this...we get five grand apiece, great residuals, *and* the use of a Fleetwood Brougham for one whole year. Can you believe that? Of course we'll have to split time with the car but—"

From behind Wayne a large hand reached around his head and cupped his mouth, the hand's forefinger and thumb clamping shut his nostrils. "Fuck your Fleetwood Brougham," said Jeff Blair, and pulled Wayne's head against his chest. "If you were any kind of a friend, you'd be telling him about Willie Slough."

Wayne was turning red.

"And you'd be telling him *now*," Blair said.

Wayne nodded.

Blair tossed him aside and turned to me. "Good to see you, Brad," and shoved at me a day-old newspaper open to Brady Young's column. "Read this shit."

I spread the column out on my lap and began to read. "I can't," I said, looking up. "This hurts my eyes."

"Read it, for Christ's sake."

I blinked. The men on the plane had mentioned Willie's outstanding play and I'd thought they were mistaken. No such luck. I blinked again, then read what I could of the column:

THE BIG GUY GROWS UP

Not physically, of course, for I am speaking here of one William E. Slough, a six-foot-nine-inch, 335-pound rookie defensive lineman. Not physically, but emotionally. The rookie jitters are gone now, the maturing process has taken hold. And surprisingly soon.

167

When Slough was drafted last spring the pundits whispered he would never be able to make the transition. No, they said. Not from the sandlot play of North Dakota's Outback Conference to the sophisticated play of the pros. It was, they claimed, just too far to come.

But was it?

Consider his performance in the New Orleans game, his first professional start. Playing in place of Brad Rafferty, Slough registered five bone-crushing tackles, three timely assists, one spectacular blocked pass, and two quarterback sacks, the second of which resulted in a safety, the crucial play in the ball game.

And consider the comments of club owner Roger Clayton as he spoke to the press following Sunday's game. "Slough," he said, "was magnificent. He turned in perhaps the finest overall performance we've ever had from a defensive lineman."

Indeed.

And so the pundits are whispering again. Only now they're saying it will be difficult to keep this young giant out of the line-up. He's just too strong, they're saying. Too overpowering.

And do you know something, sports fans?

For once they may be right.

There was more, but I couldn't read any more. I sat staring at the column. "These stats are accurate?"

"Sort of," Wayne said.

"Sort of?" said Blair.

"Well, it ain't gonna make any difference, but just so you'll know, there were, uh, extenuating circumstances."

"Extenuating circumstances?"

"Yeah," Blair said. "Big ones."

"Brady didn't mention any extenuating circumstances. Like what? Talk to me. If there were extenuating circumstances, what have I got to be worried about?"

Just then the back door swung open and in sauntered Willie Slough, wearing a full-length mink coat over some kind of jump suit, a fur hat like you see on Russians, and a pair of black, high-topped Converse All-Stars.

"Him," Wayne said as Willie approached. "He don't believe in extenuating circumstances."

And Blair said, "He *is* an extenuating circumstance."

Willie took off his coat and hat. As he hung them in his locker he looked down at Wayne. "You in my chair, twinkletoes," he said. "I gots to sit down."

"You gots to sit down?"

"Why you always pimpin' me, man?"

"I ain't pimpin' you, Bigfoot. Why you always *think* I'm pimpin' you?"

"Aww, man—you know why. Now get outa my chair."

"How you doin', Willie?" I said.

"Fine, B. You?"

"Good."

"You standin' in my locker, T? Don't you know this is my locker?"

"For Christ's sake," Wayne said. "I'll see you later, Brad." And he turned and tromped off down the aisle toward his own locker.

"Little guys and big guys, they don't mix good, do they, B?"

"No, Willie, they sure as hell don't."

"Been readin' about me, B?" He pointed to the clipping.

"Nice article," I said.

"I got some copies, you know, and mailed 'em off to my folks and stuff. They was real happy about it."

"I'm sure they were, Willie."

"Yeah, I mean, they called me up and everything. Collect, you know, but that's all right..."

I nodded.

"You mind if I ask you somethin', B?"

"No, Willie. Go ahead."

"It's kinda personal-like."

"Something about your family?"

"No, B. Somethin' about the game. Somethin' the boss man said to me after the game. I been puzzlin' about it."

"Go ahead."

Willie cleared his throat. "You, uh...you think I got big shoulders, B?"

"What?"

"Big shoulders. After the game, you know, the boss man told me I got big shoulders. He told me I was gonna carry the team on my big shoulders. That's what he said. Carry the team to Miami on my big shoulders. What I was wonderin' was, well, I'm big, you know, but I ain't that big, am I, B?"

"Oh, that's just a figure of speech, Willie."

"Oh."

"He didn't mean you'd actually have to carry the whole team to Miami. Not all at once, anyway. I mean that'd be physically impossible, wouldn't it?"

"Sure would, B."

"What he must've meant," I said, "was that you'd have to carry 'em...one at a time. I mean that's the only way you could do it. One player at a time, piggyback—you know what I mean."

"Piggyback?"

"That's the only way you could do it, Willie."

"To Miami?"

"That's what he said, isn't it?"

"Yeah, but—"

"Well?"

Willie thought on it. "The boss man...he's crazy, huh, B?"

"Sounds like it to me, Willie."

"I mean, he's messin' with my mind, ain't he? And all this time I'm thinkin' he's different." Willie shook his head.

"Different?"

"Yeah, I mean, I'm thinkin' he has respect, B. But he ain't got no respect. He's puttin' me on a joke level just like everybody and I don't even know about it 'til you tell me. It ain't fair, B."

"No, Willie." I was beginning to hate myself for having done this, but before I could make amends Phil Tanner tapped my shoulder.

"Have a nice vacation, Rafferty?"

"Gimme a break, will you, Phil?"

"It's not over, you know."

"What the hell is that supposed to mean?"

Tanner shrugged mysteriously. "Coach wants to see you. *Now.*"

170

I followed Tanner through the locker room. When we got to the staff's quarters he knocked twice at the door, then walked inside. A moment later Coach emerged, pulling a gold sweatshirt over his head. He smiled wanly, then, taking my arm, ushered me down a short corridor and into the team meeting room. He flipped on the lights and shut the door.

"Sit down, Brad."

I settled into a small desk chair as Coach began to pace.

"Are you ready to play?"

"Yes."

"Everything's all right then?"

"I'm fine."

Coach stopped abruptly, thought for a moment. Directly behind him a vast blackboard displayed our offensive game plan for Chicago, our next opponent. To the right of the blackboard a cork bulletin board held a large placard:

WHAT YOU SEE HERE
WHAT YOU HEAR HERE
WHAT YOU SAY HERE
STAYS HERE

"I'm going to have to play Willie Slough," Coach said. "I'm going to have to start him, anyway." He sat down in a chair across from me. "We didn't know when you'd be coming back."

I nodded.

"I wish to hell you'd called and let me know."

"I—"

"Look," he said. "Just bear with me on this thing, okay? I don't want to play the dumb bastard, but I'm going to have to. Mister Clayton—Christ. He's so goddamned excited about the way Willie played in the New Orleans game, I just—did you see it? The game?"

"No."

"Just the paper probably."

I nodded.

"That goddamn Brady Young. Sometimes I wonder what the

hell he's doing. I mean, Willie beats up a thirty-five-year-old cripple and suddenly he's come of age. I mean, of all the silly-assed
stories..."

"Their guy was hurt?"

"Hell, he could hardly walk, Brad. I mean, it was painful just
to watch him. But forget that. The problem here is Mister Clayton.
He knows damn good and well Willie can't play, and yet...I don't
know. We were just in a meeting. It's like you've upset him or
something. He wants you out of the lineup, Brad. He says you
let us down."

"By leaving? I had your permission, Coach."

"I shouldn't have given it. You shouldn't have asked. Clayton
is crazy on the subject of loyalty and the trouble is, of course, he's
right. You know it, I know it. Loyalty is everything. Just bear with
me on this thing. Clayton's been...I don't know how to describe
it...something's eating at him. I don't know what it is, but he
hasn't been himself lately—we're going to have to work around
him, that's all. We're going to have to humor him a little bit."

"Loyalty."

"Exactly. I mean, if he wants Willie to play, we'll just let him
think Willie's going to play. When he's out watching practice this
week we'll let Willie work with the first unit. When we get into
the ballgame we'll let Willie start, maybe even play some. Not
much, of course, but some, anyway. Now it goes without saying
that I can't do this without your cooperation. You're gonna have
to keep a low profile on this, Brad. You're gonna have to suck up
your pride a little bit or it won't work. Will you do that for me?
I've got to know now."

"I don't seem to have a choice."

"You can always quit..."

"That's what I mean."

Coach smiled. "It won't be that bad, I promise you. We get
into the game, let Willie play a series, that's it. One series and he's
outa there. Now clock time, that's about two minutes. Surely you
can—"

A bell rang, long and loud: the security system was back in
operation, meetings would begin in five minutes.

"Surely you can sit out for two minutes, Brad. I mean, what's two minutes, right? You sat out all of last week. Right?"

I nodded.

"Good," Coach said. "Well, that's about it, I guess. I'm under a little pressure here, Brad, and...well, I appreciate your cooperation, believe me."

We stood.

"Let's win this week, huh?"

"Sure," I said.

"How's the girl?"

"What?"

"You had some girl trouble, right?"

"It's okay now."

"Good."

CHAPTER TWENTY-TWO

I walked out of the team meeting room, back down the hall and into DeVito's Dungeon, the converted closet where the defensive linemen hold their daily meetings. It was still early, the room was dark and unoccupied. I switched on the lights and looked around. Nothing much had changed. Fastened to the wall on my right was the green slate chalkboard and above it, the retractable screen. In the center of the room a 16-millimeter film projector sat on a gray metal cart, the cart surrounded by eight folding desk chairs. I dragged one of the chairs to the back of the room and sat down.

Mister Clayton had surprised me. Not so much with his using my absence as an excuse to slip Willie into the lineup (someone had to play, after all), but with his intention to make that change permanent. Usually a changing of the guard is carefully orchestrated, and the orchestration takes time: an off-season during which the new troop is extolled in the press, a preseason during which the new troop "competes" for the position. Only then, when the fans are sufficiently familiar with the new face—only then is the change effected, never in the middle of a season.

Until now. Whoever the poor bastard was who played first base for the Yankees, who missed one midseason game and never played again, I knew how he felt. At least he could take some comfort from the fact that his replacement turned out to be Lou Gehrig. Willie Slough was no Lou Gehrig.

Coach's plan to avert all of this was beginning to make sense to me. Starting the football game was an honor I could, for the moment, do without, and I certainly wouldn't miss taking part in the week's practices. Of course I would have to get used to the pads and the hitting again, but I hadn't been gone so long that a little prepractice sled work wouldn't be in order. We'd be in sweats today, but a few licks tomorrow, a few on Thursday and I'd be fine. Willie, he could have the rest of it, with my blessing. He could have the six-on-seven drills, the pass rush drills—he needed the drudgery. I didn't. I could get ready in my mind. That was the secret, anyway. Get ready in your mind. See yourself beating some sonofabitch and you could do it. You just had to see it, that's all, and seeing it was easy for me. I wouldn't even have to think about it. It would just happen.

It was already happening.

My tackle this week, Chicago's left tackle, was a big exotic-looking black guy named Crespin Mug. I could see him, all six-feet-seven-inches of him. He had a large head out of which peered these narrow, slanted, angry eyes; he had a broad flat nose, a short thick neck and massive torso, and his arms and legs rippled with muscle. *Tsunami,* they called him. *Tsunami*—Japanese for tidal wave. I wasn't afraid of Crespin Mug. He was, as his nickname implied, incredibly large and strong, but he lacked the mobility that would make it all work, what coaches call "the good feet." Mug had "the bad feet," which was to say "the slow feet," which meant that he moved around more like a loaded barge than any kind of a wave.

To compensate for the deficiency Mug tried to intimidate you, to freeze you with fear. He did this by talking a lot and throwing his elbows around—he had a rotten mouth and hard, sharp elbows—and it was an effective ploy as long as his team was even or ahead in the game, as long as they were running the football and Mug didn't have to cover too much ground; but if they got behind and had to throw, and if you were still around by then, if you hadn't been terrorized into submission or ejected for fighting, why, you could run around Crespin Mug the rest of the afternoon. A head-fake would nail his bad feet to the turf and there you were, free and clear, the wind whistling through your helmet as you slipped the corner and bore down on the quarterback like a runaway freight.

So vivid in my mind was this scene that it took me a moment to realize that it was not the quarterback I was seeing nor the wind I was hearing but Jeff Blair, who was whistling as he entered the room. Blair. In one hand he carried a styrofoam cup brimming with coffee, in the other his copy of the Wall Street *Journal.* He was wearing his reading glasses behind which his eyebrows, when he saw me, arched expectantly.

"We worked something out," I said.

"No kidding?"

"Willie plays one series. You'll have to put up with him in practice, that's all."

"So who gives a damn about practice? Hell, that's terrific, Brad. The sonofabitch, in New Orleans I had to tell him what to do on every play. Did I tell you that? *Every goddamn play.* I mean, he was wandering around out there like a blind hog..."

I laughed.

"One series—you're sure?"

"That's what he said."

"I'm surprised Clayton would agree to something like that."

"I'm counting on it," I said.

As the other defensive linemen filed into the room Blair handed me the newspaper and coffee and began rearranging the furniture, a ritual with him. He placed one chair next to me—the spacer chair, he called it—and as I set the coffee and newspaper on the desk part of the chair he took a second chair and positioned it on the other side of the spacer, directly beneath a grease spot on the wall. Leaving the *Journal* for later, he picked up the coffee, sat down, rocked back in the chair so that the back of his head completely covered the spot on the wall.

"Am I on it?" he asked.

"You're on it," I said.

"Then let the meeting begin."

As if on cue Coach DeVito strode into the room. Looking tan and trim, he carried a stack of burgundy notebooks, our copies of the Chicago game plan. He handed the stack to Willie, who, taking the top folder, passed the stack to the next player, who did the same, and so forth.

"Personnel," said DeVito, now standing at the blackboard. "Their left tackle is Crespin Mug." He turned to the board and drew up a large circle, below which he wrote Mug's name and vital statistics. After a brief discussion of Mug's strengths and weaknesses he moved on to the left guard, then to the center and so on until he had covered every Chicago starter—but one.

"As usual," he said, "we've saved the best for last." And after erasing the diagram of the Chicago offense he wrote in large block letters the words RUNNING BACK and below them, in even larger letters, the name J. D. "DUCK" MALLARD.

"Gentlemen," he said as he turned to face us, "Duck Mallard can fly." He grinned. "We know that, don't we? Don't we, Willie?"

Coach DeVito often called on players cold to see if they were awake. Although Willie didn't know Duck Mallard from Ollie Owl, he at least was awake and nodded energetically.

"Good," said DeVito. "That's all I'm going to say about Mallard for now, but that doesn't mean I don't want you to start thinking about him, because I do. I want you to start thinking about him today. Mallard's the key to this game, men. We stop him, we stop Chicago, and I want you to start thinking about what that means." DeVito erased the blackboard and sat down. "Now turn to your tendencies," he said.

Paper rustling.

"Look at this," Blair whispered, jabbing my arm, and held out for my inspection the tendency page—the page of the game plan that showed by formation what Chicago liked to do on offense.

I nodded. It appeared Chicago relied heavily on execution and repetition. They used only two or three basic formations from which they ran only four or five basic plays. "So Lombardi lives," I said. "What's the big deal?"

"Look at the hit sheet," he said.

The hit sheet shows *where* those four or five plays are run—which holes they like to work and how often. Having found the hit sheet in my game plan I could see why Blair was so excited. Regardless of the play they were running, regardless of the formation they were running it from, Duck Mallard always carried the football, and he always carried it to his right, our left—away from me and Blair.

"Do I have your permission to take the week off?" Jeff asked.

"Absolutely," I said.

Chuckling, Blair dropped his game plan to the floor and reached for his copy of the Wall Street *Journal*. For several years now Blair had been touting stocks in the locker room, talking about PE ratios and stockholder's equity, the importance of timing, of knowing when to buy and when to sell—a gift Blair claimed to be blessed with. Suspicious of the claim, I began to track some of his stocks and found that his sense of timing was right on the mark...he was so right so often that I began to go "long" on his buy recommendations and until the oracle went quiet three months ago I'd made a tidy sum.

The reason for Blair's silence was still a mystery. Looking at him pouring through the *Journal* I was tempted to ask him about it one last time, but knowing how sensitive he was on the subject I said nothing and instead turned my attention to Coach DeVito, who was seated in front of the room, droning on about formations and hashmarks. I dropped my game plan to the floor, rocked back in my chair and began thinking again about Jack and what I would say to him when we talked that evening. I didn't want him to feel he'd been wasting his time. I wanted him to know how much I appreciated his efforts. I wanted him to understand how Sam Colton had become a blank wall, how Keith Thorley—

"Hey," whispered Blair. "GEICO's beginning to move again."

I'd never heard of GEICO.

"Yeah," he said. "Listen to this. Nine and a half on Friday, ten yesterday—got a burner here, sure as hell."

"What'd you pay for it?"

"Two dollars a share, something like that."

"Two? You ought to be ashamed of yourself, Jeff. Keeping these financial opportunities to yourself when you could be sharing 'em with us boys. I mean, we're *team mates* for Christ's sake."

"Yeah, and I'm tired of you guys riding my coattails. I mean, it's all right here in this paper, every goddamn business you could imagine, and all you gotta do is study 'em a little bit and make your own decisions. Why should I do all the work for you bastards?"

"It's all right there?"

"Yeah, I mean—"

"Funding," I said.

"What?"

"Goddammit. Look up a company called Western Funding."

"So who's holding out on who now. What's the name again?"

"Western Funding, out of Cleveland."

"Big board?"

"Hell, I don't know. Check it, check 'em all."

Blair turned to the New York Stock Exchange listings and began searching the agate columns.

"On second thought, forget it," I said.

"What?"

"Western Funding. It's privately held."

"So why ask me to look it up?"

"I'm *sorry*, I just remembered..."

Blair shook his head and turned away. In the front of the room Coach DeVito was lowering the screen. When he finished he sat down beside the projector and motioned for Willie to turn off the lights. The room went dark. As the projector began to grind through the film I went to the door, opened it quietly and slipped out of the room.

I was angry at myself for having left this stone unturned. Sure as hell Jack, when we talked, would ask me about Funding. He'd want to know if the activities of the company had some connection with Judy's work. I couldn't imagine what such a connection might be or how Judy might've handled it—she was, after all, a sportswriter—but I'd have to admit the possibility did exist—they *had* gone to bed, and that was one of Jack's theories. So it was worth at least looking into.

I'd have a peek at Western Funding, and the sooner the better. I went to the payphone in the players' lounge and called the offices of Rale & Associates. In the past, whenever I'd had financial problems or questions, I'd consulted Charlie Rale and he'd always given me sound advice. I hoped he'd do the same now.

When Charlie came on I explained that I wanted to research a small privately held firm but that I wasn't sure how to go about it or even where to begin. Charlie, true to form, assured me he could be of some help but he said, "it has to be today. As of tomorrow my, uh, research department is permanently closed."

"They got you?"

"They got me. Don't cross Roger Clayton, buddy boy."

"Maybe I shouldn't even be seen with you."

"Can you drop by after practice?"

"I guess, but—"

"Fine. I'll see you then. Live dangerously, buddy boy."

TWENTY-THREE

The offices of Rale & Associates were located in downtown McLean, Virginia, at the corner of Dumbarton and Oak streets, on the second floor of a restored Victorian house. The house, an anomaly among the strip shopping centers and fast-food franchises that otherwise populated the business district, was owned by a local real estate magnate who had contracted the restoration and whose offices occupied the first floor. ROUTH ROBBINS REAL ESTATE said the large, gold-flecked letters painted on the frosted pane of the front door; then, in much smaller print: R&A, ENTRANCE AT REAR.

I parked in front of the house, got out of my car and followed a dirt path around to the back of the building, where a tall, grated-metal staircase—the fire escape—provided the access to Charlie's offices. I climbed the stairs slowly, my left knee sore and throbbing from the unaccustomed exertion of practice.

When I got to the second-story landing Charlie was there to greet me. Effusive as always, he held open the door and made a grand, sweeping gesture with his left hand. "*Entrez,*" he said, and as I entered the anteroom, "the place, as you can plainly see, is a mess." He shut the door behind us and in mock anger kicked an empty cardboard box. "I'm moving," he said. "You want something to drink?"

"Well..."

"Help me celebrate."

"Sure," I said.

Charlie weaved unsteadily down the wide corridor that led to the front of the house and the upstairs kitchen. He had been drinking, and from the looks of the corridor he had been drinking all day. Drinking and packing. The corridor was littered with empty beer bottles, bits of string and tape and reams of packing paper. The walls were lined with various-sized cardboard boxes, each labeled with the name of a moving company, some packed and sealed, others empty. Off the corridor were three rooms, two of which were vacant, the furniture sold, I supposed, the files packed away in the sealed boxes. The rooms had once served as offices for Charlie's "associates," two young men who, when things were going well, were hired to keep pace with the growing business. They had been dismissed some time ago, but Charlie had stubbornly maintained their offices, as if their existence might somehow forestall the impending collapse.

Now these rooms were vacant, but as I walked down the hall to the third room, previously the master bedroom, then Charlie's office, I still found it hard to believe he was actually going to move. Just talk, I thought, but one look at his office told me I was wrong. Although his furniture was still in place and the telephone and teletype machine were still hooked up, his library of business books had been packed away, pictures had been taken off the wall and crated, and it appeared that at the time I got there he was about to dismantle his pride and joy—a vast collection of football mementos that covered the whole south wall of his office.

It really was quite a collection—old jerseys, helmets and cleats, four or five game balls, photographs. Photographs of Charlie with nearly every player who ever wore a Washington uniform; photographs of Charlie with politicians, of Charlie with entertainers, and whole series of Charlie with Mister Clayton: on yachts, at race tracks, on golf courses, Charlie smiling and tan; Clayton frowning, looking oafish and uncomfortable in his sporting gear, like a street kid in tennis clothes.

"He looks miserable, doesn't he?" Handing me a bottle of beer, Charlie pointed to a photograph of Clayton standing with Coach, Tanner, and Charlie near the eighteenth green at Hidden Hills Country Club. It was a candid shot. Coach, Tanner and Charlie were loitering in the background, smiling nervously, while in the foreground Mister Clayton stood holding an empty glass, staring down at the ground where his golf clubs lay scattered in front of him, bent and twisted like pretzels.

"What happened?" I asked.

"Well," Charlie said, "the first thing you've got to understand about Roger Clayton is that he's a terrible golfer, and like most terrible golfers he gets frustrated, and he gets specially frustrated when he can't cheat."

"He cheats?"

"The result, the outcome, Brad...it means everything to him, and if he's got to cheat, he'll cheat. No qualms about it, either...but on this particular day it didn't matter whether he cheated or not. He was, as they say, too far gone." Charlie took a swig of whiskey. "We were playing Hidden Hills, you know, with all those narrow fairways cut through woods like paths through a jungle and that's where he hit all day, into the goddamn jungle, and he'd send his caddy down there in the bush to hunt for the balls. By the time we get to eighteen the caddy's about had it and decides to take a little of his own out on Mister Clayton. So as Roger starts into his swing the caddy opens his mouth and out comes the logger's warning...TTIIMMBBEERR, and Clayton for the umpteenth time shanks the ball and off it sails into the woods, leaves and shit flying all over the place, and then—whack—it smacks a tree, and plops into a creek. You can guess what happened next. The club right here he wrapped around the caddy's head, the rest of 'em he bent himself. It was something to see, I'm telling you." Charlie laughed, shaking his head.

"I'd no idea he was that bad."

"Oh, he's pitiful, Brad. He's got no hand-eye coordination. Golf, tennis—forget it. He's goddamn spastic or something. I mean, the only time he has any real fun is at the ballpark watching you guys, or at the racetrack watching his nags. I think…yeah, come over here and I'll show you what I mean."

We walked down to the other end of the room. Charlie pointed to the top shelf, where lodged between an old cleat and somebody's arm pad was a snapshot of Clayton standing at the rail of a racetrack, his arms thrust over his head, his face lit up with excitement as the horses went by in the background.

"We were up in Massachusetts," Charlie said, "at Berkshire Downs. He had two horses running, neither finished in the money, but look at him—he sure loves the action, doesn't he?"

"Seems to," I said "You went with him to all these places?"

"Oh, sure. That was the best part of it—the travel, the contacts I made. The rest of it, well…" He shook his head.

"What do you mean?"

"Hey, you know, Brad. There's hooks in everything. The hooks. The bait. You know. You bite. Somebody reels you in so nice and easy you'd think you were still running free, and all of a sudden you're flopping around in the boat wondering what the hell happened…"

"So what went wrong?"

"Is that what you want to know?"

"I'm wondering what busted up the relationship."

"Yeah? And I'm wondering why we're talking about my personal life when all you wanted to do was some research or something. Isn't that why you came?"

I said it was.

"Then we'd better get to it," he said. "I got things to do."

I followed Charlie as he crossed the room to his desk. If he didn't want to talk any more about Clayton that was his business. I wasn't going to louse up this opportunity by pressing him.

Charlie sat down at his desk and swiveled in his chair so that he faced a cluttered credenza. On the credenza was the small teletype machine and beside it the telephone. Charlie picked up the phone and dialed a number. After listening for a moment, he mounted the receiver in a receptacle built into the back of the terminal. A short burst of automatic typing followed, then silence

184

as Charlie pondered the next entry. I walked around behind the desk and peered over his shoulder at the printout.

```
TELENET 415 DL9
NEW YORK TIMES INFORMATION SERVICE
TERMINAL @ ?
```

Charlie typed the response.

```
TERMINAL @ 201 24.
```

The machine clattered.

```
TERMINAL @ 201 24 CONNECTED.
NEWS SUMMARY NOW AVAILABLE ON LINE.
```

Charlie looked up. "Shall we see what's going on in the world?"

"Hey, what else can you do with this thing?"

"Well, I used it mainly for investment analysis. Some of the guys wanted to invest in stocks and...well, it was Blair. Blair came up with a list of insiders and we'd use the service to monitor their transactions. Do what they do, you understand?"

"Can you get biographical information?"

"Sure, if the guy's important. You wanna look up somebody?"

"How important would he have to be? I mean, to get into the computer."

Rooting about in the clutter, Charlie produced a promotion pamphlet for the service. Listed on a back page were the sources the computer's data base was drawn from. The list included nearly every major newspaper and magazine published in America, with asterisks for those given processing priority: the New York *Times*, the Wall Street *Journal*, Business Week, and the Washington *Post*.

"If your guy was featured in any one of those publications any time since nineteen seventy-two it's a cinch he'll be in the computer."

"Featured?"

"Yeah. They're not gonna pick up a passing mention or any-

185

thing. The guy would have to be, you know, important to a story...Okay, so what's his name?"

"Thorley, Keith Thorley."

For an instant Charlie seemed to freeze. The tendons in his neck grew taut, his hands and fingers tensed on the keyboard. But only for an instant. The next thing I knew he'd typed the name, and the machine had issued its chattering reply.

IDENTIFICATION IS UNKNOWN TO SYSTEM.

"Well, so much for Thorley," Charlie said. "Evidently a small fish."

"Try Western Funding. Thorley's chairman of the board."

"Brad, if the chairman of the board of a company's not on file, then the company's not gonna be on file either. That's just common sense, for Christ's sake."

"Show me."

Muttering, Charlie typed the query. The machine clattered and there it came again:

IDENTIFICATION IS UNKNOWN TO SYSTEM.

"So what'd I tell ya," Charlie said.

"Then I'm not doing this right, goddammit. I mean, there must be another way to get at this thing and I'm not...Okay," I said, "Funding was run with money that came from some kind of oil company...family-owned, I think—Pallas, that's it. Try Pallas Petroleum."

"Brad, for Christ's sake—"

"Try Pallas, and I'll get out of your hair."

Shaking his head, Charlie typed the name. This time, instead of issuing an immediate and negative reply, the machine groaned for a moment as if digesting the information, then began to rattle and spit. The printout said:

NUMBER OF ITEMS RETRIEVED = 3.
VIEW ON TERMINAL: EARLIEST = A LATEST = B
UNSORTED = C.

186

"Can we see 'em all?" I asked.

Charlie nodded. He hit the "C" key and the terminal began to print the three abstracts.

The first was a synopsis of an article that had appeared in a May, 1974, edition of the Wall Street *Journal*. It told how Pallas had pleaded guilty to criminal charges of concealing from federal regulators the transportation of natural gas. Included in the abstract were Pallas's comments on the charges and the statement of a Department of Energy spokesman who said that related investigations were continuing. These investigations must have proved out because the second abstract, from the November 6, 1974, issue of Business Week, reported that the Department of Energy had filed suit against Pallas charging violation of Section Four of the Energy Code—"a controversial law that requires oil companies to reinvest a substantial percentage of profits in oil and gas exploration, or other energy-related ventures." I interpreted this to mean that Thorley had illegally diverted funds from Pallas—but to where? And for what purpose? Thinking this all might somehow relate to Judy's work, I leaned forward to read the third abstract as it rolled off the platen.

3 OF 3 WSJ 1975 1–5
U.S. DISTRICT JUDGE JAMES T. HARTE DISMISSES
DEPARTMENT OF ENERGY LAWSUIT AGAINST PALLAS
PETROLEUM. THE SUIT CHARGED VIOLATION OF
SECTION FOUR OF ENERGY CODE, THE SO-CALLED
"DIVERSIFICATION STATUTE." IN HIS RULING JUDGE
HARTE NOTES THAT ALTHOUGH PALLAS OVER THE
PAST SIX YEARS HAS FAILED TO REINVEST THE
APPROPRIATE PERCENTAGE OF PROFITS IN OIL AND GAS
EXPLORATION AND HAS INSTEAD ATTEMPTED TO
DIVERSIFY THROUGH INVESTMENTS IN UNRELATED
AREAS, THE COMPANY DID SO ONLY AFTER GAINING
FULL EXEMPTIONS FOR THEIR PROGRAM FROM FORMER
DOE ADMINISTRATOR FOR REGULATORY PROGRAMS,
RICHARD AUBRY. IN GRANTING THE DISMISSAL JUDGE
HARTE RECOMMENDS CONFLICT OF INTEREST CHARGES
TO BE LEVELED AGAINST AUBRY WHO RESIGNED HIS
DOE POST LAST MONTH TO BECOME PRESIDENT OF

MIDLAND DRILLING, A SUBSIDIARY OF PALLAS.
INCLUDES PHOTOGRAPH OF PALLAS ATTORNEY RALPH
JAMESON EXITING COURTHOUSE FOLLOWING DECISION.
END OF DISPLAY

Turning the platen knob I removed the printout and reread the third abstract. "Not much help," I said, slumping onto a corner of Charlie's desk. "I mean, 'unrelated areas'... Now I've got to go down to the Department of Energy, dig through their goddamn files, and I haven't got the time, or maybe even the inclination."

"So don't go," Charlie said. "What's the big deal?"

"You got a phone book? Maybe I should call down there."

"It's after six, Brad. They're probably gone for the day... You want to grab a bite somewhere? I'm kinda interested to hear what's happening with you and Willie."

"Don't get me started on Willie."

"No, I wanna hear about it. I mean, what are they doing with you guys?"

"I'd better get home, Charlie. Really. My knee's beginning to slosh and if I don't get it iced and elevated—"

"But you have to admit it's interesting... I mean, how they think Willie's such a world-beater when he can't play a lick, and it's my guess they're gonna play him anyway. They say anything to you yet?"

"You're pumping me again, Charlie."

"I'm askin' you who's playing, that's all."

"You're pumping me, goddammit. Like you did in Philadelphia. I don't like it."

"So what am I supposed to do, Brad? A guy's hurt, he's not hurt. A guy's gonna play, he's not gonna play. What the hell am I supposed to do? Read about it in the newspaper?" Charlie got up and reached for his bottle.

"I owe you for the computer time," I said.

"Yeah, you do."

"So send me a bill," I said, and started for the door, but Charlie got in front of me.

"We had a deal here, Brad." He gulped whiskey, reeled. I tried

188

to step around him but he recovered. We were in the hall now, Charlie backing up as I pressed for the exit. "You fuckers, you make me sick—"

"Hey, look—"

"What are you, a fucking virgin, Brad? You play this game like you're still in high school. Like you're some true-blue college hero. You wanna act like it's for fun but you're up to your ears in shit. You're a dog race. You play so they have something to bet on."

"Hey, Charlie—"

"It's the biggest fucking thing they got. Don't you understand that? It's bigger than numbers, for Christ's sake—it's bigger than dope. And you wanna act like you're in it for the thrill of victory?"

I pushed him out of the way and headed for the door.

"You're an *asshole*," he shouted.

I opened the front door.

"You *disgust* me."

I was gone.

CHAPTER TWENTY-FOUR

Wednesday, 10:30 A.M.

"Will you hold for Mister Roberts, please?"

"I am holding for Mister Roberts."

"Pardon me?"

"I've been holding for fifteen minutes."

"Oh. Will you continue to hold?"

"I've got him, I'm not about to let him go."

The secretary laughed. "Well, he should be with you in a few minutes. I'm sorry for the delay."

She punched off. A moment of silence followed, then Muzak, an old Rolling Stones tune orchestrally reinterpreted for play in elevators and doctors' offices and over open telephone lines. I nudged the receiver against my shoulder, and while listening to the saccharine, nearly unintelligible strains of "(I can't get no) Satisfaction," pondered the sprung ligaments and shattered cartilage in the plastic knee that rested in front of me on the trainer's desk.

"Are you still there?" The secretary again.

"Yes."

The line went silent, no Muzak this time, and the next sound I heard was the smooth, even voice of Carl E. Roberts, the Department of Energy's Deputy Associate Assistant Administrator for Compliance.

190

"May I help you?" he asked.

"I hope so. My name is Brad Rafferty, and I—"

"Excuse me, but—Brad Rafferty?"

"Yes."

"You said Brad Rafferty?"

"Yes."

"This is *amazing*. Are you a football fan?"

"What?"

"Do you follow Washington? There's a great player for them with your name."

"That's me." I almost smiled.

"Brad Rafferty?"

"Yes," I answered. "I'm *him*. Okay?"

"Brad Rafferty, the ballplayer? Well, how about that. I...well, it's a real pleasure to meet you. Or rather to talk to you. We're big fans, my boys and I. In fact we've followed your career...from the very beginning." He laughed nervously. "I'm sure you hear this all the time but we haven't missed a game in years..."

"Do you have season tickets?"

"Oh, no. We go whenever we can, of course, but season tickets, or any kind of tickets, they're pretty scarce. I meant televised games."

"Would you like to go to the game this week?"

"Are you serious?"

"Absolutely."

"Well, I don't know what to say, Brad. I mean, we'd love to go."

"Would four tickets take care of everyone?"

"Four, sure. But—"

"They'll be at the Will Call window when you get to the stadium Sunday afternoon."

"Hey, that's wonderful, Brad. Will you excuse me again? My secretary's trying to tell me something." After a moment he was back. "She was just reminding me about the urgency of your call."

"Yes, well, I may have given her that impression. It's not entirely accurate..."

"I understand," he said. "Now, how can I help you?"

"I need some information, Carl. That's the most direct way of putting it. I need some information about a man named Keith

Thorley and a company he controls, Pallas Petroleum. In November of seventy-four the DOE filed suit against Thorley and Pallas charging violation of something called the diversification statute. I'm interested in finding out the specifics—where the money went, for what purpose, things like that."

"Do you know what became of the suit?"

"It was dismissed, I think, by a U.S. District Court Judge named James T. Harte."

"Harte, yes...third district. Do you remember the date of the dismissal?"

"January, I think. January, seventy-five."

"Well, that shouldn't be any problem, Brad. I'm not familiar with the case myself, but I'll send one of our clerks to the computer and we'll see what we've got. I'll write you up a summary of the pertinent facts and either drop it in the mail or, if you'd prefer, send it along by messenger."

"Messenger would be quicker, wouldn't it?"

"Assuming everything goes smoothly I could have the memo in your hands sometime late this afternoon."

"That would be terrific, Carl."

"Then messenger it is," he said. "If you'll just give me an address..."

When I got off the phone with Carl E. Roberts the team meetings were just breaking up. Players were spilling into the training room for treatment or prepractice taping; those who had been taped before the meetings or who didn't need taping were streaming by the equipment room picking up clean socks and jocks. I found the swirling surge of activity a great relief.

At my locker as I happily dressed for practice, Jeff Blair pulled up a chair and filled me in on what I'd missed of the morning meeting. Wednesday being offensive day, when the defensive unit plays the opposition's defenses, Coach DeVito had delivered the usual pronouncements about how we were to give the offense a "good picture," how we were to use *their* drills to improve *our* skills, and so on. He'd then devoted the next hour to teaching Willie Slough what to do when he heard a "pinch" call, and had ended the meeting with a discussion of the pass rush stunts he

192

felt would be most effective against Chicago's offensive line.

"And," sighed Blair, "as usual he likes the limbos..."

A limbo being a stunt between the defensive tackle and end where the tackle, sacrificing himself, slams into the offensive guard-tackle gap and grabs both offensive linemen so that the end, looping behind and to the inside, can proceed unimpeded to the quarterback, to the glories of a quarterback sack.

"I kind of like the limbos, Jeff," I said. "I really do."

"Reverse is better," he grumbled.

"Come on. You want me to go first? I'd get killed in there."

"They *overplay* the limbos, Brad. I mean, we can set 'em up with the limbos, but when we need something big, the reverse'll deliver, I swear."

"Let you get the sack, huh? You've been thinking again, Jeff."

"Brad—"

"How many times has Coach DeVito told you? He doesn't want you thinking out there, he wants you *reacting*..."

"Goddammit, Brad—"

"But it's a good idea."

"You like it?"

"Yeah, yeah—c'mon," I said, picking up my helmet. "If we're gonna use the reverse we'd better get out there and work on it and we'd better do it now, before DeVito sees us and accuses us of being pussy intellectuals..."

Jeff followed me out the back door, but as the door closed behind us we both stopped in surprise. When we had arrived at the compound that morning the day had been quiet and clear with a brilliant sun—the beginnings of another unseasonably warm winter's day, the latest in a series of such days. Since then, however, and unknown to us, the weather had changed dramatically. To the northwest an ominous wall of anvil-black clouds rimmed the horizon like a cloak. In the already howling wind the canvas sheeting on the hurricane fence flapped like five hundred yards of luffing sail, and the stands of hardwood beyond the fence swayed and moaned like a warning.

"Norther," said Blair, the word hanging in a billow of breath-fog, then blowing away as he indicated the clouds. As he spoke

193

the air took a sudden chill that made me shiver. We looked at each other and without more words, turned and hurried back inside the locker room.

At the equipment-room cage we told Tony about the weather and asked for appropriate gear.

Tony laughed.

"What the hell," I said. "We need long johns, Tony. It's cold out there."

"Yeah," put in Blair, "you don't believe us, call the goddamn National Weather Service."

Tony, who never goes out, laughed. "If it'll make you feel better, I will," he said, "but I'll tell you right now it ain't gonna make a bit of difference."

"What the hell is that supposed to mean," I demanded.

"They'll be no long johns."

"What?" said Blair.

"Orders," said Tony.

"Orders? What the hell are you talking about?" Blair began to rattle the cage.

Tony just laughed again. "You'll see," he said, then pushed aside a support pole and down crashed a heavy plywood panel that would have crushed Blair's hands if he hadn't let go of the cage in the nick of time.

A few minutes later, as Blair and I scavanged for cold weather gear, Tony's garbled voice came over the public-address system.

"For those of you who ain't been out," he gleefully began, "I'm gonna read the National Weather Service long-range forecast for Washington D.C. and surrounding vicinities. And it's a good one, too. Snow flurries tonight and tomorrow, snow squalls on Saturday...blizzard conditions by game-time Sunday afternoon."

The announcement touched off a flurry of activity as players raced outside to see for themselves what was happening, then returned, talking excitedly as they scrambled for sweats and gloves, for whatever protection they could muster against the cold. It wasn't much. Tony, though confronted with overwhelming demand, still refused to open the equipment room and dispense our long johns.

194

Having donned sweat jackets and golf gloves, having wrapped towels around our throats and taped shut the ear holes in our helmets, Blair and I, in advance of the rest of the squad ventured back outside. We stepped onto the soggy brown turf, jogged the length of the practice field to the D-line staging area, where, for the next ten minutes, we ran through our stunts, the weather deteriorating all the while.

By the time practice began the sky overhead had gone near-black, the temperature had dropped ten or fifteen degrees and the first snowflakes were beginning to fall. Yet, strangely, no one seemed to mind. Despite being ill-equipped, the players, frisky and enthusiastic, had bounded outside as if there were no place else they'd rather be. The coaches had followed, clapping and shouting encouragement, and as we formed a grid for calisthentics and the cadences began to sound across the fields, the day no longer seemed bleak at all, but warm and festive, filled, somehow, with a sort of Christmas spirit.

The good cheer vanished abruptly fifteen minutes later when Mister Roger Clayton paid his customary visit to practice. Wearing a burgundy tobogganer's hat and matching monogramed sweat-suit, he strode from the locker room to the edge of the field and there planted his feet and crossed his arms, a scowl already etched on his ruddy face. As he surveyed the activity in front of him, shifting his gaze from drill to drill, I unobtrusively eased myself from a first-unit line drill and, in accordance with Coach's plan, eased Willie in. After a few minutes Mister Clayton was joined by another man, a tall, distinguished-looking type wearing a dark cashmere overcoat and fedora, with a knitted muffler draped insouciantly around his neck, the fringed ends streaming in the wind. The men shook hands like old friends. Then they began to talk, conspiratorially at first, the tall man bending to hear and be heard, then as Clayton gestured toward the field the tall man straightened up, nodding occasionally while Clayton explained what was happening in the various drills.

A whistle sounded, high and shrill, a signal to change drills. It seemed early to be changing drills and we turned for an explanation to Coach DeVito, who, apparently as puzzled as we were, was studying his copy of the afternoon practice schedule. After a moment he nodded, then refolded the schedule and slipped it back in his hip pocket. "Buckle up, gentlemen," he said, "and follow me." We did, slogging upfield to the fifty-yard line, where we were soon joined by the linebackers, the offensive linemen, an odd assortment of second- and third-string running backs and Rutledge, our starting quarterback.

"This is for them," DeVito said, indicating the offensive huddle as we reassembled. "They're going to work on their deceptive game, but we all know they won't really work unless we make 'em work and that's exactly what we're going to do. We're gonna go after 'em, gentlemen. We're gonna go hard and tough like those bastards from Chicago are gonna go, and we're gonna make 'em work." DeVito wiped his mouth with the back of his sleeve. "We'll start with the first unit," he said. "Brad, you others, change it up every four plays."

We, the "others" and I, moved behind and to the right of the offensive huddle, kneeling there for an unobstructed view of the drill. We were apprehensive. Though this drill was normally a noncontact exercise run at half- to three-quarters speed, we knew that if conditions were right it could quickly escalate into a full-go, balls-to-the-wall, gut-check scrimmage. And today conditions seemed right. It was clear that Mister Clayton wanted to offer his guest a down-and-dirty private performance; the running backs who were second-string fodder seemed ready to show their stuff, and the coaches, who would normally control the tempo, were already boiling. Red Keane, in fact, seemed about to explode.

Kneeling in the offensive huddle, Keane was railing at the offensive linemen, for what reason we couldn't make out. Neither, apparently, could Coach, who, having walked over to the huddle and listened for a moment, interrupted Keane: "Let's go to work." Rutledge, taking advantage of the sudden silence, leaned in and called a play, but when the huddle broke Keane started in again.

"Hold it!" he yelled. "Hold it, hold it, HOLD IT."

The players stopped dead in their tracks.

"For Christ's sake, men," Keane said, "break the goddamn huddle like you *mean* it."

The players rehuddled, Rutledge called the play again and this time the break came clean and crisp—a loud, dry clap.

"At least we sound like a football team," Keane said to no one in particular as the unit hustled through the swirling snow to the line of scrimmage. "Now let's see if we can play like one..."

Rutledge, having set the team, his hands now resting on the flank of the center, began looking over the defense, but slowly, slowly and casually—a technique he used to lull the defense whenever a play was to come off on a quick-count. Now Rutledge moved under the center. I shot a glance at Jeff Blair to see if he'd been fooled by Rutledge. He hadn't, he was poised in his stance, ready to strike at the next sound. And when that sound came, when Rutledge barked the signal and the ball was snapped, I looked at Willie to see if he'd been fooled, and, of course, he had...he was late off the mark, days late. The play was a pass, and instead of moving upfield Willie was still standing on the line of scrimmage looking befuddled, like a lost tourist. Surely, I thought, that wouldn't go unnoticed by the coaches.

Unbelievably, it did. When Willie, having finally figured out the play, started upfield for the offensive tackle, he inadvertently slammed into the left offensive guard, who was sliding outside to set up, of all plays, a screen, and the force of the collision knocked Willie into the second-string running back, who had just caught the screen pass and turned upfield, and the force of that collision not only leveled the running back but caused a fumble as well. So now, when there should have been jeers for Willie, there were cheers, cheers from Coach DeVito, who had run up from his position deep in the secondary to clap him on the back and congratulate him, and cheers from Mister Clayton, who along with his friend had stood watching from the sidelines. And while Willie was taking all of this in, while he was shuffling back to the huddle, grinning his toothless grin, Red Keane knelt once more in the offensive huddle and began chewing Lee Fair's ass, Fair being the offensive tackle whose assignment it was to block Willie. Fair tried to explain what had happened but Keane cut him off. Frustrated, Fair started shouting at Keane, which went on until Keane, tired of the argument, said, "Yeah, well, next time you cut him."

And Fair, stammering, said, "Cut him? But—"

"Yeah," Keane said, "*cut him. Like a goddamn tree.*"

But there must have been some confusion about who was to cut whom, because on the next play, an inside draw-trap, not only did Fair cut Slough but the trapping guard cut the defensive tackle—a terrible mistake since the defensive tackle happened to be Jeff Blair, a man with a very short fuse.

Blair scrambled to his feet, looked about for someone to hit. Seeing the guard lying in the dirt, he let out a scream and would've kicked the guard in the head if the guard hadn't moved at the last instant. "You dumb bastard," the guard yelled. "They told us to cut—" Blair dove on him anyway and they wrestled in the mud and snow. They were soon separated and hauled off to their respective huddles, but the fight didn't end then, it had merely begun. The escalation we'd feared from the start had now happened, the pattern of attack and retaliation had been established and it could end, as uncontrolled scrimages often ended, with a serious injury.

Which happened on the next play. As the offensive unit approached the line of scrimmage, Blair switched positions so that he could line up over the guard who had unnecessarily cut him. Nostrils flared, back foot raking the dirt, Blair settled on his outside shoulder and at the snap exploded, slamming the guard across the head as he slashed inside and cut upfield. The guard, reeling, desperate to stop him, extended a leg and with a rolling, thrashing movement whipped the leg into Blair's shins, tripping Blair but not bringing him down. Blair stumbled now into the backfield, headlong and out of control, straight for Rutledge, who had set short to throw a flanker quickscreen. Players gasped as Blair's helmet smacked the inside of Rutledge's distended left knee. There was a sickening crunch as the knee buckled and Rutledge collapsed to the turf in a writhing heap.

"Oh my God," Blair said when he realized what he had done. He tried to unbuckle Rutledge's helmet and remove it, but Coach had arrived and pushed Blair out of the way and screamed for the trainer. And while someone ran to get the trainer, who was not on the field but inside making bouillon, and before Rutledge

198

could be surrounded by concerned teammates, Red Keane moved forward and began herding us away from the twitching Rutledge, downfield and away, so that we could continue with practice.

As we moved downfield I looked around for Mister Clayton. It was his presence, I felt, that had provoked all this, his angry presence and contemptuous gaze, and I wanted to see the look on his face as our quarterback, our hope for a Sunday victory, lay squirming in the dirt.

But he was not on the sidelines where he and his friend had stood watching the drill.

"Brad."

Nor was he with the group that hovered over Rutledge.

"Brad."

Nor was he anywhere on the practice fields.

"Brad, damn it."

"Yes, Coach."

"Take a couple, will you, please?"

"Yes, sir," I said, and trotted into the reforming drill, wondering....

TWENTY-FIVE

Nor was Mister Clayton in the locker room, standing where he usually stood after a midweek practice, near the entrance to the showers, inspecting the naked bodies as they trooped past, stamping his approval or disapproval with his eyes, with a wry look and a subtle shake of his head—he wasn't there. And maybe that's why the players, as they stepped from the showers and, toweling off, approached the lavatory mirrors, seemed so relaxed and high-spirited, why they lingered now in front of the mirrors, shaving and blowdrying their hair, why they lingered when they usually had to bolt—Mister Clayton wasn't standing there staring at their cocks.

"He's got his reasons."

"That's what I'm afraid of."

"This goddamn weather..."

"I don't give a fuck about his reasons. What I want to do is see *his* cock."

"He don't bring it around here."

"He leaves it at home."

"Locked in his safe."

"There is a certain amount of scientific evidence that a football player's ability varies inversely with the size of his cock—"

"Take that back."

"I read it."

"Where?"

"I don't remember."

"In team orientation?"

"You take it back or I won't block shit for you."

"There is a certain amount of irrefutable, highly scientific evidence that Owner Clayton studies our cocks because he's some kind of pervert."

"That sounds more probable as a hypothesis than the first one."

"Shut up."

"I mean, it was cold out there."

"Fuck you."

"It was cold. It's gonna stay cold."

"And no quarterback. I'm sick."

"He's fine."

"I hit him so hard he could die," Blair said.

"He'll be lucky, as cold as it's gonna be..."

As practice had wound down the temperature had stabilized, the snowflakes had grown larger and begun to accumulate, and now what everyone began to murmur about and then shout and look worried about as they stood grooming was whether or not Camaraderie would be canceled—Camaraderie being the weekly team fall-down-sloppy-drunk at Lefty's, a local bar.

"I'm not going," I said as I stepped out of the shower. "How can you worry about getting drunk when Rutledge is hurt?"

"I can worry about getting drunk any time I want."

"We don't know how hurt he is."

"That's what I mean."

"So why worry about it now?"

"I nearly killed him," Blair said.

"Enrico!" Regis left me. "Enrico, my man! You're going to Camaraderie, aren't you, Enrico? I mean, you wouldn't let a little thing like the...Holy shit," said Regis, and for a moment all went quiet.

Then someone whistled and someone else hollered and presently everyone was whistling and hollering, and I turned to see what had caused the commotion. It was Wayne Law. At the far end of the room, on a small wooden table, he stood poised and prim, like a fashion model. He was wearing nothing but a pair of black, translucent pantyhose.

"Like 'em, boys?" he taunted, pirouetting; all hooted and whistled their approval.

"You'd better like 'em," Wayne said, his tone changing as he stepped down from the platform. "Tony tells me we ain't wearin' no long handles in the game this week."

"What!" A chorus.

"Too bulky," Wayne said. "Tony says we can't move when we're wearin' long johns so he's bought us something we can move in, and you're lookin' at em." Wayne grabbed the nylon about his thighs and pulled the fabric away from his legs, curtsied. "Fat girl's pantyhose," he said. "Tony says we wear these or go without."

"I ain't wearin' no fat bitch's underwear."

"Fuckin' Tony's perverted too."

"This is Clayton's degenerate work."

"I'm gonna kill Tony."

"Tony can wear this shit."

Regis was tearing a box of pantyhose to shreds.

"It's Clayton hot to see our cocks through pantyhose."

"Of course we could make our own arrangements," Wayne shouted, a glimmer in his eye. "In fact, I was over at Harry's Hardware this morning and it just so happens that he's having a big sale, Harry is, on your genuine, Duofold, long-handled underwear."

The players were relieved to hear this and began talking among themselves, making plans for secret purchases, smuggling operations, at Harry's as soon as they left the compound.

Wayne sauntered over to me. "So what d'ya think," he said, curtsying again. "Nice, huh?"

"You fucker," I said. "How much of this deal do you have."

"That ain't the point, Brad. I mean, take a look. You gonna wear pantyhose in a football game? Come on."

"I might. If they keep me warm."

"Come on," he said, "do you realize what'll happen if the press gets hold of this?"

I picked up another towel and walked into the locker room.

"So you goin' to Lefty's?" Wayne yelled, following.

"No," I said. "I—I've got some personal business to attend to." I only wanted to get the last word from the Department of Energy man Carl Roberts, take a Seconal and get deep into sleep.

"Oh. Personal business, huh?"

"Yes."

"Kinda like Willie, I guess."

"Nothing about me is like Willie."

Wayne pointed down the aisle. He was laughing, and when I saw Willie I knew why. He was attending to some personal business, too. Seated in front of his locker, naked from the waist down, hunched forward, legs splayed, Willie was digging around in the explosion of wiry hair just above his genitals.

"Mister Guinness ought to be notified, don't you think?" Wayne had the giggles. "I mean, look at the size—"

"Will you be quiet?"

"Sorry," he said.

We had arrived at my locker. Unhitching the towel from my waist, I dropped it in a laundry basket and reached for my underwear. I was in a hurry to get out of there, but as I began to dress Willie groaned and it was such a plaintive, painful sound that, although I knew I shouldn't, I glanced down.

"What's he doing?" Wayne whispered.

Willie had pulled back the hair in his crotch and with one finger was gently rubbing what appeared to be a rather large seed mole.

"I don't know," I said. "He's found a mole or something." I turned away.

"A mole?"

"I don't know. What—"

"You'd better take care of that, Willie," Wayne said sternly.

Willie looked up, startled, then concerned.

"I'm not kidding," Wayne said. "Something like that could get out of hand. You'd better see the trainer right away."

"You really think so, T?"

"I mean it," Wayne said.

Willie, nodding, stood and ambled off to the training room.

"Come on," Wayne said. "This is going to be great."

Wayne and some other players, who apparently had overheard the conversation with Willie, crept up to the door of the training room. Inside, the trainer was putting an ice pack on someone's swollen right ankle. As Willie approached, the trainer looked up and, catching sight of the snickering players at the door, gave a knowing nod. "I'll be right with you," he said to Willie, and after wrapping the ankle led Willie to a taping table in an unoccupied part of the room.

"So what's the problem?" he said gently as Willie scooted up on the table. "Have we got a problem today?"

Willie nodded, lips pursed.

"You wanna show me?" said the trainer.

Willie nodded nervously. Hunching forward, he pulled back the hair in his crotch and pointed to the mole.

"Jesus Christ," said the trainer, bending as he peered into the jungle of Willie's crotch. "Jesus H. Christ."

Willie moaned. "You mean there's something wrong down there?"

"Crab's eggs, Willie." The trainer straightened. "What you've got there is the biggest goddamn sac of crab's eggs I've ever seen."

"You mean—"

"Don't touch it! For Christ's sake don't touch it. You bust that thing, those little bastards'll be crawling all over everywhere." The trainer opened his doctorlike bag and removed an aerosol can. "Pull up your shirt," he said, shaking the can. "We'll spray you with this stuff just in case."

Willie stood and pulled up his shirt, and the trainer sprayed the middle third of his torso, front and back, with mercurochrome.

"Now that oughta hold 'er for a while," he said, "but you'd better let me check you again...tonight. Yeah. You can never be too careful with something like this, Willie."

204

"But—I mean, tonight?"

"Tonight," he said. "I'll be here, I want you here. Nine o'clock sharp."

"But my girl's comin' in tonight, trainer—all the way from Dakota. I can't be—"

"Then you'd better be changing your plans, Willie. Shape you're in, you can't be seein' no girls."

"But—"

"And that's an order," said the trainer.

Willie nodded despondently. As he turned to leave, the group at the door scattered, then after he passed reassembled behind a bank of lockers to see what would happen next. Oblivious to all of this, Willie crossed the locker room to his locker, pulled off his T-shirt, picked up his soiled jock and socks, then, muttering, carried the bundle to the equipment-room cage. Tony, emerging from behind some boxes, reached across the counter for the laundry, then hesitated.

"You sick, Willie?" he inquired. When Willie did not respond Tony drew back, suddenly, as if the clothes were crawling with vermin. "You're sick, aren't you," he said.

Willie nodded glumly.

"I thought so," Tony said. From a drawer beneath the counter he produced a straightened wire coathanger. Using the hooked end of the hanger, he snagged the soiled clothes and turning, being careful to hold the clothes a safe distance from his body, dropped them in a trash barrel.

The watching players exploded with laughter.

"What?" Willie turned, confused and for a moment just stared at them. Then he began to tremble. "Why you doin' this?" he sputtered. "Why you doin' this to me?" And he coiled as if to lunge, but before he could the players stifled their laughter and scurried away. Willie then wheeled to confront Tony. "*Tony*. TONY." But Tony had dropped and locked the heavy plywood panel. Willie sulked back to his locker, slumped to his chair. After a long brooding silence he looked up at me.

"Why they doin' this to me, B? 'Cause of my girl? Is that it?

'Cause my girl's comin' in and I can't see her so they all have to laugh?" Willie's eyes were wet. Rivulets of mercurochrome had run down his legs.

"Joke level," I said as I buttoned my shirt. "They're putting you on a joke level, Willie."

"They puttin' me on those levels, B?"

"That thing you've got, it's just a mole, Willie. You can see your girl."

"It's just a mole, B?"

"That's all," I said. I picked up my coat, clapped his broad bare shoulder and started for the door.

"You mean my mole's got crabs, B?"

"No, Willie. Jesus." I stopped and turned around. "I—"

"My *crab's* got moles?"

God help him, I thought. "You were right the first time," I said, and turned and walked out the door.

CHAPTER | TWENTY-SIX

Carl E. Roberts had come through in fine fashion. As I hurried up my front walk I could see the brown manilla envelope jutting from my mailbox, the DOE seal in prominent display. Flipping the lid on the box, I grabbed the envelope and after stomping wet snow from my shoes, unlocked the door and walked inside. The apartment was cold and dark. Feeling my way down the hall, I found the thermostat and adjusted the settings, then walked into the diningroom and turned on the overhead light. The light was mounted to a retractable fixture, and I pulled the fixture down from the ceiling so that the circle of illumination encompassed only the diningroom table. I shed my topcoat, sat down at the table, tore open the envelope and took out Carl Roberts' letter.

Brad:
Let me first express my appreciation for the tickets. The boys are thrilled and we are looking forward to the game with keen anticipation. Good luck! Play well! And thanks again.
Now. You were interested in the specifics about Pallas's divestiture. Our records indicate that the divestiture was accomplished in three distinct steps, which taken together spanned a period of six years. In chronological order they were as follows:

(1) In February, 1969, Thorley appropriated $7,000,000 from Pallas to capitalize a financial services company called Western Funding, Incorporated. The company, located in Cleveland, Ohio, specializes in high yield, short term loans and has had remarkable success considering the extraordinary risks inherent in that type of business. Thorley's secret? Quite simply, he has found a way to *guarantee* repayment of his rather expensive loans. In the financial world, when a lender possesses such leverage, he is said to have a "hammer." Thorley's "hammer," according to our investigators, is the organization of his long-time friend and associate, Vincent DeAngelis. You may have heard of him. DeAngelis, along with his two sons (Michael in Miami, Bobby in Los Angeles), controls one of the most powerful organized crime families operating in America today.

Thorley and DeAngelis. I knew this name, DeAngelis. Not Vincent, but the son, Bobby. Bobby DeAngelis. *He* had been the Los Angeles client Judy was to travel to Mexico with, he had been part of her lie—so she must've known who he was. And not only that. Because of her position with Western Funding, she also could've known what he was doing for Thorley.

I felt like I had swallowed something heavy and leaden. My hands began to sweat.

Now I must stress here the speculative nature of the investigator's analysis. Vincent DeAngelis is a notorious character, yes, and his relationship with Thorley is well-documented. Yet in all their dealings no *evidence* of malfeasance has ever emerged. In fact in all other respects Thorley's reputation virtually glitters. I mention the relationship only because it *may* relate in some significant way to the third step of the divestiture, about which more in its proper place. First:

(II) From 1970 to 1973 Thorley, again using Pallas funds, acquired on the open market the securities of various communications companies, but with a penchant for those of the Capital Broadcasting Group. According to documents on file with the SEC, Thorley, by January of 1974, had obtained nearly four percent of the outstanding stock, becoming in the process the third largest individual stockholder in the corporation. CBG, incidentally, is the parent for the local ABC affiliate, several FM radio stations, and the Beckworth chain of newspapers, the largest of which, in terms of circulation, is the Washington *Herald*.

The *Herald?* Slowly, I reread the paragraph. Judy had never mentioned Thorley having influence at the *Herald*. She'd just shown up one day with this job, this wonderful job—how easily it had come...a parting gift, she'd said. Just a parting gift.

Retrieving paper and pencil from the kitchen counter, I went back to the table and made this diagram:

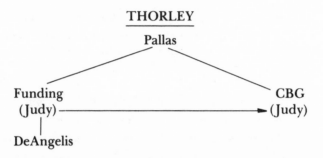

THORLEY

Pallas

Funding   CBG
(Judy)   (Judy)

DeAngelis

A parting gift, sure...the job looked to me more like the second phase of a goddamn executive training program. Could it have been that Judy, having mastered one aspect of Thorley's operation, had been assigned to learn another? That even after leaving Cleveland she had still seen him, and talked to him—and maybe even slept with him? Fighting an assault of nausea, I got up and started to pace. When she'd called me at the hotel in Philadelphia and told me things were going to be different, I'd thought she meant between us. But maybe she didn't. She could have spent time with him and I might not have known. We only lived together a little while, and after she moved out, although we saw each other a lot, the opportunity for contact with Thorley did exist. She was living alone in Arlington, in a nice apartment—too nice? In fact it was a pretty extravagant apartment, now that I thought about it. How had she managed the rent? Tenth floor, river view, two bedrooms. Suddenly I thought of Sam. I could call Sam. He would know. According to Judy it was his dissatisfaction with our living arrangements that had prompted the move. Maybe it was his money that had financed it. At least that's what I always believed...

I started for the bedroom, for the telephone, but then veered to the kitchen. What the hell was I thinking? I turned on the tap, made a cup of my hands, splashed cold water on my face. Of course it was Sam. Sam, who hates my guts.

I dried my face with a dishtowel and returned to the letter:

> —and the Beckworth chain of newspapers, the largest of which in terms of circulation is the Washington *Herald*. Finally:
>
> (III) In May, 1974, for $4,000,000, payable over ten years, at interest, Thorley, again using Pallas funds, purchased 25% of the stock in the Washington Professional Football Club, Incorporated. Because of—

I nearly came out of the chair. *Thorley and Clayton*... But then as I reread the paragraph and the rest of the letter, everything came clear. The dates. Thorley had purchased his interest in the club in May of 1974. At that time Judy had been at the paper nearly three years. If she'd known then that Thorley had become the newest member in what she derisively called "the world's most exclusive men's club," she would've written the story, or tried to write it—I was certain of that. And if for some reason the paper had quashed her efforts, if, for instance, Thorley's influence had come into play, she would've railed about it for weeks, because that was precisely the kind of scratch-my-back influence peddling that rankled her most. And she'd never said a word.

On the other hand, if she'd found out about it later, say this year—earlier this year—and if she'd then connected Thorley's ownership in the club with some crooked bullshit incident, or associate, from their shared past...

I picked up the telephone in the bedroom and dialed the number written on the scrap of paper that lay on the nightstand.

"Ramada Inn, Orangeburg—may I help you?" The sing-song voice of the hotel operator.

"Jack Rafferty, please. Room three-twelve." Holding myself together like a china cup, I nudged the receiver against my shoulder and quickly reviewed the letter and the chart, the telephone ringing in my ear, four times, five times, before Jack finally answered.

"Hello," he said dully, as if roused from sleep.

"It was her work, Jack," I said.

"Brad?"

"It was her work, just like you figured."

"Where the hell have you been all day? I've been trying to call you since this morning."

"Jack—"

"There's nothing more I can do here, Brad. I'm heading for Wasco tonight."

"What?"

"Hold on," he said. In the background I could hear ice cubes clinking in a glass and the sounds of rapid swallowing. "From the top, huh?"

"Yes," I said.

"Well, we checked out fine with the toxicologists, Brad. Sure as hell did. No way, they said, could sixty-seven milligrams of Nembutal put this girl to sleep." He belched. "And my theories about the steering wheel, why it was bent like it was? They checked out, too. Not only with B. F. but with a local guy here, a physis-something who's interested in the, uh, dynamics of, uh...you know."

"Right."

"Yeah. I can't even read my own goddamn writing."

"So she was awake when she hit the bridge abutment?"

"We could prove it in court if we had to. That's what they tell me, anyway."

"So what's the problem, Jack?"

"The den's," he said flatly.

"What?"

"The den's."

"What den's?"

"In the right rear fender and bumper. You remember the den's."

"Dents...right. You were going to send the parts to a lab."

"No. No, I didn't. It's a fuck-up. When I got back to Dunson Ford I got to poking around and found a copy of the rental

211

agreement. The den's were already there when she picked up the car."

"What?"

"They were already there, they weren't caused by the accident. I checked with Hertz, they confirmed."

"What the hell are you telling me, Jack?"

"I don't know, Brad. Maybe it happened different than we thought. I mean, maybe...maybe she hit the goddamn bridge on purpose...?"

"Oh, for Christ's sake."

"I don't know. It happens."

"You're drunk, Jack. Now listen to me. When are you leaving?"

"I was just packing when you called."

"You've got a stopover in Los Angeles, right?"

"I'm tired, Brad."

"You're drunk, Jack. Goddammit. Now *listen* to me. In Los Angeles there's a man named Bobby DeAngelis. Got that? Write it down. Bobby DeAngelis. Okay?"

"Okay."

"I want you to take a couple of days and find out everything you can about him. Who he is, what he does—he's crucial. Judy mentioned him—I'll explain later. You got the name?"

"You're on to something?"

"Yes. Jesus! I've been trying—"

"Bobby DeAngelis?"

"Yes, write it *down.*"

"And you want me to find this guy?"

"Right. Now I've got a buddy down there who should be able to help. His name is Larry Roblaine. Soon as you hit town call him, tell him who you are and what you want. He'll know about DeAngelis. If he doesn't he'll have ways of finding out. Larry Roblaine...we were roommates in college. He's in the District Attorney's office."

"This DeAngelis—"

"He's connected."

"And Judy knew?"

"I don't know, I think so."

212

"Well, we'll find out, won't we?"

"Don't get near him, Jack. Okay? All we need is information."

"Let Roblaine handle it, huh?"

"Jack—"

"I'll call you," he said, "when I get something. Give me the names again."

I did.

CHAPTER TWENTY-SEVEN

Thursday, 7:35 A.M.

Wayne Law approached the counter of the fifth floor nurses' station, spoke briefly to the head nurse, then turned and motioned to me. "This way," he said, and we started down one of three brightly lit corridors that spurred from the nurses' station like spokes from the hub of a wheel.

Rutledge had been assigned to room 560, a private room, the last room on the right side of the corridor. A linen cart was parked in front of his open door, and as we approached it we could hear the rustling of sheets and the cheerful humming of whoever was working inside. A maid. She looked up in surprise as we walked in.

"Where's the patient?" asked Wayne noting the empty bed.

"Mercy," said the woman, "your momma teach you to knock?"

"I'm sorry. We—"

"You part of the team too?"

We said we were.

"Well, don't you move," she said. She hurried out to her cart, came back with some hospital stationery and a pen. "Sign for my kids?"

Wayne accepted the paper and pen and after scribbling his name, handed the materials to me. I did the same.

214

"Now let me see," said the woman, examining the names as I gave her the page. "Wayne Law. I know you, Wayne Law." And she shot a wet, admiring glance at him. "Sure do, you got good hands and quick feets—I hear 'em talk about you all the time." She looked back at the paper. "But you, honey," she said to me, "you sure you with the team?"

Wayne laughed.

"Where's Rutledge?" I said.

"You must be a linemans," she said. "Is he a linemans?"

Wayne nodded, laughing.

She studied the page. "Oh, I'm sorry," she said. "I do know you, Brad Rafferty. You Willie Slough's back-up, ain't you?"

Wayne guffawed.

I sighed. *"Where is Rutledge?"* I said.

"Oh, he be along, you jus' make yourself comfortable." And casting one long last look at Wayne, she left the room.

"At least he's not in surgery," I said.

Wayne nodded, tossed the sack he was carrying at a chair and collapsed in the freshly made bed. As he began toying with the controls that operated the bed I walked over to the window, pulled back the drapes and looked outside. There wasn't much to see. A brick wall, part of a new wing of the hospital, filled the window. It was no more than two feet away and I could've touched it if the window hadn't been sealed shut.

"Great day," I said.

"What?" Wayne was riding the bed like a horse.

"Never mind." I took off my coat, sat down and picked up Wayne's sack. Inside were fourteen cellophane packages, each containing a pair of Duofold, long-handled underwear. "You and your fucking merchandising," I said. "Why do you do it?"

Wayne shrugged. He was sitting upright in the bed now, examining the items on the nightstand beside him. There were paperback books, a water pitcher and glass, pills, a football, a vial of DMSO and a packet of playing cards. Wayne picked up the cards. "You wanna play?"

"Might as well."

"Gin?"

"Okay."

Wayne tore into the pack as I moved to the end of the bed. "Draw for deal," he said, fanning the cards. I drew a two, Wayne an ace off the top.

"Shuffle 'em," I said, "or I don't play."

Wayne smiled. As I positioned the hospital table between us he began shuffling, shuffling and melding, quickly, as if to test the dexterity of his hands. "Had a little chat with Coach yesterday," he said as he began to deal. "In case you didn't know, we're pulling out all the stops this week, and I mean all of 'em."

"He's under a little pressure, Coach is."

"You're telling me," Wayne said. "I haven't returned a kick in two years."

"You're returning kicks?"

"That's what he said. Kick-offs, punts—until the game is decided. The way he was talking, we lose this one and he's out of a job."

I picked up my hand and began arranging the cards. "Doesn't make much sense, does it?"

"What?" Wayne said.

I discarded the king of clubs. "I mean, why this game is more important than the last one or the next one when it's not. They're *all* important and we should've uncorked three weeks ago against Philadelphia."

Wayne said nothing. He picked up the king and discarded the five of diamonds.

"I mean, three weeks ago you couldn't even get on the field and now, in addition to your regular duties, he wants you to return kicks like you're invaluable or something. If you're invaluable now, why weren't you invaluable then?" I drew a card from the deck, glanced at it for a moment, dropped it on the pile of discards.

"He's just responding to pressure, Brad. And it's coming from Clayton."

"You buy that?"

"He wants to win, that's all. Sure." Wayne picked up my discard. "What are we playing for? Quarter a point?"

"I don't know...You mean Clayton wants to win."

"Quarter a point?"

"I don't know. Sure."

"Quarter a point?"

"Yes, goddammit. Wha—"

"Gin," Wayne said.

Rutledge laughed. He'd been watching from the door and now, laughing, hobbled into the room. "I should've warned you, Brad," he said. "Let me see your hand."

I showed him the cards.

"You owe him thirty-seven fifty."

"What?"

"And I quit," Wayne said.

When the laughter died down I told Jan he was moving pretty good. "We thought you'd had it."

"So did I," he said, "but it was only a dislocated kneecap." He sat down beside Wayne and rolling up the left leg of his pajamas, unwrapped an Ace bandage and removed an icepack. The knee was discolored, as though bruised, but only slightly swollen. "And maybe some torn cartilage," he added. "Needles isn't sure. He said something about doing an arthrogram."

"When?"

"Well, today, I think. Later this morning. They want to see what's in there for sure. You know."

"You wanna play, don't you? I mean, if you can," I said.

"Goddamn right. But—"

"Then hold off on the arthrogram, okay. It's uncomfortable as hell. They blow up your knee like a balloon. They pump it full of air and dye and it takes about a week for the sloshing to go away."

"Needles said a couple of days."

"Wait, I'm telling you. At least until Saturday. What's the hurry? If the knee hasn't improved by Saturday, then sure, go ahead and do it. But why eliminate yourself now?"

"Yeah," Wayne said, "we need you, for Christ's sake."

Rutledge thought on it.

"We do," I said. "You're better on one leg than that air-head rookie we've got. He plays, we might as well stay home."

"But what if he insists?"

"Needles?"

"You know how he is."

"Get your wife down here. Have her in the room with you. He won't—"

"I don't know."

"Jan—please."

"You guys better get to practice, huh?"

"But—"

"Thanks for coming down," he said "I'll, uh...I'll do something. Don't worry about it."

It seemed pointless to press the issue so we left. In the hallway I felt my own knees quiver. I'd been there, my knees pumped up and poked and cut. We got on the elevator to the parking garage.

"Clayton shows up at practice and everybody goes nuts," I said. "Everybody goes crazy. It's a feeding frenzy and we end up maiming ourselves. He puts us on display like a bunch of horses or dogs he owns—he puts us on display for some passing scumbag and we end up maiming our own guys."

"Thorley is no passing scumbag."

The air went out of me. I nearly reeled against the elevator wall. My stomach felt like we'd dropped ten floors straight. "What?"

Wayne laughed. "It never fails," he said. "Whenever he shows up, Clayton puts on the big-dog. You saw him out there yesterday, all puffed and explaining everything."

"That was him? At practice?" I tried to sound casual.

"Yeah," Wayne said, "the tall guy in the nice clothes. It's not for everybody Clayton breaks out the monogrammed sweats. No wonder all this shit's coming down."

"I didn't know...Christ, he might come back."

"Yeah, well, if he does, you'd better pad up real good. Yesterday was just a deceptive drill, you know. He comes back today, there's no tellin' what we'll do..."

"Thorley," I said. "That was Thorley..."

The elevator stopped, the doors opened. Thorley had been at practice. Aloof and distant, superior to his friend yet politely solicitous of his attention—he had been at practice and he might come back. The prospect scared me. As we started for the car I started to worry about what the hell I should do.

"Are you thinking what I'm thinking?"

"What?"

"About Jan. He's gonna be putty in Needles' hands."

"Oh. Yeah."

"We're gonna have to help him out."

"Yeah," I said.

"We're gonna have to call Janie. Old Janie, she'll understand. Did I tell you she's already made hotel reservations for the you-know-what in Miami?"

"No."

"And not only that," he said. "She's also booked a Caribbean cruise for the week after the game, and, after that, a month's stay at one of the best hotels in Saint Croix. Jan tells me that just in clothes and deposits she's already blown the six grand we'll get if we beat Chicago."

"Right," I said, sweating.

"Right," Wayne said as we climbed into the car. "If Janie can't do it, no one can. Don't worry about it."

"I'm not."

"You look like you're gonna shit yourself," he said.

I was sure I did.

CHAPTER TWENTY-EIGHT

When we got to the compound Wayne went straight to the telephone and dialed Janie Rutledge, Jan's wife. When she heard that if Jan underwent the proposed arthrogram he wouldn't be able to play Sunday she agreed to go to the hospital right away.

"Let us know what happens," Wayne said.

"I'll call you as soon as I get home."

Wayne and I went on to our respective meetings. Taking my customary chair against the back wall of the storage room, I tried to settle down and listen to Coach DeVito, but as usual on Thursday he was repeating verbatim what he'd said on Wednesday and I couldn't keep my mind on it. I kept going back to Thorley, thinking about him, debating what to do if he should show up at practice again. A part of me wanted nothing to do with him, another part—a bigger part—needed, demanded a confrontation. It was the part where Judy lived. It was as though she were in there telling me I was such a big strong guy I should do something, and after a while I said yes to her. I decided I'd ask Thorley straight out about Judy, ask him quick and unexpected and maybe that way surprise an answer out of him he'd never give otherwise.

After the meeting I went straight to my locker and slipped into my practice pants and cleats. I was nervous and beginning to sweat.

I wondered if he were already here, maybe touring the facility or something. Pulling on a longshoreman's wool hat, I went outside and looked around. He wasn't out back, anyway. There was no one on the grounds except two members of Tony's ground crew riding snowblowers across a thirty-yard stretch of Astroturf at the far end of the compound. I watched for a moment as in tandem they crossed the field, their machines spewing towering plumes of snow. During the night there had been an accumulation of some three or four inches and it was still coming down, quietly but steadily, in great goosefeather flakes. The wind had let up some, though.

Back inside Wayne was waiting near my locker. He nodded as I approached and gave me the thumbs-up. "Janie called," he said. "Needles didn't even mention the arthrogram. Not a word. In fact he said Jan was coming along remarkably well."

"Great. So when's he getting out?"

"They're gonna keep him 'til Saturday afternoon. As a precautionary measure. But as soon as he gets out he's heading for RFK to throw some. I'm supposed to meet him."

"After practice?"

"That was Coach's idea. He doesn't want the guys to get all excited about Rutledge playing, then be disappointed if he can't. So he's keeping it under wraps. Coach'll check him out Saturday, let us know something Sunday morning. If he can play, you know, that'll give us a helluva lift."

"Did Coach know about the arthrogram?"

"Doesn't sound like it, does it?"

"Fucking Needles."

I glanced at the clock. There was still twenty-five minutes before practice—plenty of time to find Thorley and talk to him...I was beginning to wonder if it was such a good idea. By confronting him I'd reveal my suspicions, mark myself as someone for him to be worried about. Still, I didn't know if I could trust myself to stay away from him if he did show. Maybe he wouldn't. If he were coming it would be with Clayton, who was habitually in the building by nine and it was nearly eleven—I could check the parking lot.

I changed back into my street shoes, took my wallet from the hip pocket of my pants. I walked through the locker room, down the corridor that led past the team meeting rooms, out a double steel door and into the administrative section of the building. At the end of another corridor, through another set of double steel doors, I entered the lobby of the building where game tickets were being sold from behind five plexiglas windows. Packed against the windows, an impatient crowd in heavy winter clothes and smelling of wet wool was clamoring for tickets. The room was hot, the people rowdy. A policeman was trying to keep order, a difficult task that became impossible when a local television sports reporter waded into the throng and in the harsh white glare of an arc light began taping a segment for the evening news. Like moths to a flame, people began jostling and fighting one another to get on camera.

I stepped up on an endtable. Looking over and beyond the crowd and through the condensation on the floor-to-ceiling windows I caught a glimpse of the parking lot. In the section nearest the building a beat-up old Volkswagen squatted in the reserved space usually occupied by Mister Clayton's burgundy-and-gold Cadillac. Relieved, I stepped off the table and approached the player ticket window and after ordering and paying for Carl Roberts' tickets returned to the locker room to finish dressing for practice.

Neither Thorley nor Clayton made an appearance that day, nor the next, and by Saturday I had pretty much decided to shelve the whole thing until after the game—that is, if we lost. It would have to be shelved till after the season if we won. It was an unencumbered block of time that I needed to maybe approach the whole thing differently. Maybe I could work back to Thorley from the DeAngelis connection, maybe even get official help from somebody like Roblaine and the Los Angeles County District Attorney's office. If there was hard evidence to be found, that might be the way to find it.

Besides, the football game was shaping up to be much more than just a battle for a spot in the conference finals. It deserved my full attention. It seemed that Coach, with his subtle mustering of "his players," was preparing now, finally, to take over operational control of the club from Clayton—at least in matters of attitude and personnel. It was a gamble, no question, and the stakes were high, but the potential benefits justified the risks. If we could put together a string of play-off victories, if we could give Clayton just a whiff of a world's championship, then in the future, instead of dictating from on-high what would be, he just might defer to Coach. Then staff positions wouldn't be occupied by imbeciles; high draft choices wouldn't be wasted on players who couldn't play. Because the success of this plan and Coach's future, and mine, would hinge on Sunday's outcome. I spent most of Saturday evening with my playbook, reviewing the tendencies of the Chicago offense, psyching myself for what I knew would have to be the game of my life.

That's what I was doing when the telephone rang. It was ten o'clock and I'd been at it for nearly three hours. Eyes aching, mind dancing with images of Crespin Mug, I closed the book, pulled myself up from the couch, went into the bedroom and picked up the receiver.

The phone line crackled with long distance static. When the noise subsided a voice said, quietly, "He's dead, Brad."

It was Jack. "What?" I pressed the receiver hard against my ear. "I can't hear you, Jack. Who's dead?"

"Bobby DeAngelis," he said louder. "Is that better?"

"Yes, I...Jesus Christ. DeAngelis? You're sure?"

"It's been about a year now. They found him in a hotel parking lot stuffed in the trunk of his car. He was a real mess. Tied up. Skull crushed. The murder weapon was a baseball bat."

"Jesus Christ."

"No suspects."

"A family affair?"

"They think so, yeah. They called it an execution."

"I wonder who else is dead. Judy. DeAngelis. I wonder who else."

"I don't know, Brad. But I got an idea who might be next."

"You do?"

"A guy named Richard Farrell. He and DeAngelis were partners in a car-leasing business."

"What's the name again?"

"Farrell, Richard Farrell."

I turned the name over in my mind. It seemed vaguely familiar.

"He's a bank officer in Westwood," Jack went on. "When one of his car-dealer clients went bankrupt he sold the inventory to DeAngelis. That's how he got involved with him. Sold him cheap, I might add, which really pissed off the bank—but that came later. Anyway, to pay for the cars, DeAngelis borrowed five hundred grand from a Cleveland outfit called Western Funding, Incorporated. Farrell cosigned the note. When DeAngelis died...you get the picture?"

"What's Farrell make at the bank?"

"Thirty, thirty-five."

"He still owes the full five hundred?"

"Well, no. He unloaded the cars. It's more like two, two and a quarter. But like I was saying, you know...I mean, if you ask me, he's dead. A walking-around dead man."

"Jack, let's—" All at once I knew where it was I'd heard the name. "Holy shit."

"What?"

"I..." Or rather had it on the tip of my tongue.

"You were saying?"

"I had it, the name."

"You know this guy?"

"I don't know. I can't...let's put it on the back burner, Jack. I've got a big one tomorrow, you know what I mean? I can't be thinking about this stuff tonight. I'm going nuts. Okay? I'm going fucking nuts."

He was silent. I could feel his confusion, even anger coming through the phone at me.

"Look," I said, "why don't you go home, watch the game, and I'll call you after or something. We'll go from there. It's going to be a great game."

"What the hell's going on here, Brad?"

224

"I got a game to play, Jack. I got a goddamn game to play, don't I?"

"You want that ring, don't you."

"What?"

"The goddamn ring. Not that I blame you. All that gold, them diamonds sparkling like a clear night...it's a real handsome trophy."

"Sure I do, I want it—"

"You gonna kick some ass. All right."

"That's *right.*"

"Fuckin' bury Crespin Mug."

"I'm ready."

"Kick his black ass, right? Be a champ of the world."

"It'll be our ring, Jack, yours and mine—"

"Now don't be talkin' foolish. I wanna see it, that's all."

"You got it."

"Just lemme touch the sonofabitch, right."

"You got it."

"Lemme wear it."

"You got it."

"I'm not talkin' about I keep it, just wear it."

"Jack," I said, looking around the room. "Jack, it's late."

"The ring," he said. "Gonna get us a ring."

I hung up. I slammed down the phone. I couldn't wait. I whirled around. I wanted to be playing now. I wanted to be in the game now. I dropped into my stance and ran into the couch, hurled it sideways. The game, I thought, the game. I've got to get ready, I've got to be prepared for *everything*...

I grabbed up my playbook, crouched over it on the floor. The diagrams, page after page of X's and O's, diagonals and curls blurred out of focus. I dropped the book as if it weren't what I thought but something else. Sleep, that was what I needed. I needed sleep. The week's practice had been brutal, practice and worry about things that if they kept me distracted would make me raw meat for one Crespin Mug. Except I was ready, if only I could sleep...that was what I needed because aside from rest it was the quickest way to get me to the game. I would be unconscious from now till the game. I went off my feet and into my bed, hit the covers hard and everything groaned, including me. Sleep was coming over me, a weirdness in it, as if I might have been drugged. I rolled onto my back, hoping sleep was only sleep, and saw the ceiling like the pale sole of a giant's foot about to press down on me. And I went out....

When I woke up, the night was not over but merely deeper and darker. In the gloom nothing seemed closer, least of all the game. I longed for it...like an old best friend. And not only was I unrested, I was more tired than I'd been. And I had this kind of hot place in my head and this kind of crawling sensation on my skin that I couldn't seem to get rid of no matter how hard I rubbed and scratched. Suddenly I realized it was only the residue of the dream I'd had just before I woke up. Still, it seemed crazy that what had happened to me in a dream could be happening to me when I was awake. But it was happening...I had these goddamn sticky things all over me and I couldn't get rid of them. What the hell was going on? In the dream I'd been creeping through this crumbling old house after some kind of ghost I wasn't even sure was there, which was logical because of course I didn't believe in ghosts. I'd followed it into this dark little room where I thought I'd had it cornered, but when I'd lunged for it the ghost had disappeared and left me flailing around in a net of cobwebs, tearing at them, covering myself with their itchy stickiness—with the same itchy stickiness that covered me now...

I was in the livingroom, walking around in tight little circles, clawing at my arms, at my legs—just as I'd done in the dream. Could the ghost have been Judy? Could she have led me into the goddamn cobwebs for some reason? Jesus Christ. Was I now supposed to make something of these tangled little bits and strands? Was that it? Was I now to glean from them some kind of pattern— the pattern of the original web?

I went into the bathroom and knelt beside the bathtub and turned on the hot water. The itching had suddenly intensified, it had become unbearable. I had to do something about it before I seriously hurt myself. I had to stop it, or at least exchange it or override it with some other sensation that would be in my body

226

and not in my head because I didn't seem able to do what Judy wanted me to do. To reconstruct a whole from fragments and then to act on the fragmentary reconstruction was crazy...it was fucking nuts. And that's what she wanted me to do. Just like in the locker room. It had happened then with Thorley and it was happening again now—she wanted me to get some sonofabitch. But Thorley *had* been at her funeral...I hated him, resented him, but that didn't mean he hadn't cared about her, was maybe as confused about her death as I was. So who the hell else? Charlie Rale, because he might have been caught and punished for doing nothing more than betting against the team? Clayton, because he might be in business with somebody who might be in business with somebody else who might be a bad guy? What kind of logic was that? Was being bad contagious, like a goddamn disease? Could it be picked up from shaking hands at a cocktail party or from having your name next to somebody else's name on a goddamn business deal? Hadn't that government guy Roberts said in his letter that between Thorley and DeAngelis no evidence of wrongdoing had ever been uncovered? Hadn't he said that in all other respects Thorley's reputation virtually glittered? So what if Clayton was in business with Keith Thorley? Wasn't it possible he was just using Thorley as an entrée into a more glamorous and richer world than the one he was in? Didn't every businessman want to move in the kind of exclusive circles Thorley seemed to live in and to have the kind of clout he seemed to have? So who the hell was I supposed to get? Bobby DeAngelis, because Judy had mentioned his goddamn name and maybe he...maybe she'd screwed him? Well, they already had him anyway, he'd already been got. So who?

I closed my eyes, took a deep steamy breath, thrust my arms into the scalding-hot water and waited for the tingling sensation that would tell me the itching had been beaten, thrown back to whatever murky place inside me it had come from. There were too many damned patterns I could construct from my fragments, some suggestive of some things, some of others, each about as valid as the next. I was no goddamn superspy. I was no goddamn social reformer, it wasn't my job to set things right. How could it

227

be? How could I get the bastards when I couldn't even say for sure who the bastards were?

It came then, the tingling sensation I'd been waiting for. I withdrew my arms from the hot water and dried them off. They were red and raw and they hurt but I didn't mind. I almost enjoyed the pain. Good. It reaffirmed something about me, my sense of myself. My toughness. I was, after all, a professional football player—I was tough. I was a football player, and I was very fucking tough.

PART THREE

CHAPTER | **TWENTY-NINE**

I woke up Sunday morning to the hollow smack of newspaper hitting concrete. Turning over on my back, I lay for a moment and listened, the next smack coming shortly, then the next, the sound receding as the paperboy moved down the block. Above me, embedded in the ceiling, bits of glitter reflected the uncertain light. Glitter, yes. In the ceiling. I remembered how Judy had laughed when she'd first noticed. I smiled, remembering, and rubbed my eyes. I threw back the covers and sitting up on the side of the bed squinted at the dim, luminous face of my electric clock. Eight-thirty. This surprised me...the room was still dark and the paperboy, who lived nearby, was just beginning to deliver his route. Leaning forward, stifling a yawn, I pulled back the curtains and with my fingernails scraped a circle in the condensation frozen on the window. Outside the world had gone gray-white, its features obliterated by the swirling, wind-driven snow of Tony's blizzard.

I showered and dressed, and after warming and eating a Stouffer's frozen breakfast, started for the stadium. Usually a forty-five minute trip, on this morning, in spite of light traffic, it took nearly an hour and a half. I hardly noticed. Though many of the streets were unplowed, I found roaring through the untracked snow a curiously invigorating experience.

Near RFK traffic intensified. Snowplows, roadgraders and jeeps equipped with scrapers were busy clearing snow from parking lots and access roads, while in the stadium men with snow shovels and bags of salt were clearing sidewalks and ramps, salting them, making the way less treacherous for our fans, some of whom—the tailgaters—were already beginning to arrive.

I parked in my assigned space, clambered out of the car and hurried across the exposed lot and into the shelter of the stadium. Once out of the wind it seemed not quite so cold, in fact altogether tolerable, a feeling enhanced by the warm wishes of good luck shouted out by the vendors and snow crews I passed on my way to the locker room.

Taped on the double steel doors that opened into the locker room was a large plastic sign:

HOME TEAM LOCKER ROOM
POSITIVELY NO ADMITTANCE
(EXCEPT FOR PLAYERS, COACHES, CLUB OFFICIALS,
AND ACCREDITED MEMBERS OF THE PRESS)
BY ORDER OF THE COMMISSIONER

The doors, of course, were locked.

"Tony?" I pounded on the steel. "Tony. Open the goddamn doors."

Nothing.

"TONY. GODDAMMIT—"

The doors swung open. Tony looked at me and sniffed. "Players only," he said. "Can't you read?" He pointed at the sign.

"Where's the coffee?" I said.

Clean and brightly lit, cozy and comfortable, the locker room was as familiar to me as my own home. As I followed Tony to the equipment room he pointed to a wooden table where he'd laid out some of the special equipment he'd gotten to help us cope with the cold. There were plastic bags for the feet, skindiver's

232

sheer rubber gloves for the hands, and for the skin a frostbite preventative to be rubbed in before donning any of the afore-mentioned gear. In addition, on the folding metal chair in front of each locker, there were small boxes of inch-and-a-half mud cleats that had been shaved sharp as pitons, and beside the boxes, cellophane packages containing pairs of Madame Broussard's "for the full-figured woman" pantyhose.

"No long johns," said Tony, as if anticipating a protest. "I got my orders."

I nodded, hardly hearing, because I'd noticed a slight but sig-nificant change in the usual locker room decor. Above the lockers, in place of the customary adhesive strips marked with players' numbers, were attractive gold-on-scarlet placards bearing not only numbers but full names, position and years in the league. They gave, it seemed, a kind of air of permanence and substance to each player.

"They come right out," Tony said, watching me. He reached up and slid Blair's placard out of its slot. "You can take 'em home after the game."

I had coffee and Polish sausage in the equipment room with Tony, then went back to my locker, undressed and slipped into a T-shirt and jock. From the wooden table I took a jar of Vaseline and a can of powdered fungicide, and after mixing the ingredi-ents, applied the salve to the insides of my thighs, which had been chafed raw from the season-long contact with the jock—an oc-cupational affliction cured only by retirement. As I walked into the training room the trainer looked up and, noting the way I walked, laughed.

"You wet your pants, Rafferty? Already?" He was standing in front of his taping table, tucking his shirt in his pants.

"I—"

"Stone crabs," he said. "I love stone crabs, Rafferty, and there's only one place in America you can get 'em. You know where that is?"

"Is that what Willie had? Stone crabs?"

"Up," he said, irritated. "We got work to do."

I scooted up on the table. As the trainer sprayed my ankles with tape adherent I said, "It's Miami, isn't it? Where they have stone crabs."

He nodded.

"I wanna get there as bad as you do."

"I know." He smiled. "The usual?"

"Sure."

The trainer worked quickly, tearing the tape, wrapping it around and smoothing it over my feet. He took pride in the speed with which he worked and the appearance when he finished off the neatly packaged joints, particularly the way the stark white of the tape contrasted with the faint blue of one's feet, and the way the blue darkened as the tape cut deeper and deeper into one's flesh—he must've taken pride because I'd yet to see an ankle that, when he'd finished with it, wasn't blue and throbbing—a prime candidate for a case of gangrene.

"Up," he said when done, and I stood up on the rickety white table and with my head crooked against the low ceiling and my feet beginning to swell, extended my right leg a half-step and lifted my heel. Under the heel the trainer slipped a roll of adhesive, then, as I rested my heel on the tape, he set to work on the knee, slowly now, carefully measuring the strips of adhesive before cutting them and applying them in parallel layers over the badly stretched ligaments in my right knee. He didn't talk. Neither did I. Not until he'd finished.

"Have a good one," he said as I grabbed his shoulder and vaulted down from the table. "You need anything else?"

"Thanks," I said. "I'm fine."

In the locker room an equipment boy moved from stall to stall, placing game programs on the unoccupied chairs. On the cover of the program was a cartoon picture of Chicago running back "Duck" Mallard soaring like a kite over a packed RFK Stadium. On the field below, guiding the kite, stood a grinning Crespin Mug. Shaking my head, I set the program on the floor, stacked the box of cleats and the package of pantyhose on it and sat down. After slitting the ankle tape along the inside of my arches and the knee tape along the back of my calf I pulled a rubber skidder over my left knee, then dusted both legs with baby powder. The powder served as a lubricant so that my game pants would pull on without rolling up the tape and the skidder. Next I rubbed my toes with frostbite preventative, then, horror of horrors, reached for the package of pantyhose.

I was too goddamn tall. The elastic waist hit me just below the hips, leaving some five inches of slack material hanging from my crotch. I sat down and peeled them off. With a peculiar, panicky feeling I pulled them on and peeled them off again. Jesus. In a kind of frenzy I grabbed a pair of scissors and began cutting away the nylon legs.

Just then the double steel doors banged open and in walked Wayne Law, carrying an armload of long underwear and looking uncharacteristically tense. He went to his locker, where he quickly stowed the smuggled goods in his equipment bag. As he stood to begin undressing, the double steel doors banged open again and Jan Rutledge came in. He was wearing a full-length suede coat, fur-collared and belted across the middle, and one of those Russian hats that were all the rage that year. He looked like a general or something. And I was quick to notice that he was walking with only a slight limp.

"Can you go?" I asked as he crossed the room.

"Goddamn right," and shedding his topcoat and hat, Rutledge disappeared into the training room.

Now other players were arriving—Willie Slough, who for a change was early, Blair, Regis and Enrico Monte, and as they filed by Wayne's locker to pick up long underwear or pills, more players arrived, and then members of the coaching staff, and pretty soon the locker room was reverberating with loud music and shouted conversation.

I wriggled into the altered pantyhose. I'd cut off the legs just above the knee and now I taped the ragged ends to my skin and very carefully pulled on my socks and game pants. Then I picked up my copy of the game program and retreated to the relative calm of the equipment room.

"Tony?"

No answer. Good, I thought. I walked around a bank of footlockers, removed an unread Sunday newspaper from a folding metal chair, sat down and, after pouring myself another cup of coffee, rocked back in the chair and began leafing through the program.

The usual stuff. Scouting reports, statistics, stadium information, pictures of our players and staff—stuff I'd seen ten thousand times. The feature was on J. D. "Duck" Mallard and his offensive line. More of the same. Mallard credits success to the big guys up front...Mallard buys dinner for the big guys after every game...Mallard buys *bracelets* for the big guys after *every season*...complete with pictures of Mallard doing all of these grand things "for the big guys." I flipped through it, I was getting mad.

Past the pictures of the Chicago players and staff, past the blurb on the bands that were going to perform at halftime, in the center of the program, flanking a four-color ad for Coca-Cola (Look up America, enjoy the real things), were the starting lineups for today's game. I ran my finger down the left-hand column, our lineup. Sure enough there I was, under DEFENSE, fourth name down:

68 BRAD RAFFERTY RE

I supposed they didn't have time to make the change and put Willie in my place. I was grateful for that.

Below the lineup, in smaller print, was the club's numerical roster, and I ran my finger down this list too, counting veterans, seeing how many players were older than me, how much longer I could expect to play. Three or four years as it turned out, a whole goddamn college career. An eternity. At the very bottom of the page, in very small print, was another list giving the names of the officials scheduled to work today's game.

All at once from the locker room came an abrupt, explosive roar, then another. Compressed as they echoed through the tiny room, the sounds startled me. Moving slightly in the chair, I looked out the equipment-room door to see what was happening. The roars were cheers for Rutledge. He was standing at the far end of the locker room, smiling as he flexed his heavily taped left leg.

Each movement brought an explosive roar from his teammates, all of whom had gathered around him. Then, suddenly, the room fell silent and the players began backing away from him in an ever-expanding circle. Someone had handed Rutledge a football. As he stood staring at the ball, turning it over in his hands, slowly, as if memorizing every crease and grain in its hide, Wayne Law broke from the group. He jogged toward me, turned in front of the equipment-room door and, like a baseball catcher, settled into a crouch.

Rutledge straightened. Eyeing Wayne, he raised the ball to his shoulder, stepped gingerly onto his left foot and, grimacing, threw. The ball squirmed off his hand, skidding twice on the concrete before reaching Wayne, who had to lunge to make the catch. Raising slightly, Wayne rifled the ball back to Rutledge who, after flexing his leg once more, vigorously threw again, this time a fluttering spiral that at least went straight to the mark. The players, who until now had been watching in deathly silence, began talking excitedly among themselves, their excitement growing as, with each subsequent throw, the spirals tightened, the velocity increased, and the grimace faded from Rutledge's face.

Smiling to myself, I glanced once more at the list of officials, then closed the program and set it on the floor, the glossy paper sticking for a moment to my wet hands...my hands were wet because I'd started to sweat. Dark stains were spreading from my armpits across the front of my gray T-shirt. An acrid smell was filling my head. And it wasn't because the referee for today was Al Pasco, the official I'd had the confrontation with in the Philadelphia game. He'd made an honest mistake, I believed that, and even though I'd popped off to the press about him it wasn't because of any leftover apprehension I felt at his working this game. No, it was because of another name further down the list...a name I'd glimpsed as I closed the book—the name of the umpire... *Richard Farrell.*

I'd never noticed this list before, but then, the print was very small and I'd never paid much attention to the officials anyway. How many games and how many programs, and in every one of them this little list I'd never noticed? Who were these guys anyway,

I'd always thought, just a faceless bunch who picked up a few dollars officiating pro football games in their spare time...What did they make? Five hundred dollars a game? Something like that. Not bad for an autumn weekend. Just like everybody else, is what I thought, regular guys with families to support and bills to pay and one of these regular guys today was Richard Farrell, the former partner of Bobby DeAngelis, the California banker who owed Keith Thorley a huge amount of money. Thorley, the financier and partial owner in the club with direct ties to one of the most powerful Mafia leaders in the country. The Mafia, whose business and chief source of income was bookmaking.

I was up and pacing. I knew now where I'd heard Farrell's name before. It was in the staff meeting room the day after the Philadelphia game. Coach had mentioned him during our discussion of the drive-killing holding penalties. "It could've been worse," he had assured me. "Farrell could've flagged *every* play." Yes, but he hadn't, he had been very selective in the plays he flagged, or so it had seemed to me...that's why I'd picked up the canister of offensive game film, to see those plays for myself. But the canister had been empty. Red Keane had had that reel. Keane, who had initiated the manipulation of Wayne Law. I felt sick. If Wayne had sat out just one series we might've been all right. But Keane had turned Wayne over to Needles and one series got to be a whole goddamn half. That killed us. When Wayne was put back into the game early in the third period it was already too late, we were too far behind to come back and win—Farrell had made sure of it...

Fighting nausea, I grabbed the newspaper and pulled out the sports section. I was sure now that the Philadelphia game had been rigged. It made sense, too...We had been favored to win. To make the favorite play poorly would be much easier for Farrell than to make the underdog play well; it would give him much more direct control over the outcome of the game...*And* we were favored to win again today—by one point, according to Brady Young. On the strength of our defense and the home-field advantage.

I turned to the back of the section and searched the agate

columns for the injury report. One point wasn't much to work with unless Mister Clayton had neglected to report Rutledge's dislocated kneecap as he had Wayne's pulled hamstring. That way the point spread would be blown to hell before the game even started, and even without Farrell—

In the small column that listed the names of our injured players there was no mention of Jan Rutledge. I read it again. His name was not there.

I dropped the newspaper and bolted from the equipment room. At my locker, after searching briefly for Wayne and Rutledge— they were nowhere to be seen—I slipped into my street shoes. As I pulled on my coat Willie Slough, who was seated beside me wrapping clear packing tape around the tops of his burgundy stockings, looked up and smiled.

"Hey, B," he said warmly, "where you been hidin', B?"

I turned and started back across the room for the double steel doors.

"B?"

I ignored him. My eyes were riveted to the blank gray face of the doors, through which in a moment I would pass, if only I could avoid Phil Tanner, who, clipboard in hand, was lurking nearby.

I wasn't getting off the hook, they weren't letting me off the hook. Judy...shit, shit, *shit*...

"Where the hell you goin', Rafferty?" Tanner alert and yapping as I approached. "Out for a little walk, huh? That's what you—"

"Shit," I said.

"What?"

"Shit!" I yelled.

The doors banged open, Needles came in. I stopped. Needles, lugging a large black doctor's bag, was wearing a greatcoat and alpine hat, beneath which his eyes, when he saw me, narrowed, as if in suspicion—or fear? But of what? I watched as he disappeared with Tanner into the coaches' dressing room.

And then I remembered the arthrogram.

"TEN MINUTES FOR SPECIALISTS," Tony called out.

With the arthrogram Needles had tried to eliminate Rutledge

239

as a participant. The bastard. He'd fouled up once, but he would try again. They would make him try again. But when? During the game, like with Wayne? Earlier?

"TEN MINUTES," Tony called out.

I didn't have time to wait around and find out. I had to get to Pasco. I wanted to tell someone in authority. He was my only hope. And maybe Coach...if I could trust Coach...But Pasco first, and I had to get to him soon, before he went out on the field or he wouldn't talk to me. Christ, he probably wouldn't talk to me anyway—league rules prohibited our talking—still, I had to try. But first I had to see what was up with Rutledge.

I rushed back across the room and knelt down in front of Willie Slough. "Willie," I said quietly, grabbing and shaking his arms, "I want you to do me a favor. Will you do me a favor?"

"Jesus Christ, B, *Jesus*," he said, wrenching free of my grip. "What's the matter, B? What is it?"

"I'm sorry, Willie. Nothing. I'm very sorry." After a steadying pause I asked if he were almost dressed.

"Dressed? You mean for the game?"

"Yes," I said. "For the game, for Christ's sake."

"Oh," Willie said. Then, as if to be certain of his answer, he began looking himself over.

I sighed and glanced once more around the room, saw Wayne and Coach as they moved from behind a blackboard near the door of the training room. After a moment they were followed by Rutledge.

"You want to talk to me, B?" Willie asked.

"There's Rutledge," I said.

"What?"

"Over there. See him?"

Willie looked.

"Now listen to me, Willie. When Rutledge goes out to loosen up, I want you go with him. Okay? I want you to go out with the specialists."

"Out? You mean out on the field? But I ain't a specialist, B. I'll get fined."

240

"You don't have to go out on the field, Willie, just down to the end of the tunnel. What I want you to do, I want you to watch Rutledge warm up. But from a distance, you know what I mean? From a distance is fine. So just go down to the end of the tunnel and watch him from there. Okay? That's all you have to do."

"Like a sentry or something?"

"Exactly," I said. "Now listen to me. If Rutledge comes in early, before warm-ups are over, he'll have to pass you. If he does, I want you to put your big old arm around him and go wherever he goes. Understand? *Don't let him out of your sight.*"

"But, B—I mean, what if he be goin' to the crapper, B? You want me to be goin' in the crapper with him?"

"Willie, for Christ's sake."

"Serious, B. I mean—"

"Please just do what I've asked you to do."

"But—"

"*Please.* Okay?"

Willie considered it for a moment, then, reluctantly, nodded. "You swear to me on sweet Jesus you ain't doin' this to put me on a joke level and I have lost you as a friend, B?"

"I swear it, Willie."

I got up and hurried back across the room, out the double steel doors and into the concrete corridor, then turned right, away from the public area, from the system of ramps and walkways that could take you either outside to the parking lots or inside to the spectator seating. Sprinting through the cold, dimly lit passage, I came to a long flight of stairs, took them three at a time, hoping all the while I was headed in the right direction. A few feet beyond the last stair the corridor ended, and I paused to get my bearings. I was at field level but beneath the movable stands that had been wheeled into place after baseball season. The steel I-beams supporting the stands were bolted to the stadium along a concrete retaining wall that curved gently away from me in either direction. Along the base of the wall, visible in the shafts of light that filtered through the narrow space between the permanent and portable stands, ran a crumbling track of asphalt. Down it to my left, maybe

241

fifteen yards, sat an old man in visored cap and green uniform. He was guarding a door with the sign:

OFFICIALS' DRESSING ROOM
POSITIVELY NO ADMITTANCE!

I was not meant to go in that door, he was there to stop me. That old man was there to keep people like me out. Crouching, I tried to shrink myself into the cover of the shadows. From far off behind me came a ringing, resonant clank, and then a groan as if the whole stadium above me had shifted. I was under the stadium, and felt someone watching me from behind. I peeked, then whirled to look down a hallway disappearing in tiers of shadow. Something tickled my face, and I looked up into dripping beads of water and realized the water had spread as it broke against my cheek into a weblike tracery that I wanted to brush away. My arms began to itch. Oh, no, I thought. I buttoned my overcoat, pulled a stocking cap out of my pocket and along with it, tangled in the knit, a pair of sunglasses that I put on after tugging the stocking cap down over my ears and lifting up the collar on my overcoat. Stuffing my hands into my pockets, I strode toward the door.

THIRTY

"No sir," said the old man, standing, palms up, head shaking as I approached. *"No sir."* Authorized personnel only."

"Al Pasco," I said. "I have to see Al Pasco."

"I don't know Al Pasco. Authorized personnel only—"

"He's the referee, goddammit. He's in that room and I have to see him. It's an emergency."

"An emergency, huh." The old man regarded me skeptically. "What kind of emergency?"

"His wife, she...there was an accident. This morning. Christ, *you* tell him."

"No, no. She hurt?"

"Bad. Yes."

"You shoulda said so sooner."

The old man walked back to the door, raised his right hand, rapped twice, paused, rapped twice more. Like a code. Except nothing happened. He put his ear to the door and listened for a moment, then rapped once more—hard. "A gentleman would like to speak to Mister Pasco," he called out. "It's important."

A deadbolt clicked, the door swung open, and out stepped Pasco. He was tall, perhaps forty-two years old, with sharp features, dark hair and beneath the clingy knit fabric of his uniform a decidedly athletic build.

"What is it?" he said in an authoritative tone that had the security guard nearly snapping to attention.

"This gentleman would like to speak to you, sir." The guard pointed at me. "It's important."

Pasco peered into the shadows.

"In private, sir," I said. "I would like to speak to you in private."

After studying me for a moment Pasco came forward, warily at first, then with a disarming confidence. He reached out and unbuttoned my coat, pulled back the lapels and read the number marked on my T-shirt.

"I thought I might see you today, Rafferty. But certainly not here. This is highly irregular." He let go of the coat.

"I...I know that, sir." I took off the glasses.

"So what can I do for you? I suppose you're still upset about that call. Philadelphia, wasn't it?"

"Listen, sir—"

"I was a little quick with the flag. I admit it."

"I don't care about that, sir. I mean, I appreciate what you're saying, but I—I'm here because of your umpire. He's in trouble," I said. "The worst kind of trouble."

"Dick? What the hell are you talking about?"

I took a breath. "I believe he's involved with some...some organized crime people...financially...he owes a big debt—"

"Just what are you telling me, Rafferty?"

"I'm telling you, sir, that I think he's in a helluva bind. I'm telling you he'll do whatever those people want him to do whenever they want him to do it..."

"This is some kind of bad joke—"

"No. Believe me. I wish it were."

"I assume you have some *proof* of what you're saying? Because otherwise—"

"You've got to keep your eye on him, that's all I'm saying—"

"And you're sure it's this game? Rafferty, what the fuck is this, you speeding? You coked up? You gone paranoid?"

"*No,*" I said. Obviously he wanted more. He'd asked for proof.

244

"I have the loan agreements," I said. It was a lie, of course. And I was about to take it back, to tell the truth, that I knew about Mister Clayton and Keith Thorley, but my lie had made him smile. I went on, elaborating, as if to make his smile bigger. "I have the loan agreements. Not here. Not with me. I didn't know until this morning he would be working this game—"

His smile vanished. He shook his head. "I can't...you should've taken this to league security. I don't—"

"There wasn't time for that, sir. I just found out, I told you. You've got to do something."

"What? I can't pull him for the alternate without a solid reason. He'll fight that, he'll deny the whole thing and then—"

"Al!" One of the other officials had come out of the dressing room. "It's about that time, Al!"

"I'll be right there," he said, and as the official ducked back inside the room a prolonged, shattering roar came from above.

"There go the specialists," I said. "We haven't got much time."

Pasco was pacing now. "I can watch him, Rafferty. That's about it. I can watch him and overrule anything blatantly suspicious. But you've got to do something for me. Two things. First, keep quiet about this until we can figure out how the hell to handle it. I mean, any kind of publicity...I'm sure you understand. Second, meet the supervisor of officials after the game. I'll arrange it. Meet him at the top of the stairs near the entrance to your locker room and tell him just what you've told me. We'll work from there. You may have to go to New York."

"New York?"

"You're sitting on a powder keg, Rafferty. The commissioner, league security, they'll want to know how you got there."

"Right," I said. It seemed a curious statement on his part, but my thoughts had already turned to Rutledge and time was short. "Right," I said again, and ran like hell for the locker room.

CHAPTER THIRTY-ONE

The locker room was empty. The players had gone, except Willie Slough, who had gone but come back. He sat in full gear straddling a folding metal chair in front of the training room door. He was watching the door like a terrier watching a rathole.

"They in there?"

Willie gave a start. "Oh, B. Yeah," he said. "They wouldn't let me in." He got to his feet.

"Needles with him?"

"Yeah, B. How'd you know?"

I tried the door. It was locked. "Kick it in, Willie."

"The door?"

"Kick the sucker *in*, Willie," I said, indicating a spot just above the door knob.

Willie raised his right leg and with a short swift jab hit the spot with the flat of his foot. Nothing happened. Just cleat marks on the door. "Again," I said. Willie recoiled and hit the spot once more, harder, and this time the door flew open, its latch-bolt ripping the strike-plate from the jamb, its knob punching a hole through the inside of the adjacent wall.

Rutledge, lying flat on his back on a treatment table, raised his head to see what had happened. Needles, who was standing over him, remained intensely concentrated. Inserting the needle of a large syringe into the cork top of a small glass vial, Needles held the instruments up to the light and began drawing the vial's clear solution into the syringe. Then he smiled. "What is this, some new warm-up drill? You boys break down doors?" He looked at Rutledge. "Pull up the leg," and as Rutledge drew up his injured leg, from which, around the knee, the tape had been cut away, Needles slipped the syringe from the vial, set the vial on the table and with his free hand began probing the joint for a suitable place to make the injection.

By this time Willie and I had come over, and as Willie got himself up on the table next to Rutledge, I clapped Needles on the shoulder and asked him how the hell he was doing.

"What the fuck," he said, "you guys—*leave that alone.*"

I was picking up the vial.

"Gimme that, you can't—"

"Take it easy, doc," I said, and fending him off with my left arm, I read the label on the vial. "Tetracycline?" I gave him a hard shove. "You're gonna inject his knee with *tetracycline?*"

"Let me see that," he said.

I showed him the vial.

"Well, uh..." He turned to Rutledge. "Look, Jan—"

"You been paying your malpractice premiums, doc?"

"Now listen here, Rafferty—"

I threw the vial against the wall, smashing it. "His knee hurts, give him some Empirin," I said.

"Holy shit," Needles said. "That's what I meant. I meant to give him Empirin. Boy, am I nervous about this game. I meant to give him Empirin..."

"Oh," I said.

"What the hell is going on here, Needles?" Rutledge said.

"Thanks," said Needles, "I nearly fucked up here, Jan. Sorry..."

"You're welcome," I said. "C'mon, Willie." We left the room.

At my locker, nerves jangling, I pulled on my shoulder pads and game jersey. As I slipped into my game shoes my teammates, strutting and shouting, began trooping in from the field. They came singly and in pairs through the door at the end of a short corridor that began on the left side of my locker, the side away from the training room. The staff would soon follow, I knew. Grabbing my helmet, I hurried across the room to Wayne's locker, shook a cigarette from his pack and picked up his matches. Then, shouldering my way through the arriving players, I rushed down the corridor and into the bathroom, where I locked myself in one of the stalls.

The moment of reckoning would come soon, I was sure, as soon as Needles told someone what I'd done. Then Tanner would come for me and take me to Coach, and Coach would demand an explanation. But there was no explanation. There was nothing I could say that would prove anything. Mostly it had all been a bluff...hell, I didn't even know what tetracycline was.

I lifted my legs off the floor, bracing them against the door of the stall, fired the cigarette and waited, listening over the gutteral flushing of toilets for Tanner's booming voice. And after a while it came: "Let's finish up in here, Coach is about ready." I strained, listening for more, waiting for a search of the stalls. Neither happened. He left. By the end of Coach's speech, snatches of which I could hear, along with the occasional punctuating cheers from the players—by the end of the speech, when still no one had come, I stopped worrying. It seemed the bluff had worked. Needles hadn't told anyone what I'd done because he couldn't afford to tell anyone. The team was praying now and I was wondering how Needles had smoothed things over with Rutledge and Willie. I'd find out later. I stood up and buckled on my helmet. Things were bad but not hopeless...they had Farrell on their side, we had Pasco on ours. And we had the advantage of knowing what Farrell was up to while at least for the moment they had no idea that Pasco had been alerted...

The prayers from the other room were over and the amens were sounding. I banged my hands against the sides of my helmet. Time to go.

Outside, light snow was falling from a dark, overcast sky. Though the wind had abated snow still swirled and eddied as it descended into the stadium, perhaps because of the convection currents generated by the blazing stadium lights. The swirling snow and the blazing lights were all I could see from the covered dugout where we stood waiting for the end of the Chicago introductions.

"AND AT RUNNING BACK..."

A thermometer on the back wall read 22 degrees Fahrenheit, but the nervous energy discharged by the players as they stretched and bounced and fidgeted made it seem much warmer. This was what I liked.

"FROM THE UNIVERSITY OF TEXAS..."

Suddenly the players stopped squirming.

"NUMBER THIRTY-ONE..."

"Here it comes," came an excited whisper. And as "DUCK *MAL-LAAARRDD*" boomed through the stadium, the players craned their necks and listened, intent not on the announcement itself but on how our fans would react to the announcement, and in a moment it came, what they had hoped for, a silence so deep and long and vast that Mallard must've thought he had run into a goddamn vacuum.

"PLEASE, LADIES AND GENTLEMEN," the announcer implored, "*PLEASE*, A GREAT BIG WASHINGTON WELCOME FOR THE REST OF THE PLAYERS AND STAFF..."

But nothing came, not a smattering of recognition, not even a boo. Laughing, slapping palms, we waited in the dugout until the silence became a low rumble of anticipation. Then at a signal from a man standing on the top step of the dugout—he had a walkie-talkie pressed to his ear—and as the public-address announcer took once more to the airwaves..."AND *NOW*, LADIES AND GENTLEMEN..."—we surged up the dugout steps and, to the most tumultuous welcome ever given a Washington team, out onto the field behind our bench. There, as if pressed together by the sheer force of the roar, we huddled in a tight circle and began jumping up and down and beating on one another, the roar swelling as we moved en masse toward our bench to greet our offensive players, who were being introduced from the far end zone, the roar now an impenetrable din wiping out names and colleges, impenetrable and swelling, reaching one final crescendo when Jan Rutledge, hobbling to midfield, was met and enveloped by the circle of players and literally carried to the sidelines.

"Bring it up, men, bring it up!" Coach hollering and gesturing over the roar of the crowd as the team bounded off the field. "BRING IT UP, GODDAMMIT." The coin toss had been carried out during pregame warm-ups, we had lost, and now, as we gathered around Coach, he gave final instructions to the defensive unit—"SET THE TEMPO."—and to the kickoff coverage team— "DON'T GIVE 'EM ANY LIFE." After which we all made a pile of our hands and with a gutteral "RAH" broke the huddle.

As the coverage team deployed, the crowd still roaring, I walked down to the end of the bench and began shaking hands with the defensive starters. "Let's go, Jeff. Frank? Have a good one, huh?" A quick shake, a slap on the ass, all greeted with a distracted nod or a muttered, "You, too." I knew how they felt.

"RRRRAAAHHHHHH…"

After making a final check of my equipment I turned for the first time to the field. Bathed in the glare of the stadium lights, surrounded by shoals of soiled snow, it seemed weirdly small, almost surreal. Cameras were everywhere, and it was for the cameras that the dormant brown turf had been sprayed with a thick coat of bright green paint, smudges of which could already be seen on the backsides of many of the players.

As Stoufer raised his hand to signal his readiness, I looked around for Richard Farrell. Nearly invisible against the banks of mottled snow, he was standing across the field at the 35-yard line, hands on knees, cap pulled tight, apparently composed and confident as he inspected the alignment of the receiving team. And why not? Throwing a game wouldn't be such a difficult assignment for him…

"AAAHHHH…"

My eyes darted to the end zone where, near the goal posts, Al Pasco stood keying the network liaison, on whose signal the game would begin. He was staring fixedly upfield at Richard Farrell as if to detect some visible sign of what he'd just been told. He must have felt outraged at his associate's treachery, and determined to guard against its possible effect on the course of this game. There was something in the precise way he moved, the set to his jaw, that said to me he'd accepted responsibility for the knowledge I'd given him and that this game, at least, would be played as it was supposed to be played.

I watched as the network liaison, clipboard in hand, headphones in place, stepped forward and pointed at Pasco, as if to say, "Action." As the liaison returned to the sidelines Pasco looked upfield for Stoufer, and when he had his attention gave a shrill blast on his whistle and made a gesture like an infantry officer leading a charge. Stoufer dropped his arm and with the roar of the crowd peaking once more, approached the ball and smacked a low, line-drive kick that was fielded on the short-hop by the upback on the near side. Sidling to the middle of the field, the back hesitated as the wedge went by, then cut in behind them and started upfield, only to slip down, untouched, on the lacquered surface. He should have stayed down but didn't. Defenseless and vulnerable, he was on his knees when three players hit him simultaneously from three different locations. When the players unpiled, the ballcarrier lay still and limp. Time-out was called. The band began to play, the cheerleaders began to dance, the doctors hurried out onto the field and after a cursory examination called for a stretcher crew. All of which excited the players who had made the hit. As they came off the field they were jabbering about the "carry-off" and how they were going to spend the hundred-dollar bill they would find in their lockers in an unmarked envelope come Monday morning. "What happened to him?" I asked as they passed, but they knew the cameras were on them, they were mugging and couldn't be bothered.

"Change your cleats," an equipment boy shouted as he moved through the swarm of players. "Coach says change your cleats."

On our bench other equipment boys were already kneeling in front of seated players, replacing their half-inch, flat-topped knobbies with the inch-and-a-half mud cleats that had been shaved into sharp conical spikes that could puncture a thigh or a calf as easily as they could the encrusted, frozen field.

"Change your cleats," the boy shouted. "It's a fine if you don't."

I turned back to the field. The paramedics were positioning the injured player on a collapsible stretcher. When they had him where they wanted him, one of the paramedics wrapped him in a blanket while the other cinched the straps that had been thrown over the blanket across the player's chest and legs. They lifted the stretcher, locked the stainless steel struts in place and wheeled the player off the field, hurriedly, his head bouncing as they crossed the rutted surface.

When they'd cleared the sidelines Pasco gave a short blast on his whistle and marked the ball for play. It was on their 22-yard line. Nearby, Willie stood rolling his neck and swinging his arms as he waited for the first play from scrimmage. He looked tight as hell.

"Ready, Brad?" Coach DeVito took my arm.

"Willie's not," I said.

"I know, but check with Coach, huh? Before you go in? Just so we're all on the same page."

"Sure."

DeVito smiled and clapped me on the butt, then turned and walked to midfield, where he joined the other assistants, all of whom were clustered around Coach, their eyes riveted to the playing field.

"DEE-FENSE, DEE-FENSE." The crowd chanted as the Chicago offense broke their huddle and deployed. They were in a far left formation, their favorite—the tight end was on the near side, the fullback directly behind the quarterback, Mallard on the weakside directly behind Crespin Mug.

"Set," called the quarterback, and Mug dropped into his stance. He had taken an abnormally wide split—perhaps a yard separated him from the offensive guard—which meant the play would probably be run to the opposite side, the strongside. What Mug wanted Willie to do, he wanted Willie to split out with him. That way Willie, who was responsible for backside containment, would, by virtue of his alignment, eliminate himself from the play. But we had prepared for this. On the weakside of the far formation the defensive ends had been instructed to line up on the tackle's inside shoulder and pinch.

252

"BLUE, FORTY-EIGHT."

But Willie was on Mug's outside shoulder and aimed upfield.

"HUT."

Head down, back foot raking the dirt, Willie was intent on one thing and one thing only, and that was getting off on the football.

"HUT—"

And that he did beautifully. As the quarterback accepted the snap and pivoted toward Mallard, who was flowing strong, Willie exploded across the line of scrimmage, head down, low and hard, like a battering ram. Mug, however, had stepped to the inside and there was no one for Willie to hit. Like a man whose foot finds an abyss instead of pavement, Willie hurtled upfield, stumbling and lurching until, finally, he fell flat on his face at the 10-yard line. Mallard, meanwhile, though headed wide and to his right, had spotted the opening, stopped, and cut back. Mug smashed the weakside linebacker, the cornerback overcommitted, and suddenly Mallard was breezing up the far sidelines, free and clear, five yards at a bound, headed for a sure quick six. But then, unaccountably, Mallard slowed to a jog, then stopped completely. Apparently there had been a whistle. Near midfield the head linesman stood toeing a spot on the sidelines, his arms waving frantically over his head.

Out of bounds was the call, at our 48. There was no argument from Mallard or from the Chicago coaches...the call had been made right in front of them. In fact, their coaches seemed more concerned about the next play than anything else—they were urging their charges to hurry upfield—and in a moment I knew why. As our players hustled onsides the Chicago offense deployed without having huddled. They were in a far left formation again. Regis hollered at Willie to tighten up. He did. He shifted to Mug's inside shoulder and pointed his head toward the guard-tackle gap. But neither Regis nor Willie had noticed that Mallard had switched positions with the fullback. When Mallard switched positions with the fullback their tendency was to run weak instead of strong. It was all in the game plan. "Mallard," it said, "is a lousy blocker. The fullback," it said, "is an excellent blocker. Therefore," it said, "they will always run to the side of the fullback."

But Willie hadn't noticed, and at the snap he took a hard inside charge. Mug coiled. As Willie took his second step Mug drilled his helmet into Willie's exposed ribcage and drove him down the line of scrimmage, their combined bulk caving in the entire left side of the formation. The fullback kicked out the weakside linebacker and once more Mallard was loose in the secondary, picking up eleven yards and another first down before being hammered to the turf by the free safety.

Pasco marked the ball for play at our 37, and again Chicago chose not to huddle. They were in far left again, but this time the backs were in their normal slots.

"BLUE—"

Quick count. Mug set short as the quarterback took the snap, turned and offered an open hand to the fullback, who was plunging into the line. While Willie and the weakside linebacker charged in to tackle the fullback, the quarterback, the ball stashed against his hip, dropped deep, set and lofted a soft spiral toward Mallard, who had circled into the vacated flat. As the ball came fluttering down Mallard shot a glance upfield to assess the defense, and was so stunned by the vast open plain that lay in front of him—there was not a defender within thirty yards—that he was late in looking back for the ball, which with a dry smack ricocheted off the curved side of his helmet and caromed into the dirt. Our fans, who had been silent through most of this drive, erupted with a great cheer and once more began to chant as Chicago, abandoning their hurry-up offense, formed their first huddle.

It was second and ten at the 37.

"DEE-FENSE, DEE-FENSE."

A passing down, according to Chicago's tendencies, and when the huddle broke they did indeed deploy in a passing formation. Red, we called it—a running back behind each offensive tackle, the backs split this way so they could get quickly into their routes.

"GREEN. THIRTY-SIX."

Willie widened on Mug, anticipating a pass, and at the snap charged upfield. The quarterback, dropping two quick steps, set, pivoted to his left and launched a missile at his flanker, who was slanting for the middle of the field. It seemed for a moment that

Willie would deflect the pass. Having glimpsed the short set of the quarterback, he had, on his first step, climbed high in the air and extended his arms, and it seemed that the ball would hit him squarely in the chest. At the last possible instant, however, Crespin Mug, who had also set short, exploded into Willie's legs, and the blow sent Willie spinning like a pinwheel. As the football sailed high and hard into the secondary—fortunately too high and too hard to be caught—Willie turned a rapid, thrashing flip and, with a sickening thud, landed flat on his back on the frozen turf.

For a long moment he lay very still. Then, as the crowd applauded the incompletion and the impending third down, he rolled over on his stomach and pushed himself up to all fours. Grimacing, he sat back on his heels and very slowly began to rotate his torso. Thinking he might have to come out of the game, at least for a play, I buckled on my helmet and ran out on the field...and the crowd started to boo. For a moment I thought they were booing me, but then as I cleared the Chicago huddle I saw a yellow penalty flag on the ground near the line of scrimmage. I stopped running. Just beyond the flag Al Pasco was conferring with Richard Farrell, who apparently had made the call.

"Hey," I yelled.

Pasco gave me a look.

"Goddammit," I shouted, and started toward him. As I did Pasco left Farrell and rushed to meet me. He was irritated.

"Relax," he said. "For Christ's sake, *relax*. I told you I'd handle this. Now let me." He wheeled and hurried back to Farrell.

Feeling more than a little foolish, I walked over to Willie. "So how you doin'," I said as I knelt down beside him. "You hurt?"

"I didn't do it, B. I swear I didn't."

"You didn't do what, Willie."

"I didn't use no illegal head slaps."

"They called it on you?"

"That man right there, B." He pointed at Farrell. "He says I used illegal techniques when I was flying upside down through the air..."

I couldn't help laughing.

"Is that in the rules, B?"

"No, Willie, it's not. But don't worry about it. You see the referee there? He won't let him get away with it."

"You kiddin' me, B?"

"Watch him," I said.

Pasco had left Farrell and was walking toward our bench. Midway between the hashmarks and the sidelines he stopped and switched on his transistorized microphone, then looked up at the pressbox.

"NO FLAG," he said calmly, his voice echoing through the stadium. "IT IS THIRD DOWN."

Willie looked at me and grinned.

"Can you go?" I asked as we got to our feet.

"It's third down, ain't it?"

"Get you one," I said, and I turned and hustled off the field.

Faced with a third and ten from the 37, Chicago deployed once more in a red formation. To bolster our pass defense Coach had replaced the middle linebacker with a fifth defensive back, and to muster a pass rush had signaled for line stunts—a double limbo. It was the perfect defense. At the snap Willie Slough and left end John Reese cut underneath the looping defensive tackles and stormed upfield. Confronted with these two lumbering hulks, the Chicago center chose to block Willie, which left Reese free, a fact quickly perceived by the Chicago quarterback, who flushed to his left, eluding Reese but not Jeff Blair, who had circled wide in containment. Blair collared the quarterback and like a hammer-thrower began whirling—once, twice—but before he could let fly Al Pasco blew the play dead.

The crowd, which had risen cheering to its feet, booed lustily as Blair released the quarterback, but their displeasure didn't last. Although Pasco had deprived them of a spectacular play, they knew he was just doing his job, and besides, the sack *had* counted, it *was* fourth down, and Wayne Law, one of their favorite players, had come onfield to return the punt.

"Wayne Law, Wayne Law..."

The chant started somewhat feebly in the west end zone with a group of fans who had draped a bedsheet banner over the retaining wall—"*WAYNE* WILL ENFORCE THE *LAW* ON CHI-

CAGO." When Wayne, who had settled in at the 10-yard line, turned and waved at them, they shouted with increased vigor, and the chant quickly spread throughout the stadium: "WAYNE–LAW, WAYNE–LAW, WAYNE–LAW."

The punt came low and hard, a line drive with a wicked spiral. Barely clearing the line of scrimmage, the football skipped like a stone at the 25, again at the 20, then came leaping and tumbling toward Wayne, who, giving ground, sidled to his right and waited, his eyes locked on the dribbling ball. He shot upfield, took the ball on a high-hop, split the first wave of coverage and, cutting hard to his right, swung wide, downshifting as he skirted the contain man and approached the corner, then accelerating, moving up the sidelines behind a series of blindside, peelback blocks that came off like a string of firecrackers.

Pandemonium as Wayne, hardly breaking stride, hurdled the last defender and highstepped into the end zone.

"WAYNE–LAW, WAYNE–LAW..."

As our players mobbed Wayne in the end zone I limbered up and took a few starts, then went looking for Coach and found him after a moment on the sidelines, but upfield from the other coaches and with a pair of headphones pressed to his ear. Head bowed, right foot raking the dirt, he seemed disturbed. Thinking this odd, particularly in light of the preceding play, I turned and looked up at the stadium's mezzanine level. In a small booth just to the right of the pressbox were our spotters. There were two of them, both seated, both wearing their brightly colored club jackets, but neither speaking to Coach. They couldn't. Their headsets had been usurped by a frail man in suit and tie who was pacing the floor behind them. It was Mister Clayton and he was doing all of the talking.

After a while Coach said, "Yes, yes, I understand," and with a look of resignation took off the headphones and handed them to Keane, who was standing nearby. Then, slowly, hands thrust deep in his pockets, Coach walked downfield toward Wayne Law. I followed, watching as Coach put a hand on Wayne's shoulder, listening as Coach, after congratulating Wayne on his return, said casually, "Let Monte take the next one, huh? Like we talked about?"

Wayne said, "Sure," at which point Coach patted his arm reasuringly, then returned to the midfield sidelines and dropped to his haunches to watch the kick-off.

I knelt beside him. "Don't let him do this," I said.

He looked at me. "Willie's got the next series, Brad."

"Don't let him do this, Coach. We've—"

He got up.

"Coach—"

"I don't know what you're talking about," he said. "Willie's got the next series." And he walked away.

CHAPTER | **THIRTY-TWO**

I walked over to the bench and sat down. It was cold. I wrapped myself in a cape and tried to keep warm. I didn't know what else to do.

Though I couldn't actually see what was happening on the field I could tell by the silence of the crowd and by the periodic shifts of the chain crew that Chicago was moving the football. They had started at the 20 after an unreturnable kick and now were lining up at midfield. It was second and five at their 49. Our coaches were hollering instructions and I found myself listening very carefully to what they had to say. I was listening because I could never hear them from the field. It was always too noisy. So I was listening out of curiosity, and as I listened, I began to giggle. I couldn't help it. While Coach DeVito was bellowing at the defensive linemen, "Watch the run," the secondary coach was bellowing at the defensive backs, "Watch the pass." Watch the run, watch the pass...back and forth it went, a counterpoint of confusion, and after several rounds I felt compelled to join the chorus. "Don't forget the draw," I hollered. "Watch the screen." And I laughed and hollered until the secondary coach turned and gave me a hard look.

But then something else funny happened—or it seemed funny

to me, and I started laughing again, but softly, so no one could hear. What it was, the first quarter ended. And when it did the Chicago team, which had fought and clawed and scrapped for every yard of the 28 they'd gained, had to turn around and re-capture the same holy ground. I thought this was very funny. It was as though some capricious demiurge had put a halt to the game and said, "Sorry, fellas, there's been a big misunderstand-ing...you've been going west-to-east when you should've been going east-to-west." "Oh," everyone seemed to say, and as if it didn't make any difference, the two teams politely changed sides and after a commercial time-out resumed the battle with the same old fervor and intensity. Crazy.

Fantasy time...Chicago drove for the end zone they'd just struggled so valiantly to escape, while we were trying so desper-ately to stop them, it had been a joke, hadn't it? The change in direction? Weren't they headed the wrong way? Let them score, for Christ's sake *let them score*... It was not until they actually did score (five minutes later, on a naked bootleg around a bewildered Willie Slough) and the resulting six points were credited not to us, as I'd expected, but to them, that I came rattling back to reality.

Rattling because Coach DeVito had grabbed my arms and was shaking me violently against the back of the bench. "Did you see that dumb bastard," he was screaming. "Did you see what he *did?*" He let go of me and gestured wildly toward the field.

"Who?" I said.

"Willie." He was screaming. "He lost containment on the quart-erback. He—" DeVito broke off as all at once the stadium erupted in an ovation. "What the hell," he said, and stepped up on the bench to see what had happened.

"Well?" I said.

DeVito stepped down. "The dumb bastard," he muttered. "He's driving me crazy."

"Willie?"

"Willie," he said, slumping to the bench, burying his face in his hands. "He just blocked the extra point."

I laughed.

"He's driving me crazy, Brad. I swear he is." And as Willie came dancing off the field, surrounded by jubilant teammates, his arms thrust to the heavens, DeVito got wearily to his feet and with a shake of his head wandered back to the sidelines.

"Just like Kong swattin' airplanes, B. You see me?" Willie sat down beside me and pulled off his helmet. The steam venting from the neck of his jersey veiled his broad grin and began melting the drops of perspiration that had frozen in his pencil-thin moustache.

"Who had containment on the bootleg?" I said.

"Kong," Willie said, ignoring the question. "I kinda like that name, B. Maybe you guys could start calling me that."

"Kong?"

"Sure, B. I mean—Oh!" Willie lunged forward and clutched the calf of his left leg.

"Willie, wha—"

He yelped and shot back against the bench, writhing as his leg went stiff as a ramrod and rose quivering in the air.

I knelt in front of him, grabbed the toe of his left shoe, pressed it back toward his shin and began kneading the constricted muscles.

"Cramps?" said the trainer. He leaned in to take a look.

"Yeah," Willie said. "That's what happened on the bootleg, B. That self-same thing."

I nodded.

The trainer rummaged in his doctor's bag and produced a packet of thick pink pills—muscle-relaxers of some kind. Tearing the top from the packet, he shook two of the pills into his palm and offered them to Willie. Willie leaned forward and nibbled the pills off his palm like a horse taking sugar, chewed them up and swallowed.

"Good God," I said.

"He did the same thing in training camp," the trainer whispered. "With a suppository."

"What's that?" Willie said.

"Jesus Christ," I muttered.

"You need to loosen up a little, Willie. Before you go back in."

"Oh," he said.

The trainer folded the packet and tucked it into the top of one of Willie's sweat socks. "If you have any more problems," he said, "just...you know," and he patted the lump in Willie's sock.

Willie nodded. We watched as he got up and jogged downfield, cutting occasionally to test the bad leg. He seemed all right.

"A suppository?" I said.

The trainer was closing his bag. "It was about the size of a small hand grenade," he said, making the shape with his hands. "I don't know how he ever got it down..."

"Did it work?"

"Come on, Brad."

"No, really. I mean—"

"*Rafferty.*" It was the special teams coach. "You on punt coverage?"

"No," I called.

"Be ready," he hollered. "Punt coverage be *ready.*"

"I guess he didn't hear me," I said to the trainer. "Where—" I broke off. The trainer had gone to tend another injured player, and I was sitting alone on the bench. Alone.

CHAPTER THIRTY-THREE

I spent the rest of the quarter in self-imposed exile on the bench, and halftime too, having locked myself once more in a bathroom stall, passing the time there smoking cigarettes and drinking coffee. Fear kept me from joining my teammates. Fear of what I might say to them. Unaware of what was going on with me, enthused by Willie's blocked kick, they were thinking we could win merely by playing well. They were convinced of it. You could see it in their faces and hear it in their voices and I didn't want to poison their true excitement. Though Clayton's roster manipulations had hurt us, the score was still 7–6, Rutledge had been reasonably effective, and Farrell hadn't made a call since being overruled by Pasco in the first quarter. So we had a chance. A slim one, maybe, but still a chance, and I didn't want to be the one to spoil it.

When we went out for the second half I wrapped myself in a cape and took up a position away from the other players but with an unobstructed view of the field. The snow had stopped falling and in the blazing stadium lights everything seemed unnaturally clear and precise with a foreshortening of time and distance. Surrounded by shoals of snow and by hundreds of spectators who somehow had gained access during intermission, the field seemed as small and intimate as the cluttered neighborhood vacant lot where we used to gather on autumn Sunday afternoons after the pro games to play in idolatrous emulation of our heroes—Jimmy Brown, Johnny Unitas, Raymond Berry. Their magic sent us to the scrabbled lot and for a while we were them. But only for a while. It was strange how quickly we abandoned our imagined identities for the sheer exhilaration of the action. It was overwhelming, running full tilt through a brisk November day, dry leaves thrashing at our feet, the nip of the cool air in our throats. Other than a building wall, a grassy bank, there were no formal boundaries to our field, no lines or stripes, and we never kept score. We didn't have to. The movement was enough. The movement *was* the magic. It made us feel a way we never felt, and it made time disappear...

When I looked up at the scoreboard clock less than a minute remained in the third period. Nothing had changed, except our chances for victory, which with each passing second seemed an increasingly real possibility.

The score was still 7–6. Both teams had had a series of short, unproductive drives, each ending in the inevitable punt. We'd been sparring with each other, searching for weaknesses. Or, in Chicago's case, new weaknesses. In the first half they had discovered and exploited Willie, a plan pursued through the third quarter but with less and less success. Resistance had stiffened. Not because Willie had settled down to play good football—on the contrary he seemed even more sluggish and out of synch than before—but because Jeff Blair, acting on instructions from Frank Regis, had been slanting toward Willie on nearly every play, thereby shoring up the vulnerable position.

As play began in the fourth quarter Chicago quite logically shifted their attack to our left side. An end run netted five yards, an off-tackle attempt three more, but Regis, sensing the change, stacked the defense on third and short and Chicago failed to make the first down.

It was fourth and two at the Chicago 44 and the clock was moving at 13:20. As the special teams deployed for the punt, I could sense a queer sort of tension gathering around me. Sharp, almost palpable, it was embodied in those fans who had made their way down to the field and in whose midst I now stood. They were touching me, these people, cautiously at first, as someone might touch a caged animal, but then, when I didn't immediately protest, with increasing confidence, their fingers becoming probes with which to tease and taunt, and finally I gave out with it. "*Excuse me,*" I said, wrenching my cape from their grasp, and as the punter launched a towering spiral that would fall like a bomb in the far end zone, I started upfield for the relative safety of the players' bench, which had been cordoned off by the green-suited rent-a-cops.

But the fans wouldn't let me go. They began tugging at me and shouting and when some bare-chested drunk tried to pull off my helmet, I threw him to the ground. "Oh!" The crowd gasped and drew back as I turned and faced them, heart pounding, ready to fight. For a few tense moments they were silent, then someone laughed and said, "Go get 'em, Brad." "Yeah," they all said, "go get 'em..." And with "Go get 'em" ringing in my ears I hurried upfield and slipped through the cordon...

On the field our offense had assembled informally at the ten yard line waiting for Rutledge, who was still on the sidelines taking instructions from our coaches. On the bench our defensive players were sitting singly and in pairs, heads bowed, elbows on knees, feet tapping the dirt as they waited for the next call. Behind them was a wall of policemen, and behind them, stretching from the bench area to the upper deck, was an unbroken expanse of fans, on their feet and beginning to chant as Rutledge, briefed to the shorthairs, hobbled out on the field.

"Reverse limbo looks good, Brad." Jeff Blair sidled up to me and put his arm across my shoulders. His face was twitching in four or five different places, his neck muscles were contracting spasmodically. He'd been in the jar and seemed on the verge of exploding. "Real good," he said, twitching. "But I can't get the genius over there to run one." He pointed at Willie. "You gonna play today, or does our coach wear panties?"

"Panties," I said.

Blair shook his head and turned to the field.

I couldn't take my eyes off Willie. There was something odd in the way he was sitting. It was his hands, I decided, the way they were folded so casually in his lap. And his head, the way it hung so limply from his neck.

"There's something wrong with him," I said.

"Willie? You're telling me."

"No, I mean—"

"GODDAMN SONOFABITCH."

Rutledge had mishandled the snap. He had backed away from the center too soon and the football had squirted up in the air. "GET IT," Blair screamed as the ball bobbled on a sea of outstretched hands, but they were linemen's hands, thick-fingered and heavily taped—none supple enough to make a catch—and the ball dribbled through them and dropped gently to the turf, where it lay for a moment, a golden egg unclaimed. Until it vanished beneath a mass of players. Al Pasco waded into the squirming heap, sorted through the players, whistle shrieking, and began searching for the football. We watched anxiously until Pasco straightened and moved clear of the pile. "We've got it," Blair said hopefully, "*we've got it.*" Not so. With a single crisp gesture Pasco signaled a Chicago recovery. Blair muttered and took a mighty kick at the dirt. A painful groan rose from our fans, and an explosion of obscenities erupted from our bench. All of this, however, was quickly overriden by Coach DeVito, whose cries of "*Defense, we can do it, defense*" was meant to rally the troops. After a brief sideline huddle and more exhortations Blair and the other defensive players buckled up and trotted out on the field.

Willie, however, had yet to move. He was still sitting limply on the end of the bench. I walked over and sat down beside him. "Willie?" I reached out and shook his arm. That was all it took. Willie keeled off the end of the bench and landed with a muffled thump in a pile of snow. For a terrible moment I thought he had died. But then I saw the heaving of his chest and the vaporous condensation of his breath. So what the hell had happened? I felt his sock for the packet of muscle-relaxers, and when I found it empty I knew Willie had fallen asleep. Whatever concern I'd felt for him was swamped by the single thought...this was my chance to play. There was no one else who could handle the position and I didn't waste a moment getting to it.

"Howdy boys," I said, out of breath, as I slipped into the huddle. "What've we got?"

"Hey Brad." Blair pounded my back. "Wha—"

"Quiet," Frank Regis snapped. "We've got a special, Brad. But watch that goddamn trap. They've been killing us with the goddamn trap."

When the huddle broke I moved out to my position and began loosening up—running in place, circling my arms, trying to break a sweat. As I did Crespin Mug raised up out of his huddle and gave me a look. I nodded, startled at his size. Next to Willie he hadn't seemed so big, but now…Christ, he looked like a coke machine wearing a helmet. I reminded myself that this was the fourth quarter and he was probably tired, and tired or not, he was slow as molasses. After checking the down-marker—it was first and goal from the nine—I turned to Jeff Blair.

"The trap, it comes out of red?"

"Yeah," he said. "Weakside."

"I'm gonna crash it."

Blair nodded.

"Cover for me?"

"Sure."

When the Chicago offense deployed I found myself on the weakside of a slot formation, but it was an I, not red. They liked the inside stuff from an I-formation, so as Mug settled into his stance I positioned myself on his inside shoulder and got ready to pinch. But then, when the quarterback started his cadence, the running backs shifted to red.

"Brad!"

"I see it, I see it…"

I widened and canted my stance so that my head was pointed at the left cheek of Crespin Mug's big ass. At the snap I would charge through Mug to a point three feet beyond the quarterback, where, if the play was indeed a weakside trap, the quarterback, running back and trapping guard would, for the briefest instant, come together like targets in a shooting gallery. It was possible then for one man to take out three, and that's what I intended to do. Poised and quivering a little in my stance, I imagined myself as an arrow taut on a bowstring, about to be launched.

"No," called out their quarterback. "This way, *this* way." He was yelling at someone on the opposite side of the field. It was the slotback. After the shift of the running backs the slotback had gone in motion, but apparently had settled in the wrong position. As he adjusted his alignment there was a pause in the cadence, during which the right offensive guard very slowly turned his head toward Crespin Mug.

"*Psst, Crespin,*" he said.

Mug looked at him out of the corner of his eye. Any obvious movement would have brought a procedure call and a five-yard penalty.

"What's the count?" whispered the guard.

Mug muttered something under his breath, then glanced at me and Blair to see if we were listening. We were. Mug shook his head. He thought for a moment, then very slowly turned back to the guard. "Dos," he said.

Blair giggled. "You stupid bastard, Crespin."

"Hut," called the quarterback.

"We *speak* Spanish, Crespin. God-damn, we're *fluent*—"

"Hut—"

I shot across the line of scrimmage, low and hard, like the arrow I'd imagined myself to be. Mug vanished to the inside, there was a flash of color and bone-jarring jolt, and the next thing I knew I was sprawled face down on the turf, eyes shut tight, praying to God no 270-pound pus-gut would drop on my legs and snap them like twigs. When none did, I relaxed. It was then that I noticed the dull, throbbing ache in my left shoulder, and of more immediate concern, the crushing weight that now bore down on my neck and head. I opened my eyes. Someone was sitting or lying or somehow pressed against the back of my head, and only the bars on my helmet kept my face from being mashed into the green turf. A blade of dead grass tickled the inside of my nose, the taste of the paint was in my mouth. Then the weight shifted, and able now to move, I swiveled my head to the right. Not three inches away was the grinning, stubbled mug of Frank Regis.

"Hello, Frank," I said as the bodies unpiled above us. "How are you?"

"Very well, thank you," he replied. "Lookie here." And he gazed lovingly down at his stomach where, nestled like a baby in his thick, hairy arms, was the football.

"What?" I could hear the crowd beginning to roar. "We've got it?"

Regis nodded and grinned. The crowd was roaring, and I could feel someone pulling at my legs.

"Brad!" It was Jeff Blair. "Brad, you did it, you wiped out the whole goddamn play..." He helped me to my feet. "The whole goddamn *thing*. And Mug—did you hear what I said to Mug? I told him we spoke Spanish. Get it? I told him..." Blair's words were lost in an avalanche of sound that swept us up and carried us to the sidelines.

"Way to go, Brad, way to go..." Players pounding my back as Blair and I made our way to the bench.

"Yeah, you should've seen him, Brad. I mean—"

As we sat down on the bench television cameras descended on us from all directions. "Say something, will you, Brad? Say something for the home folks!"

I smiled wanly, and waved.

"No, *say* something. Show us you guys—"

I got up and went to the utility table.

"Come on, Brad..." They followed, cords dragging. "You can talk, can't you?"

I picked up a cup of water and went where they couldn't, to the sidelines.

"You all right?" The trainer took my arm.

"We don't need 'em," I said, indicating the cameramen who were still lurking behind our bench. "We'd be here without 'em and they can take a flying fuck."

"I didn't mean that, Brad. That guard caught your head with a knee and I thought you mighta got your bell rung."

"I'm fine."

"Well, good," said the trainer, "cause you're all we got left, big

269

fella. Willie, you know, he had an allergic reaction to those pills and we had to take him in."

"You mean he fell asleep."

"Yeah, well, that's what I wanted to talk to you about. Needles says it was an allergic reaction. Sleep might be a symptom of the kind of reaction he had, it might not. The truth is we're just not sure yet and until we are, we wanna be careful what we say about it."

"Oh?"

"It wouldn't look too good in the papers, you know what I mean?"

I turned away.

"Brad, hey..."

"You know something, trainer?" I stopped and turned around. "We don't need you either. You or Needles or the goddamn own-ership—we don't need any of you bastards. You get in the way. You and those goddamn cameras and broadcasters, you're fucking shit between us and whatever it is out there we can do and it's like you don't want us to have it. You can't have it and you don't want us to have it so you get in the way. You fuck us up, with the cars and the money and the people who watch us and know our names and you tell us that's what we want when it's not what we want. That's what *you* want. But we're not like you. We want something else. And today, you little sonofabitch, in spite of all you bastards, we're gonna get it."

"Have a tranquilizer, will you, Brad."

"Fuck you."

"Your bell got really rung. Are you dizzy?"

"I'm sick of you. That's what I'm sick of."

"You feel nauseous? You're talking like a nauseous man. Sit down."

"I'm sick of you."

"Sit down."

I moved away from him. There's a feeling a victory comes from and we had that feeling. You could see it in the team and the way they were playing and you could see it especially in Jan Rutledge. Roger Clayton had underestimated him. Sure he was hurt and he

270

couldn't set up quickly to pass, but goddammit, he could still handoff and he could still lead. And that's what he was doing. He had the offensive unit operating with the precision and efficiency of a military drill team. Wherever they went, they went quickly and confidently, Rutledge always at their heels, obviously hobbled but giving off confidence, his commands crisp and clear as a drill-master's. It was beautiful to see, the way those linemen popped out of the huddle and charged to the line and snapped into their stances, asses high, weight slung forward, nostrils venting twin jets of steam as they waited and waited for the sound that would set them free. And then, when it finally came, how they surged into the opposition and, with their scythelike bodies, felling the opposition like great stalks in a plowed field, shredding them.

When the drive finally ended, at our 34-yard line, after a failed third down pass, one minute and 59 seconds were all that remained in the game. After each coach was notified of the two-minute warning and when the accompanying television time-out had expired we punted out of play and Chicago took over, first and ten, from its own 20.

Once more, it started. The chanting rhythmic explosions of sound, louder than anything I'd ever heard, louder and more powerful, sounds that seemed, as we took the field, to penetrate and set vibrating every cell in our bodies. They were very close to us, the fans. Four or five deep, they lined every available yard of sideline, from the bench areas down to and across both end zones. They were so close and so loud that Regis had to use hand signals to call the defenses, and Chicago had to try three times before the crowd finally settled down and allowed them to get off the first play of the final drive.

It was a screen left to Mallard, good for eleven yards up the sidelines in front of our bench and a first down. Mallard, however, had failed to get out of bounds and the clock was moving at 1:37 as both teams hustled to and deployed along the 31-yard line, neither team having huddled. Chicago couldn't afford to huddle; they'd squandered a time out early in the third period and another during our last drive. They had only one left and now was not the time to use it.

"Hut," called the quarterback, and taking the snap, he dropped, set and fired a six-yard quick-out to his flanker, who as he made the catch ducked out of bounds at the 37, the clock stopping then at 1:19.

Players coming and going, pointing and shouting, trying to communicate over the roar of the crowd, the roar now high, steady and continuous.

"Reverse!" Blair screaming in my ear as we leaned into the huddle. *"Brad, reverse!"* On the next play he wanted to try a reverse-limbo, the stunt we had worked on in practice.

"Too soon," I hollered.

"What?" Blair leaned even closer.

"Straight-rush," I hollered. "Set 'em up."

Blair nodded, and the crowd roared as the Chicago offense broke their huddle and deployed.

Perhaps a yard outside of Crespin Mug, and canted so that both Mug and the football fell within my line of sight, I settled into my stance. Mug was sitting back on his haunches and angled out so that his shoulders nearly paralleled mine. Which meant that the quarterback would probably take a deep drop and, correspondingly, the pass receivers would probably run deep pass patterns. It also meant that Mug was worried about blocking me, about losing me at the corner. So, as the quarterback moved under the center and started his cadence, I widened even more, glancing as I did upfield, at a spot nine yards behind the quarterback, the spot where he would set to throw and where, if I could elude Mug, the quarterback and I would meet. Tensing in my stance, I shifted my attention back to the football. When it moved, I moved.

Mug leaped in front of me. It was an odd, lurching movement, sort of like a desperate frog, and at the very instant of his leap he was off-balance and vulnerable to a quick inside charge. Giving up that opportunity, I rammed my hands into the meat of his upper arms and clamped them in a vice. Locked in this posture, we danced for a moment, and Mug seemed to relax. At the instant he did I shot my left arm under his, and using his body as a kind

272

of fulcrum, launched myself at the quarterback, who had arrived at the magic spot and was just setting to throw. And I had him. Though Mug was hanging all over me, I had the quarterback; the fingers of my outstretched right hand had snagged the fabric of his jersey, and I could feel him twisting and turning and trying to get away, and for one glorious moment I had him.

And then I let him go. I couldn't hold on. Mug's vectored force had overridden my tenuous grip, and now Mug had me. As the quarterback stepped up to throw his pass, Mug rode me to the turf and rolled me over and with his crushing weight bearing on my chest began punching me in the ribs, short, swift jabs that might have been painful if I hadn't been listening closely to the fans, listening for their reaction to the play, and when I heard them groan I knew the pass had been completed.

"Get off me, you fat fucking slug," I said, and wrapped both hands around Mug's thick neck and pushed until he rolled off. I got up and along with Mug and the other players, and the officials and chain crew, hurried downfield to the new line of scrimmage, our 44-yard line, where the receiver had been tackled after the reception.

"RED SIXTY-NINE Y-OUT." The quarterback shouted the next play as everyone hustled into position. "RED SIXTY-NINE—"

"MAN-WEAK, MAN-WEAK." Regis interrupting, shouting the defensive signals.

The quarterback glared at him. "RED SIXTY-NINE—"

"*MAN-WEAK*," snarled Regis, and leered defiantly at the quarterback, who, out of frustration, turned to Al Pasco.

"He's jamming my signals," the quarterback complained. "He's jamming my *goddamn signals.*"

Pasco shrugged. The clock was moving at :43.

Once more the quarterback shouted the play, this time without interruption. But then, as he moved under the center, he noticed a flaw in his club's alignment. "Billy Bob. Goddammit, you're supposed to be *in motion.*" Billy Bob Haslett was flanked to my right—he was the receiver who earlier had lined up on the wrong side of the field. "BILLY BOB," screamed the quarterback, but Billy Bob couldn't hear him and the quarterback panicked. "Red, uh—no, shit. Time out," he wailed, wheeling, flashing the T-sign at Pasco. As Pasco nodded and signaled the Chicago time-out, the quarterback ran over to Billy Bob Haslett, grabbed his arm, dragged him to the sidelines and left him there with a group of angry coaches to be verbally dismembered. Meanwhile our players and coaches were busy plotting strategy, our band was playing, our crowd was roaring, and out of this flux one could sense the building of a victory, the biggest victory in the history of the Washington franchise.

As Al Pasco marked the ball for play we huddled, and into our huddle stepped Frank Regis, who had been on the sidelines conferring with our defensive coaches.

"THIRTY-SIX SECONDS AND NO TIME-OUTS," he shouted, jerking his thumb at the scoreboard. "WE GOT 'EM BY THE BALLS AND WE *AIN'T* GONNA LET 'EM LOOSE."

Players nodded excitedly as once more the crowd began to chant.

"THEY GOTTA WORK THE SIDELINES TO STOP THE CLOCK, BUT WE'RE GONNA SHUT THAT SHIT OUT WITH FORTY-EIGHT MAN-WEAK. UNDERSTAND? FORTY-EIGHT MAN-WEAK WITH STUNTS." Regis looked at me. "Whatever you want, Brad. DeVito says for you to call it."

"Reverse," said Blair.

"Brad?"

"Right," I said.

"REVERSE," shouted Regis. "EVERYONE GOT IT? FORTY-EIGHT MAN-WEAK WITH A DOUBLE REVERSE LIMBO." And we broke the huddle.

Being careful not to look at Blair and thereby give any indication of what we were planning, I wandered out to my position, did a few quick toe-touches, ran in place for a moment, then banged myself on the helmet. This was it. A reverse limbo would get us a sack, and a sack would end the ballgame. All we had to do was execute.

The Chicago huddle broke, and Crespin Mug came running to

274

the line, gut lurching, jaw set, eyes vacant—a steer to slaughter, I thought—and as Mug dropped into his stance I dropped into mine and I hoped it wasn't lost on him that I was aligned precisely as I was the play before. It wasn't, he was still worried about losing me at the corner...at the snap he repeated the same desperate froglike leap—only this time I wasn't headed for the corner. As he plopped in front of me, off-balance and vulnerable, I planted my right foot and cut hard beneath him, to the inside, into the guard-tackle gap. And though Mug, with a frantic lunge, was able to hook my waist and so slow my charge, he had reacted too late, I was already into the guard, I had him locked in a bear hug, and Jeff Blair, looping behind and to the outside, was free.

The quarterback never knew what hit him. He had set deep, with his back to Blair, and he was just stepping to throw, his arm was in motion, when Blair smashed him. Blair, running full speed, had rammed his helmet into the quarterback's kidneys; at impact the quarterback's head had snapped back and his helmet had flown off, and for an instant I had watched the flying helmet thinking the poor bastard had been decapitated. Then someone yelled and I looked up and here came the football tumbling out of the sky, end-over-end like a bad punt. I couldn't get to it. Crespin Mug was hanging off my waist like an anchor and I couldn't move. As I pulled and stretched and strained against him, I saw that Chicago's left guard had settled under the football and I relaxed. The guard was hardly an eligible receiver and if he wanted to catch the football, I should let him, I shouldn't interfere. The penalties for such a play were stiff. They'd have the same effect as a sack—the game would be as good as over. So I relaxed and watched and the moment he caught the ball the line judge, who was positioned in front of our bench, threw his flag, and the moment he turned upfield the back judge, who was positioned fifteen yards downfield from the line judge, threw *his* flag. I was so confident of the impending penalties that when Mug turned me loose, instead of giving chase I stepped off the ten yards myself and at the Chicago 46 turned and knelt to wait for the inevitable recall.

Downfield, a flurry of activity. Near our 22-yard line, where the Chicago guard had finally gone down, Al Pasco was conferring with the other officials, a tight little group in animated conversation. Our players were milling around nearby, chatting casually as they waited for official confirmation of what they already knew. Meanwhile the Chicago coaches were using the delay to get their field goal unit in the game. One at least had to admire their resourcefulness...with nine seconds left and no time-outs, there was little else they could do but line 'em up and hope for a miracle.

Now Pasco left the other officials and jogged toward the press-box side of the field. The crowd, which had been buzzing in confused anticipation, became silent as Pasco stopped and switched on his transistorized microphone. "LADIES AND GENTLE-MEN," he began, but the transmission was garbled with static. As he paused to adjust the knob on the black box clipped to his belt I got up and buckled on my helmet and began once more to loosen up. When the action resumed, and it would in a moment, I wanted to be good and warm.

"LADIES AND GENTLEMEN," he began again, and this time the words came loud and clear. "LADIES AND GENTLEMEN, A DEFENSIVE LINEMAN TIPPED THE FOOTBALL *BEFORE* THE RECEPTION..."

I stopped what I was doing.

"NUMBER SEVENTY-FOUR," he said.

74...

"AND THE MOMENT HE DID..."

No. There was some mistake.

"*ALL* OFFENSIVE PLAYERS..."

He didn't. Blair didn't—

"BECAME..."

This wasn't happening.

"*ELIGIBLE RECEIVERS*..."

As the words boomed and echoed through the vast silent stadium, my mind began to roar at itself. While one part said wait, Pasco's words are merely sounds that will be absorbed in the heavy air and when they are everything will be as before, another part said *move,* and though I found the first argument compelling, my legs did start to move, and for an instant I experienced the odd sensation of acting and not acting all at the same time.

And then my loping gait became a sprint.

CHAPTER THIRTY-FOUR

But even while I was still far upfield Blair was rushing at Pasco from much closer. As Pasco switched off his microphone, turned and started back for the line of scrimmage Blair pulled up in front of him, helmet in hand, arms flailing. Pasco took it for a moment, then stepped around him and continued on his way. Blair, red-faced, frothing, wound up and threw his helmet at Pasco's head. Fortunately for Pasco, the helmet stuck for an instant to Blair's hand and instead of striking Pasco in the head, bounced and clattered across the field and clipped him harmlessly on an ankle. Pasco stopped and spun and made a threatening gesture at Blair, who, perhaps frightened by what he'd done, suddenly turned meek. Nodding sheepishly, acting as if nothing unusual had happened, he walked over and picked up his helmet. Pasco watched him for a moment, then, satisfied the threat had been put down, turned and started once more for the line of scrimmage.

But the threat had not been put down. I had been sprinting for Pasco. Now he was within my range and I intended to hurt him. I intended to drive my helmet through the small of his back and stick him squirming in the dirt like an insect. My eyes riveted to the black-and-white stripes that ran down the back of his shirt, the stripes distending and bending and joining one another in a

278

series of concentric circles, the circles looming larger and larger, I accelerated and stretched out and though now dimly aware of some distant screaming voice, closed for the kill.

And then the voice exploded in my consciousness. "YOU GOD-DAMN CRAZY SONOFABITCH..." And there was a flash of color and a deadening jolt as someone stepped in front of me and smashed a forearm into my chest and head. The blow stopped me cold, stood me up. A bolt of pain shot down my spine and set me tingling. Then I went numb.

"You wanna make it easy for 'em?" Frank Regis had me locked in his arms. *"You wanna give 'em the goddamn field goal?"*

I mumbled something unintelligible. I'd gone numb, senseless.

"Look," he yelled, releasing me. "It's a thirty-nine-yard kick. He might miss the goddamn thing. We might block it..."

"Thirty-nine yards..."

"YES."

But as I looked at the grid and all of the numbers I realized there were too many of them. There were big chalk numbers on the field and small electrical numbers on the scoreboard and big fabric numbers on the backs of all the players and in my confusion I began out loud to add them together.

"Jesus Christ," said Regis, and grabbing me again, he turned and shouted at someone, "Where's Slough? Get Slough in here."

And the someone replied, "Slough? He's asleep."

And Regis returned, "Well, goddammit, so is Rafferty."

But I wasn't asleep, I was counting, and I couldn't stop. Convinced now that the sum of all these numbers would yield some immutable truth, I continued with the calculations, only faster, faster and faster—and it was all Frank Regis could take.

"Goddammit—*stop*," he screamed, and whacked me sharply across the earhole of my helmet.

It was then that I noticed the crowd. Those fans seated high in the stadium were on their feet and booing. The sounds came rolling down in great waves and the stadium was awash with their anger and hostility. Swept up in this, those fans who stood packed along the sidelines began to riot. There was no other word for it. While a few of them, the drunkest of the lot, ventured out onto the playing field, most of the others surged into the far end zone and charged the fluorescent yellow goal posts. Determined to prevent the Chicago field goal, they began shaking the structure, trying to tear it down. As Regis dragged me toward the line of scrimmage I watched them, praying they might succeed. And for a short time it appeared they might. But then the policemen, who had massed nearby, waded into them, nightsticks thrashing, and in a few minutes were able to secure the goal posts. Though the fans continued their rampage—now smashing chairs and ripping down banners—they did so as individuals, in a random way, and it sickened me to realize the game would continue...

"There," said Regis, indicating my position on the line. "Get down there and block the goddamn kick."

I stood for a moment, staring down at the space. It was a slit, really, a dark little slit between two filthy people who in tattered knickers and knee socks and with strange plastic globes on their heads and with odd lumpy growths on their shoulders were squatting in the dirt, and I wondered if these were the kind of people I should be associating with or if they were really even people at all—

"Get down there," said Regis, and he gave me a shove.

"Yes, okay," I said, but wary now, I only knelt.

What stopped me was this idea that the people around me weren't really people at all. I was really beginning to think they weren't. Because in front of me, stretching away from me in either direction, was a row of thick muscular legs so tightly arrayed that they seemed all of a piece—the lower extremities of some monstrous, centipedal creature that had been captured, somehow, and tamed, and dressed up, and positioned center-stage in this extravagant sideshow, as if to perform, all uniform and in unison, except the pair of legs to my immediate left. They were different. They were not of the creature but somehow superior to it—straddling, as they were, the leather orb that was the center of the creature's organization—and I studied them for a moment, wondering how they fit. The shoes were black and ripple-soled, the legs were slim and hard, and the uniform was...it was a trainer's. That was it. The one who works with exotic animals...

I looked up at this towering figure and opened my mouth. Or I should say my mouth opened itself, because I wasn't conscious of having anything to say—but I spoke anyway. Or rather moaned...what came out of my mouth had the protracted, plantive quality of a cow's moo.

The trainer looked at me as if he couldn't quite believe what he had heard.

I'd better explain, I thought. But when I opened my mouth to do so, out it came again, an involuntary "moo," even longer and louder than the last one, and this so distressed me that I sat down in the dirt.

The trainer smiled then, in a pitying way, and shook his head. I managed a smile in return, but I couldn't help wishing he'd get the hell away from me and leave me alone. Then, thankfully, he did, he stuffed his whistle in his mouth, blew it, and moved out of the way so that the creature could perform. As he did the air filled with numbers—shouted numbers from the creature, flashing numbers from the distant scoreboards—and I started counting again, counting and watching, taking it all in.

It was quite a spectacle. Especially when the creature snapped to life, burst apart, shattering into a tumult of armor-clad fragments that tore in a vicious assault against its own midsection, a horizontal attack that with the sweet smack of leather-on-leather suddenly turned vertical, the attackers leaping high up in the air to swat at the orb as it sailed over their heads. Then there was a long moment when everyone stopped what they were doing and turned to watch the orb, their bodies twisting and bending as if to influence its flight. Then bedlam. Half of the creature erupted in a spontaneous cheer and began to dance while fragments stomped and swore and writhed on the dirt, and a low rumbling roar rose up as thousands of spectators spilled out on the field.

And there I sat, mesmerized by all the legs. It was fascinating, actually, what was happening with them. As the prancing legs and the shuffling legs of the creature separated and attempted to move off the field, they were swarmed by the short, stubby legs of the spectators. It was as though the spectators did not want these curiously costumed beings to leave the arena even though the event that had been staged in the arena had ended. It was as though *this* was the event—these moments of direct contact—and everything else had been only a prelude. That's the only reason I could think of to explain why so many of them had gathered around me. Because they had, in scary numbers, like iron filings gathered around a magnet.

Then I heard from my right a delicate voice, and looking over, found a young boy on tiptoes whispering into the ear of the man who stood next to him. After a moment the man nodded, as if in encouragement, and the boy broke from the circle and ever so slowly stepped forward. He was wearing bluejeans and tennis shoes and a corduroy coat, its flaps hanging well below his knees. His steps were tentative.

"Excuse me, sir," he said, drawing close.

I was staring at his neat little shoes. Judy was rising in my consciousness, I couldn't keep her out.

"It looked kinda rough out there," the boy said.

I nodded vacantly.

"Did you hurt yourself or something?"

"No," I said, and thought: *they killed her.* It was out now, no more denying it. And still staring at his little feet, I saw Judy and the wreck and the fact of the matter: *they had killed her.* I was sure of it. Jack had been fooled by their cleverness into thinking the wreck had been an accident or a suicide. Actually they must have drugged her somehow, or sabotaged her car. They had killed her, it didn't really matter how. But then the boy startled me by kneeling down and reaching to touch my arm. I had no choice but to look at him, and what I saw was a young man of some nine or ten years whose slightly insolent features had gone soft with concern.

"Do you want me to get someone?" he asked. "Do you need some help or something?"

I smiled, embarrassed, shook my head, no, and wondered if I could explain to him...to anybody...how frightened of her they must have been, how big it really was, this thing that had crushed her—how far beyond help she...we...really were. I wondered if I could make him or anybody understand and believe...

The boy brushed away the loose dirt from the trampled earth between us. "You guys really played your hearts out," he said, tracing now a design in the smooth place he'd made. "We, uh...we beat 'em, you know, really. Well, that's what my dad says. We beat 'em everywhere but on the scoreboard, my dad says."

A kind of groan sounded through the fog in my head. As I stared at him, I could feel myself sinking. He was one of them too, him and his goddamn dad and...they were every-where...they were reproducing themselves...

"Maybe we were looking ahead to the conference championship. I've read about that, you know. How a team gets excited sometimes and can't exactly...can't...I mean, they get excited about a game they're going to play so they don't pay attention to the game they're playing. So they lose the game they're playing and never get to play the game they were so excited about playing. Right? And so everything, you know, falls apart...That's what my dad says..."

"Go away," I muttered.

"Did you have a good week of practice and everything? I mean, maybe...my dad says you play like you practice and maybe if you didn't have a good week of practice then—"

"Get *lost*," I said—and immediately regretted it. "No, wait," I called, but it was too late. I'd shocked the kid. He'd already scrambled to his feet and run back to his father, which had sparked suspicion, then outrage and indignation in the faces of the people who had been watching us. They were sore as hell at me—I could feel their anger, and I knew I'd have to do something.

When the father came toward me, I unbuckled my chin strap and held it out, a feeble peace offering. It worked, though. The father snatched at the strap, knelt in front of the red-eyed boy. "You see? I told you he'd give you something to remember him by." The boy accepted the strap as though it were a piece of buried treasure.

"What about *my* boy," a gruff voice from behind said as the father and son wandered off.

"Yeah, and what about mine," another said.

"And *mine*," said a third, "we got kids too."

"It ain't fair," they said. The circle closed around me.

"I guess..." I took off my helmet. "I guess—"

"*Gimme* that." A big hand darted out, clamped the helmet and wrenched it from my grasp. Other hands were quickly on the helmet.

"You realize how much money I lost on you, you lazy fuck? You played like pussies. Pussies."

"Bums..."

"I lost eighty fucking dollars."

"You got an arm pad, mister?"

"What?"

"*This,*" said a man as he grabbed the pad on my left elbow, gave a mighty jerk and off it came.

"Bums. A buncha goddamn prima donnas."

"Bums."

"Can I have one, buddy?" This man was on the other side of me, and he already had the thing off and was waving it in my face. "Thanks a lot." I could feel someone tugging at my feet.

"Let *go,*" I managed to get out, and kicked the sonofabitch in the teeth. My right shoe came off, and there was a mad scramble for that, and now someone was pulling at my other shoe and someone else was pulling on the neck of my jersey, stretching the material, pulling it down and over my shoulder pads, and as hard as I could I swung my right arm back and tried to smash the guy who was pulling on my jersey, but someone else caught my arm and pushed it against my back and jammed it up toward my neck, and I thought I heard the click of a pocket knife and the ripping of my jersey, and then my jersey was gone and the cold air hit me like a fist and I kicked another sonofabitch, the sonofabitch who was trying to pull the skidder off my left knee, but I could do nothing to stop the bastard with the knife, and it wasn't long before he had cut the strings that held my shoulder pads together and they just fell away, in two parts, and when the guy who was holding my arm let go to grab half the pads I punched him square in the jaw and he went sprawling, but he quickly recovered and came charging back and I took him on and we rolled over and over in the dirt, but neither he in his heavy clothes nor me in my T-shirt...neither of us could get the upper hand, and as we lay

284

straining against each other I could feel again hands on my legs and this time they were rolling up my knickers and tugging at my knee pads and I began kicking at whoever was doing this, kicking and screaming and crying, and suddenly everything went still.

I was under the stadium. I was in a tunnel. It was cold and dank. There was a moth-eaten woolen blanket draped across my shoulders and a large gloved hand clamped to my right elbow. I didn't know who the blanket belonged to...the hand belonged to the policeman who was leading me up the ramp. As my eyes adjusted more to the darkness I could see that there were other people in the tunnel. We were passing them. They were wearing greatcoats and hats and were leaning against the walls of the tunnel, notepads and programs tucked under their arms, an occasional face illuminated in the dim glow of a cigarette. There were more and more of them as we proceeded, and some of them began blurting out questions. We ignored them. Neither of us knew the answers. Then we came to the place where the reporters were most dense and the policeman let go of my arm and pointed at a double steel door. I nodded my thanks. God, I just wanted to go home. But as I started for the door a little man I'd never seen before stepped forward and blocked my path.

"You can't go in there," he said.

I looked at him incredulously.

"You can't," he said. "I'm sorry."

The corridor was very quiet. I could hear the breathing of the reporters and the pounding of my heart in my chest. "Goddammit, I'm going in," I said. "I'm a player." I gave the man a shove, opened the door and slammed it behind me, hurried up another corridor past a bathroom and shower room and except for the pounding of my heart it was still very quiet, and when I came to the end of the corridor I saw why...the people in the locker room were all kneeling in silent prayer.

It was something I'd never tried in all my years as a pro. When Coach said, "Let's spend some time with the man upstairs," I always sat on my chair with my eyes open, looking around the room for someone else with his eyes open—it was sort of a pact I'd made with myself that if I ever found someone else with his eyes open I would make friends with him, because I thought he would probably understand what I didn't, could tell me how after the prayer Wayne Law could go out and fuck some 300-pound teenager and John Reese could get in his car and pack his nose with a pound of cocaine and Jeff Blair could go home and beat the hell out of his little wife—but I never found anyone else with his eyes open so I never found out the answers to those questions, and it occurred to me now that maybe the answers lay in the meditation itself, if you really seriously tried it. So I dropped to my knees and clasped my hands in front of me like the pictures of clasped hands you see painted on black velvet for sale in Mexican bazaars, and I closed my eyes and began saying to myself over and over again, "I'm praying, I'm praying..." and I was just falling into the rhythm of the thing when someone elbowed me in the ribs and said, "What the hell are you doing?"

I opened my eyes and turned my head and found myself looking into the narrow, steely eyes of some thick-necked brute I didn't know. "I'm praying."

The guy laughed. "Jake, take a look at this, will ya." And the man named Jake, who was kneeling in front of us, turned and looked and he laughed too. As he did a man in the front of the room said, "What the hell's going on back there," and all of the faces turned and looked and I got up and began backing down the corridor, now confused and disoriented, because though the room seemed very familiar to me, the faces did not, in fact I had never seen any of these faces before, and at the door it dawned on me that I was in the wrong locker room.

The reporters laughed as I came out. I hurried through them, back down the tunnel and up the dugout steps. I slipped behind the portable stands, followed the crumbling asphalt path, made my way around the stadium. After a while I came to the door that opened into the officials' dressing room. The sign had been taken down. The chair the guard had sat in was gone and the door was ajar. I opened it and looked inside. Wet towels, folding metal chairs, plywood stalls, empty but still bearing the identifying strips of adhesive. Pasco. I found his name over a corner locker and stared at it for a long time. He was one of them too. He knew I

286

was lying about the loan agreements. He knew I didn't have them because he knew *his* people had them. That's what I thought and I hoped I was right, because if I was right they wouldn't kill me.

I closed the door and continued down the path to a flight of stairs. I climbed the stairs and on the top step sat down and waited for the supervisor of officials, though I knew he wouldn't be coming. When I could no longer control my shivering I got to my feet and proceeded up the corridor to our locker room.

Inside it was quiet, most of the players had already dressed and gone. Scattered across the concrete floors were damp towels and soiled socks and husks of adhesive that along with the piles of pads had been shed and left behind—the jettisoned equipment of an army in retreat. Tony was sweeping up. He glanced at me as I crossed the room, then with a shrug continued to work. I sat down in front of my locker. I was cold and very tired and I wondered if the trainer would give me a Seconal.

"Hey, Brad." In front of a mirror near the door of the training room Wayne Law stood blowdrying his hair. "There's a seafood smorgasbord at the Hilton," he called over the whir of the dryer as he eyed me through the mirror. "They've flown in live Maine lobster and Florida stone crabs and they've got bluepoints from the Chesapeake and an open bar and we oughta have a pretty good time even if we did lose..."

I said nothing. I slid off the chair and lay down among the husks of tape and twisted jocks and the dirty towels. I was cold and very tired and I began covering myself with the towels.

"Hey, Brad," Wayne called over the whir of the dryer. "Where the hell you been anyway? And where's your goddamn shoes? Your feet are blue."

"The game was fixed," I said.

"What's that?" Wayne adjusted the setting on the dryer to low. He was still looking at me through the mirror.

"I said, the game was fixed."

"Yeah? Well, we'll get 'em next year," he said, and he put the dryer back on high.